Book two of the *Duty* Trilogy:
Duty Calls

By: James A. Haddock III

Websites
Jameshaddock.us

Copyright © 2019 all rights reserved

No part of this book may be used or reproduced in any manner whatsoever without written permission except in the case of brief quotations embodied in critical articles or reviews.

This is a work of fiction. Names, characters, businesses, places, events, locales, and incidents are either the products of the author's imagination or used in a fictitious manner. Any resemblance to actual persons, living or dead, or actual events is purely coincidental.

CHAPTER 1

The *Travis* landed beside *Duty*. "Captain Gallant, about a click away from here there are the remains of the crew we need to recover, as well as all the equipment. We'll be over shortly to meet with the refit crews and lay out the work we need done on the *Duty*." I said.

"Roger, Sir, I'll get a recovery team out ASAP," Captain Gallant said.

"Buck, how are you doing bringing *Duty's* systems back online?"

"Doing good, Sir, tankage has thawed. I found the O^2ponics-soup in supply, so we can get that mix started," Buck said.

"Good, the *Travis* is here so you'll have help over there soon. Then you can come back to the *Loki* for a break and get lunch," I said.

"Sounds good, Sir."

We all went over to the *Travis* and met with the Captain and the repair crew foreman. "Looks like you found work to keep us busy," Captain Gallant said.

I nodded, "Yes, she was a derelict, now she's ours. She's been out here for about a century. That was her crew's bodies you recovered out on the plain," I said.

"If she's been out here for over 50 years, space law says she belongs to whoever finds her," Captain Gallant said.

"That would be HMS and the crew of *Loki*," I answered. "Because of the find I'll give everyone on the *Travis* a bonus." That brought out the smiles. "Buck is over in engineering on the *Duty*, bringing the power back online. We need to get a crew over there to help him with that.

"I'd like the inspectors and the team leaders to go to the *Duty* and start their inspections, to see what repair work needs doing to get the hull sealed. She's a huge ship, so it may be better to work in pairs for the time being. Don't worry about the front drive engine room, Mal and I will work in there. I think the crew housing area is sealed, but double check me. Then we can work on getting the O^2 back online. Questions? OK, let's get to it."

I waited until the work crews had gone, leaving us with Captain Gallant. "Any word from the admiral?" I asked.

"Nothing yet. It may take a while for him to get things sorted," he said.

"Yeah, well, this will keep our crews busy and out of trouble," I said.

"Hopefully," he answered.

"Let's get coffee and talk, Archie ... we need advice from your perspective."

He nodded, "Galley?" We nodded and followed him to the galley. We all got a cuppa and moved to the Captain's table. On a ship this size, the command crew had their own table. We took our seats, "What's on your mind, Commodore?"

"Just Nic when we're alone please. All these titles get bothersome."

He smiled, "OK, Nic, what's on your mind?"

"This whole business of the corporate ships attacking us, the setup for a trap, moles in the Legion. I guess my mind is not set up to work in that direction. This playing chess with people's lives is like something out of a book or a movie," I said.

He nodded, "well, my young friends, you'd better reprogram your minds, because you are in the game and it's already turned deadly. These people and corporations play for billions of creds and power over millions of people, and they play for keeps.

"Your lives mean less than nothing to them. All they want is creds and power, and the more they have, the better they like it. Your inventions and tech is a way for them to get more of both."

I looked at Mal, "Business is war." Mal nodded.

"You hit the nail on the head, Nic," Archie said. "Business is war, and this case, literally war. They have shown they will spend money, lives, and ships to further their goals. You have to start thinking like them, and you are playing catch-up.

"You need to get out ahead of them at least five moves to survive."

"What's this thing with the ESFL? I thought they were created to stay neutral," I asked.

"They were. But again, it's power, politics and creds. If they can turn the ESFL toward their goals and use them to hinder other's, that's the way they play the game. The Legion has always had to deal with this to some extent, but it seems to have become more aggressive of late. The Admiral has been bucking their moves ever since he took over as Admiral of the ESFL. They've been trying to get rid of him since he took command."

"What a way to live!" I shook my head.

"Not really, but that's reality."

"With all this in mind, they have already come after us, our business associates, and our tech. We think the next thing they will try will be a thrust at family, business, assets, and creds." He was nodding.

"The question is how to protect them," I said.

"You have a good lawyer right?" He asked. We all nodded. "Have them move all your business assets and creds to Titan. Titan has become space's Switzerland. Nobody can touch your stuff there. Family is a different matter. You are right, eventually they will go after pressure points, and family is easiest to get to."

"Thanks Archie, if you think of anything else that will help us, we appreciate the advice," I said.

"Anytime Nic, now I want to take a tour of *Duty*, no pun intended," He chuckled.

***

They had gotten the O^{2}ponic soup working to make and refresh *Duty's* O^2. But it would take a while before we could go without our vac suits. Mal and I took a tour of the grav-cone-drive engine room and its dedicated engineering area. I understood the theory, but it was the application I was a little fuzzy on.

"We need to get an ACE and palm pads installed ASAP. We need to control access to this area," I said.

"I reset the passcodes for now. That will do until we get an ACE up and running," Mal said.

"I agree, this is definitely a close hold top-secret tech," I answered. "The girls are on the bridge learning the ops area. You get started on the ACE, I'll keep studying the drive."

We installed palm pads in engineering and the bridge. Two days later we met with the inspectors and the crew foreman. They had a good start on what we needed to do, and had come up with some immediate upgrades we could make. All the basic systems were the same as those in use today, but there had been a lot of tech advances in the last 100 years.

"We can have the holes repaired and sealed in about a week," Randy, the head engineer, said. "The O^2 soup's cooking, but it will be a week before we can open its housing to receive fresh air. We've already replaced keypads with palm pads. That was an easy fix and put the crew to work. Most of the big systems just need to be checked and upgraded. The gravitonics are the same, but the control systems have improved."

"Sounds good, let's meet again in a week unless something big comes up," I said.

I would have to figure out how many OFEs we would need to cover this monster. I planned on using the same sized OFEs as we'd used on *Loki* and Taurus. We also needed to check the drive's magnetic frequency to make sure it could operate at the same time as the shields would without producing problems.

We found *Duty's* food storage lockers full of frozen foods, and were surprised to see that they were still good, since they were at "space" temperatures. We sent a sampling of the food over to *Travis* to have the messmen test them to make sure they were still good, and if so, use them. The food tested perfectly fine, and we started using them right away.

Our calculations showed we would need 223 OFEs to cover *Duty,* so we set up the magna-flux 3-D printers to start making them. Mal had the ACE program installed, but would wait on the integration process until we had more systems online.

I asked the girls to go through the crew quarters and make notes, so we could talk about what we had to work with. They were happy to help, and it gave them something to do, since there was nothing to pilot. I was working in the GCD room when Mal messaged me, saying he wanted me to look at something on the bridge.

I went up and found Mal with his head in the computer cabinet. "What did you find?"

He sat back and looked at me, "I'm not sure."

"What do you think you've found?"

"I was going to upgrade *Duty's* computers with one of my new ones, but when I started the ACE install, she ran just fine. They are running at almost the same performance level as one of my new ones."

"How is that possible? They're 100 years old!"

"I don't know. That's what I'm trying to figure out."

"Did they have an advanced CCU as well as advanced drive tech?"

"No, these are standard, or were standard a century ago. There's nothing special about them."

I shrugged my shoulders, "Let's pull them and take them to the lab and see what we find." Mal nodded.

That evening over dinner on *Loki,* we caught each other up on the day's activities, and Jazz and Jade shared their housing notes.

"We can house 1,000 people on *Duty*. 50 percent of the quarters are singles, 25 percent are doubles, and the other 25 percent are family quarters. All of them have their own heads, and the doubles and family quarters have galleys. This thing, as we keep saying, is huge," Jade said.

Buck nodded, "Yeah, I've been looking around the factory areas. That smelter-refiner is a beast. If what I've seen and read is true, it pulls off usable gases from the smelter-refining process to use as fuel to help power itself. We need to upgrade the FEs like we did at OEM."

"I'm no closer to solving my CCU mystery, I've taken it apart down to the last screw. My next step is to magnify all the parts. I don't know what I'm looking for, maybe something will jump out at me." Mal said.

"I ran my figures on the shield covering program, it will take 223 emitters to cover this baby." I said.

Buck whistled, "that will take a lot of cable runs." "It will take a lot of everything," I said. "And to that end, Jazz can you and Jade take Taurus and look for the elements we need to keep *Travis'* holds full?" I asked.

"Sure, first thing in the morning." Jazz said.

The work crews had the hull sealed in less than a week and then moved on to repairing other systems. The priorities were the generators, engines, and force shields. Jazz and Jade kept *Travis'* holds filled with raw materials.

Then Mal messaged me, saying he thought he had found something. I found him in the lab looking at a monitor and shaking his head.

"What are you looking at?" I asked.

"The answer, I think." I looked at the monitor but saw nothing obvious. "We've gotten so used to seeing it, we overlooked it."

"I don't follow," I said.

"Mithrilium," He answered.

"OK, what about it?" I asked.

"There's mithrilium dust all through the CCU, it permeated every part. The drives, the chips, the connectors, everything." He said.

"OK, I still don't see what you're trying to show me."

"We don't use mithrilium in CCUs. There's no need, they don't need super strength, so we never used it. These have been dusted or embedded with mithrilium. The mithrilium has changed, or enhanced would be a better word, the CCU's capabilities. They run faster, cooler, and more efficiently. The drives hold more data, all while using less power."

I sat down, staring at the screen. I held a finger up and he waited. "The mithrilium has magnified electronic performance, while reducing energy requirements?" He nodded, then stopped.

Then he held his finger up and I waited.

"If that holds true with all electronics and power plants, it should act the same way with generators and engines. Everything electrical," he said. I nodded my head. "How do we test it?" He asked.

"First, let's make a CCU using mithrilium infused parts. That's a small enough project that no one will notice. We'll see what that tells us."

We went straight to one of the small MF 3-D printers and made all the parts we needed for a processing unit, with a 2 percent mithrilium additive. We took our parts back to the lab and assembled them.

To say the results stunned us would be the understatement of the year. The new mithrilium computer, or M-Comp as we decided to call it, was 50 percent faster than anything Mal had ever seen or heard of. There was absolutely no heat produced which meant even running at 100 percent, full time, it would not be damaged.

Mal ran all of his normal tests and shook his head. "It only needs minor tweaking."

"You'd want to do a minor tweak on a bar of gold!"

Mal made an ACE M-Comp for *Duty* that was half the size of normal, but twice as powerful. We took the new unit to *Duty's* bridge and installed it. Mal ran the install for the ACE program. What would have taken one to two days was done in just over an hour.

Mal looked at me, "Close hold?"

"You're dang right, close hold!" I said. "We need to wipe the MF 3-Ds after every use, so no one else catches on to this. We also need to change the cable size we are using on the shield emitters. We'll make M-Cables, and that will save us, say, 75 percent on cabling materials. We could redo the emitters themselves, but we're too far along to change production."

"Let's make a small MF 3-D printer using mithrilium infusion to take back to *Loki* right now." Mal said.

We started one of the MF 3-D printers making our new M2F 3-D printer parts and started the other one making the new M-cable for the shield emitters on *Duty*. We left instructions that the new cable was special and was to be used for the shield emitter runs.

We gathered our M2F 3-D parts and took them back to *Loki*. The M2F 3-D was the same size as the other 3-D printer but was more efficient and faster. We didn't have all the raw materials on *Loki* that we needed, so we solved the problem by adding storage areas.

***

Like kids with a new toy, we went back over to *Travis'* small MF 3-D printer and made parts for another M-Comp. When that run was finished, we ran the parts for a small generator using a 10 percent M-additive. We took our parts back to the lab and assembled them.

Mal finished with the M-Comp before I finished with our new M-power generator, so he tested it. We were hopeful of good results, but what we got was great results. It was the equivalent to a 1 to 100 ratio, or 1 watt's worth of power to turn the generator, to make 100 watts of output.

The cost of running our ships, once equipped, just dropped dramatically. We could now run our ships for 1/100th of the cost. "Oh great! I joked, more tech they will try to kill us for."

"On the bright side, they can't kill us but once." Mal said laughing.

We got Buck busy adding space for material storage in *Loki* for the M2F 3-D, while we made replacements for the generators on *Loki* and put the standard generators in the parts storage area on *Travis*, to be used elsewhere.

Mal got a wild look in his eyes, and replaced all my cyber components with new M-Components and M-Comp. I called a halt to it when he asked for my eye.

"First you make me a new eye and then we'll talk." I said.

"That's a great idea! I can add more capabilities to it!" The M-batteries, M-capacitors, and M-OFEs put my cyber gear off the charts, while *Vee* was now twice as powerful and exponentially faster. *Loki* got upgrades too.

We finally had a handle on how the new drive worked. Mal and I upgraded all the electronics on *Duty* and put all new M-gens in the GCD engine room. One thing we learned was that the cone drive took a lot of power to operate, but the new M-gens solved that issue.

We could now open *Duty's* environmental systems to supply the housing areas' O^2 needs. We opened the housing areas and started the crews running checks in all quarters, meanwhile replacing all the generators and electronics on *Duty* with the new versions.

I walked past Mal, suddenly stopped, and said, "I got an idea."

"Are they gonna kill us over it?"

"Only once."

We stopped at the cargo bay on the way to the lab, and I grabbed a grav-pallet.

"Well, crap!" Mal said. "Of course!" When we got to the lab, we set the grav-pallet up on the workbench and disassembled it, then replacing the electronics with M-tronics and new grav-plates with a mithrilium additive of 10 percent. As close as we could figure, it would now lift 10 times as much using a tenth of the power.

Over the next few days we made two more M2F 3-D printers and installed them on *Duty*, setting them to work making grav-plates as fast as we could install them. Crews would uninstall one and feed that one into the hopped of the printer and replace it with the new M grav-plate ... and repeat.

Buck replaced all the grav-plates on *Loki* with the new ones. We had been working on *Loki* like mad men, bringing it up to the new specs.

We were taking a break one day at the galley table on *Loki*, when I observed wryly "You know, Buck, a rich man shouldn't have to work so hard."

"Well, I'm not complaining about the pay, but I'm hardly rich," he said, smiling.

"Hmmm, Mal, am I wrong?"

"No, he's definitely rich." Mal said, pursing his lips. "Oh, I know what it is, it hasn't hit his account yet."

"That's right, we must take care that, we'll tell Pam's mom when we see her," I said.

"OK, what are you two talking about?"

"Well, you are a crew member of *Loki*, and we discovered and claimed a derelict ship. The split is usually 50 percent to the company, a good chunk to the captain, and the rest divided among the crew," Mal said.

Buck's mouth hung open.

"To quote my girl, close your mouth, dear, you'll catch flies." Mal quipped.

He closed his mouth, but still just stared.

"And how much did we figure a crewman's share would be?" I asked Mal.

"About 2 million creds." Mal replied.

"Are you serious?" Buck asked. "You will cut me in on all the shares? I hadn't been part of the crew but a few hours."

"True, but you were a solid contributor to the job, and now you're part of a rich crew. We hope you don't quit and retire to a life of leisure," I said.

"I ain't going anywhere, this is the best job I've ever had. And the pay ain't bad either," We all laughed.

CHAPTER 2

We had been on *Duty's* rock for three months and I was becoming concerned about what was going on in the rest of the Solar System.

"I think we need to find out what's going on at home, and any Intel we can get on what the Admiral is doing," I said.

"I agree," Mal said. "But I don't think we should all go. We can't leave *Duty* without one of us on her to retain ownership, just in case." Jazz and Jade were nodding.

"Well, Duty is ready for occupation, and the ACE is fully integrated. Not all systems have been tested but I see no problems there." I said.

"I think you, Jazz, and Buck should go home and check on things," Jade said. "Mal and I will stay on Duty, and continue testing and upgrading her,".

I looked at Jazz, she shrugged her shoulders.

"OK," I said, "we'll do that. We'll meet with Captain Gallant in the morning and let him know what our plans are. Meanwhile, as soon as the force shield is installed and ready, I want it online."

"Have you finished the shield belts yet?" I asked Mal.

"Yep, they're down in the armory."

"Jazz will take hers with us when we leave tomorrow. I think you all should make it a habit of wearing them all the time." I said.

"You got them to work?" Jade asked. Mal nodded.

"What belts?" Jazz asked. Buck's head was going back and forth like he was watching a tennis match.

"Force shield belts, battery-powered personal force shields.

You wear the belt and you have a force shield around you," Mal said.

"Cool!" Buck said, "Oh sorry, I get one, right?" We all laughed.

We met with Captain Gallant the next morning and told him our plans. "Once we have some Intel, we'll let you know what our next move is." I said.

"I think that's a wise decision, you need good, solid information to fight this war. Don't go rushing in. You have contacts there, so use them to check out the battlefield conditions. I would even use that little disappearing trick if I were you."

I nodded, coming to a decision, "Travis, Captain Gallant now has authorization to use the "Go dark" program."

"Authorization acknowledged."

"Mal will explain what it does — but use it sparingly. We don't want to show our hand. At this point even the ESFL doesn't have it," I said.

"Understood."

Mal and Jade gathered their things from Loki and move them to Duty. We hugged goodbye and got underway.

Loki went dark as Jazz brought us out of the rock field. We let Loki run the sensors. She now had twice the computer power as before, and her processing speed was much faster. In addition, with her M upgrades, Loki was a lot faster and used less fuel.

"Let Loki have the helm let's go eat," I said.

Jazz nodded, "Loki, you have the helm."

"I have the helm," Loki said.

We went to the galley and made dinner. As we ate, Jazz said "I hope everything's all right."

"I'm sure it is, if it wasn't, they would've commed us," I answered. "When we get closer, we'll call in and see how things are going. Let's also contact Aaron and get him to move everything to Titan. Hopefully that will forestall any move against our assets."

"I hope the Admiral has solved his and our problems, so we

can go back to living a normal life." Jazz said.

"Me, too, but I'm not going to bet the farm on it just yet."

We had been on course for home for a week when Loki said, "Commodore, we have an encrypted message from Invincible's ACE," Loki said.

I was afraid I knew what it was, "what's the message?"

"Vesuvius," Loki said.

"Well, that's not good," I said.

"What's it mean?" Jazz asked.

"Mal and I put tamper-proof programs in all of our tech. We sold tech, but if anyone tried to open it to reverse engineer it, it destroyed itself, leaving nothing but ash, sand and carbon."

"So, someone has tried reverse engineer Invincible's ACE comp?" Jazz asked.

"It looks that way," I said. "And if the ACE went, she took everything with her: controls, shields, everything. The Admiral wouldn't do that, so I'd guess he no longer has control of the ship. I bet someone is not happy about it right now."

"Loki … send an encrypted message to Major asking for a SitRep."

"Message sent."

"Breakfast anyone?" I asked.

***

"Commodore, encrypted message from Major. Security board is green, no overt threats, situation normal."

"Understood." I waited until we were a day away from Conclave Station before sending another message.

"Loki … send an encrypted message to Aunt J, Commander Jones, Bob, and Jocko that we are on our way, about a day out." I said.

"Message sent."

The replies came in and Loki read down the list.

"Message received from Bob: "It will be good to have you home."

Message from Aunt J: "It's about time!"

Message from Commander Jones: "Local space around Conclave Station is Amber, unsure further out. 'Our friend' is missing. Approach with care; internal security is green."

Message from Jocko: "Be careful of traffic. Lots of new ships around the station. New faces on the Promenade, and they have the same look as the ones you and Travis ran into. Travel safe."

"Acknowledge receipts." I said.

"Acknowledgement sent."

"Loki … send an encrypted message to Aaron Stein. Re-flag all business assets, accounts, and ships to Titan, ASAP. Do not wait to see me. I should be there in a day or two. Business will continue as normal for now, but we need the protection of Titan's banking system."

"Message sent."

"So, things aren't all roses, but nothing crazy, it would seem," I said.

"At least everyone's all right," Jazz said.

"Commodore," said Loki. "I have detected a ship that seems to be trying to hide in the edge of the asteroid field. It is operating on minimal systems."

"Understood, I guess that's their version of going dark," I said.

"Message from Aaron Stein, understood, a wise move. I will start paperwork and issuance immediately. This is a quick and easy paper move, and I foresee no issues. Travel safe."

"Loki … set a course for A11, one with the least chance of visible observation. Our arrival time is not as important as us arriving unseen."

"Understood, Commodore, executing course." Loki replied.

We landed in A11 at 0200. There was no need to go over to A14 or comm anyone, so we slept in. At 0600 we messaged Aunt J, telling her we'd be joining her for breakfast.

When we got to A14 I finally felt like I was home. As we walked toward the galley there were waves and greetings — "welcome home"; "the boss is back", "vacation's over." It was good to be back.

When we got to the galley, Aunt J was waiting for us. She grabbed us in the hug, teary eyed, like we'd been gone for years. We got our breakfast, finding that Chef was still in business, thank God. As we moved through the galley, cups were raised in welcome.

"I'm guessing things didn't go as planned," Aunt J said as we ate.

I smiled over my omelet, "You could say that."

"My other two OK?"

"Yep, they're fine, they send their love."

"Why didn't they come, too?"

"They had *Duty* to attend to," I said, smiling.

She frowned, "What kind of 'duty'?"

"We'll have a closed-door meeting and fill you in on everything," I said.

She nodded, glancing around, "OK."

"How's business been?" Jazz asked.

"Business has been great. The haulers have been running the mining circuit almost nonstop. The cargo ships are due in any time now. Our shares of the OEM have also been doing well. Bob says they will finish the hybrid haulers next week."

"You remember that tug family you helped a while back?" She asked.

"The Wanderer?" I asked.

"Yeah that's the one, he's become your biggest fan. He tells everyone who will listen how 'you are a man who holds to his word and will do right by folks' — his words," she laughed. It was good to hear her laugh. After breakfast we got refills of coffee and went to her office.

"OK, so what happened?" Aunt J asked. We gave her the whole story. The setup; the ambush; the ship battle and destruction; the messages to and from the Admiral; finding the Duty; the repair, refit and upgrade of Duty; the new GCD engine; the M-tronics discovery; our trip back in, and the destruction of Invincible's upgrades; the re-flagging under Titans banking system to protect our assets; and said we had heard about the Admiral being missing. She sat listening to all of it, asking a few questions.

"You kids have been busy. What's our next move?"

"Our concern is that once they realize they can't seize our assets, they'll come after family and friends. They may try piracy again and try to take our ships. But all our ships are shielded. We will use our security force to protect as much as we can.

"But that depends on how determined they are to get to us. Based on the ship to ship battle we had, they are pretty determined." I said.

"What if they come at us hard?"

"Step one would be to move everyone into A14 behind our shields. We had Chef lay in enough supplies to feed a full Hab for a year," I said.

"And if they push beyond that?"

"The last resort would be to evac everyone to the Duty and move to a new location where we can control the battlefield."

"I'm not happy about all this, but no one asked me." Aunt J said deliberately. "I think we should comm Bob and have him move all the yard work over here, along with all the workers, and get them behind our shields.

"Jocko has been keeping me up-to-date on the goings on out in the Hab rings. More and more toughs are showing up. They haven't caused any trouble yet, but it looks like they're getting ready to. The locals are getting nervous and the security police can't do anything because they aren't breaking any laws," Aunt J said.

"OK, let's get Bob over here, and make plans." I said. We had Bob fly over in the old Uncle J; it was shielded, so he was safe. We filled him in on some of what was going on, but not all of it.

"How many jobs do we have going on in the yard?" I asked.

"The only thing left is two hybrid haulers. We finished up all the smaller jobs."

"Can the hybrids move yet?" I asked.

"Oh yeah, they are done with them. They are just running

the last systems checks. We held our flight testing when you messaged you are on the way in, just in case you wanted to do the honors."

I thought for a moment. "We are closing the shipyard location for now. Load all the equipment into the hybrids and move them over here, together with all of our people. Let's get everyone moved who wants to come to work for us and be housed over here behind our shields. Let's try to do it as quietly as possible. They'll be passing through our security when they get here to keep everyone safe," I said.

"When do you want to start?" Bob asked.

"How long will it take you to load all the shipyard equipment?"

"At least two days."

"All right, put everyone to work loading equipment. Once that's done, start the move," I said.

"I guess I better get started, then," he said.

Aunt J told HR and Finance about our re-flagging on Titan. They had seen other companies do it, so they knew what to expect. We added Duty to our books, too, flagged through Titan. Once Aunt J had finished updating the business side, she met with us again and we gave her a personal shield belt.

As I fitted it to her, I cautioned, "you need to wear this all the time. Better to have and not need, than need and not have."

She nodded her head, "I will."

We went over to A12 and met with Commander Jones and Captain Smythe, bringing them up to date on the corporate ambush and ensuing battle. They didn't seem all that surprised, and I got the impression they'd seen this movie before.

"Invincible has been compromised, when someone tried to force their way past our safeguards and all the upgrades self-destructed." I added.

"I had hoped the Admiral would have been on her." Reggie said.

I nodded, "That would've been nice," I said. "We would have had one more ship on our side."

"It's gotten worse since we talked, Reggie said. They relieved the Admiral of command of the ESFL. The new commander is a puppet for the corporations and the politicians they control. Now Cole is missing. It hasn't come to actual battles yet, but they are choosing sides. There are those loyal to the ESFL Charter and Admiral Cole, and then there are those who've chosen the new regime. From what we can gather, it's about a 50/50 split so far.

"Invincible was a heavyweight for whichever side controlled her, but now she's off the board."

I told him what we felt would happen next, and the moves we were making to forestall attempts to hurt us. I warned them that they should be prepared for hostile actions.

We met with Aunt J again, "I think we need to fill our cargo ships with supplies before it hits the fan," I said.

"What do you have in mind?" Aunt J asked.

"Assign each cargo ship to buy supplies for a full-sized mining colony. They need not know which ones. Have them go to multiple places to fill the orders. Once they have a full hold, we'll meet them somewhere and unload them." I said.

"OK, I'll send the buy orders now." Aunt J said.

"Major ... comm Jocko." I said.

"Nic, glad you made it in safe. I'm assuming you're home."

"Yeah, I'm home, we need to meet, can you come here? We'll send a shielded grav-car for you."

"When?" He asked.

"Now, if you can."

"Give me an hour, then send a grav-car. The security teams know the location."

"OK."

"Mr. Aaron Stein is at the personnel hatch." Major said.

"Have him brought in." I said. Security escorted Aaron into the conference room.

"Good to see you again, Nic."

Shaking hands, "You, too, Aaron."

"I have paperwork for you to sign and then the re-flagging

is a done deal. We have already moved all financial assets into Titan accounts. Once these papers are signed that moves your company and ships under Titan government flagging."

We signed, he transmitted the documents, and that was that. "I'm assuming you will continue to use our firm for your business?"

"You assume correctly, Aaron, unless you open your own law office."

"Not yet," he said, smiling. "But I'll let you know if I do."

Jocko showed up about an hour after Aaron left and I met him as he exited the grav-car.

"Good to see you again, Jocko," I said, as we shook hands.

"You as well, lad." We moved into the conference room.

"You must've kicked over an anthill while you are out and about. The corporations are bringing in workers and union toughs like they were preparing for war," Jocko said. "They've bought off or threatened the Conclave Council into submission. And the heads of the security forces are in their pocket as well," he said.

"Whatever happened to that representative you wanted me to meet with?" I asked.

"That lowlife? That individual is a waste of O^2. Let's just say he's not the man I thought he was. He's a political coward, just a yellow belly," he said disgustedly. "The word's been put out, that anyone who has dealings with you will suffer the same fate."

"So, battle lines are being drawn," I said.

"That they are, and the pots are on high simmer."

"Who's the corporate point man on this?" Aunt J asked.

"I don't know, he stays on a big corporate ship docked over at the main port. He never leaves, just sends his flunkies out to do the dirty work."

"As far as the 'anthill' I kicked over. Well, the ants attacked, and I stomped on them." I said.

"How badly?" Jocko asked.

"Two corporate warships fired on us — that's piracy, so we destroyed them."

Jocko whistled as I told him about the setup and ambush, and how I had tried to talk them down. "They stopped talking and started shooting, and paid the price."

"What's your plan now?"

"We merged our people, and we're moving the Van Dam yards to A14. We've re-flagged everything under Titan to keep them from seizing our assets," I said.

"What if they push harder?"

"I'll be as peaceful as they let me. But I don't react well to threats, especially where my family and friends are concerned."

"Pardon the interruption, sir," said Major. "But we have a situation developing you need to see."

"On screen," I said. We all turned to watch the wall screen, and saw there was a mob gathering and moving toward A14. "Are they armed, Major?" I asked.

"Pipes, tools, some standards security batons." The scene changed to a power grid control room. "This is the main power control room for Alpha ring. They have been trying to isolate us from the rest of the Hab ring, but that's not possible as we are the main hub. They appear to be about to shut down power to the whole ring."

As we watched, that is exactly what they did.

"We are now operating on backup power, all systems normal. Alpha ring is without main power," Major said.

The scene changed to the A14 corridor where the mob was moving toward A14's cargo hatch.

"Major, increase gravity in A14 corridor. starting at 30 meters out, increase by 50 percent every 10 meters until you reach 3Gs." I said.

"Done." Major answered.

The mob stopped at the 10 meter mark, flattened by the heavy gravity, and crawled back to the 30 meter mark. Two men in the back of the mob began making a comm call.

"Major, capture that call," I said.

The speaker came on, "you said you cut their power and we could get in."

"We cut their power, we cut power to the whole ring."

"They must have internal backup generators, because they still have power, and we can't get in. You better let the boss know."

"Comms closed." Major said.

"That was obviously the brains of the group," Jocko said.

"Incoming comms from the Conclave Council." Major said.

"This should be interesting, put them on to receive video, send voice only," I said.

"Understood." Major said.

The screen came on, showing the Council's meeting room. "Good morning gentlemen, what can I do for you?" I asked.

"You've been found in violation of section 12 para 6B. You will immediately surrender yourself to the authorities until we resolve this matter."

I smiled, "to save me the time of looking that statute up, what is it I've supposed to have done?"

"Inciting riots, civil discord, and destruction of property. You have caused the main power grid in Alpha Ring to fail."

"That's interesting, I heard on the news it was widespread power fluctuations from the main Conclave fusion reactors."

Major immediately went to work spreading news about the main fusion reactors all over the net. We saw councilmen checking the net and nodding their heads at the chairman. The lights flickered in the Council room.

An aide leaned forward to the chairman, "We are on backup power, and our ring grid is down."

The chairman sat still for a moment, "It appears, Mr. Haydock, that we were in error, please forgive the intrusion."

"Channel closed," Major said.

"Well, they know I'm back now," I said.

Jocko looked at me, "Who is Major, and how did you do that?"

"The Major works in the intelligent group and he coordinates our responses."

"He and his team did an outstanding job. That put a kink in

their chain." Jocko said.

"Power restored to Alpha ring, and all other rings. It seems they have solved the problem at the main fusion reactor," Major said.

I chuckled, "Thank you, Major." I looked at Jocko, "Jocko you want to move your offices in with us?"

He thought for a moment, "Not just yet. We need to be out there being seen and keeping the wolves at bay."

I nodded, "if you need any additional support, let us know."

"I appreciate it, Nic."

"Will you stay and eat with us?"

"No, I need to be getting back, maybe next time."

"Fine, you know you're always welcome."

***

I stuck my head in Aunt J's office. "Can you get Mal's parents to move in to A14? I have a feeling things are about to heat up."

She nodded, "I'll get them in here, soonest. Oh, Doc and his brother are chomping at the bit to meet with you."

"I'll go see them now, thanks." I went to med-bay, where Doc and his brother were in a deep discussion. "Good morning, gentlemen."

"Good to have you back Nic."

"Good to BE back. So, I'm guessing from your enthusiasm you've found something from your samples?"

"Those are the most amazing things, and the possible applications are endless." DB said.

"So, they'd be safe for me to use to strengthen my hip? Because it's been giving me trouble."

"Yes, they are perfectly safe for you to use to increase your hip's strength. The nanites will also heal and strengthen the rest of your bones," DB said.

"Great, how long will it take and how long will I be laid up?"

"It should only take 3 to 6 hours for the treatment, there

should be no recovery time." Doc answered.

"We need to see the equipment to be sure and crosscheck our assumptions with the nanite programming." DB said.

I looked at him, "you need to know what you're getting into. The corporations are actively trying to steal our tech, and they are willing to kill or destroy us to get it."

"I don't care, I must be a part of this. These are history making tech breakthroughs, and the possibilities are limitless."

"I understand … that's what started this thing with the corporations in the first place." I said.

"I understand what you're telling me, but I'm still in. This is my life's work."

"OK, I'll have Buck set you up." I messaged Buck to bring the crated Auto-doc that was in Loki's cargo bay to A14's med-bay and set it up for Doc, ASAP.

CHAPTER 3

The next morning, families of the Van Dam workers showed up at A14, where Jazz and Aunt J helped get them assigned to quarters and get settled in. Bob messaged that he thought it would be safer to send the families over separately. The workers would come later on the hybrid ships, once they loaded everything.
"Commodore, the cyber-attacks on our systems have increased exponentially in the last 12 hours," Major said.
   "Any risk of them getting through our firewalls?"
   "Not in their lifetimes — although these are of higher quality than previous attempts."
   "Let me know if anything changes."
   "Yes, sir."
I dropped by med-bay to check on progress and found DB in a panic, "This is a catastrophe, we're done!"
   "What's going on, Buck?"
   DB cut Buck's response off, "The nanite auto-docs are not programmed. They will not work without that programming, and it's specialized programming!"
"Oh, is that all?" I said.
   "IS THAT ALL!" DB shouted, "ARE YOU NOT HEARING ME?" I held up my finger, and he stopped.
   "Everyone in the hanger hears you. Sit down and take a breath, and we'll fix this." I said. He clenched his fists but sat down.
I checked to make sure they had plugged the nanite Auto-doc

into the data port.

"Vee, have *Loki* download the nanite Auto-doc program from her med-bay to the new one here in A14 med-bay."

"Acknowledged." *Vee* said. We all watched as the nanite Auto-doc booted up. I ran a diagnostic program, and everything came up green.

I turned to DB, "next time, ask before you go off the deep end."

"I'm sorry, my emotions got away from me ... I apologize. I'll do better in the future."

I turned to Doc and pointed at the nanite Auto-doc, "your turn, Doc, let me know when you're ready."

"We will Nic, thank you." I left them with their heads together.

I couldn't sleep so I got a blanket and went to the observation dome and I sat watching the stars. I heard Jazz getting up. She came in the dome and I opened the blanket for her to get in. She sat down in front of me and leaned back onto my chest.

We held each other and watched the stars. "I've been thinking." I said.

"About?" She asked.

"Marriage."

She tensed a little, "Got anyone in mind?"

"I do actually, a beautiful girl."

"Oh? Tell me more." She said.

"The only thing is, I think she's got a thing for Mal."

"WHAT?" She screamed, jumping up, "I will scratch your eyes out!" She jumped on me, I grabbed her and held her tight. We were both laughing.

I looked into her eyes, holding her close. "Jasmine, will you marry me?" Tears ran down her face, she put her head on my chest, then suddenly sat bolt upright. "I can't! I mean, we can't!"

"Why not?" I asked, confused.

"Mal and Jade aren't here, they would kill us!"

"OK, we'll wait until we are all together." I said.

"In that case, I accept." She said, holding out her left hand. I took it and kissed it.

She looked at her hand, and then at me, "Aren't you forgetting something?" She asked.

"Oh yeah, you're right, we should message Aunt J right now."

"No! A ring! You're supposed to give an engagement ring when you ask someone to marry you."

"What?" I asked. She stared at me. "Is that a new rule or something?" She crossed her arms over her chest and gave me "The Look,".

"You mean like this one?" I asked, opening my left hand.

She gently took it, looking at it closely. "Your mother's?" I nodded, choked up. "That means more than any ring you could have bought me." She fell back into my arms and we both fell asleep.

It must be a woman thing, because the ring was the first thing Aunt J saw when we entered the galley at breakfast.

She grabbed Jazz's hand, looking at the ring, "Finally! You know, to be as smart as that boy is, sometimes I wonder!"

"I was hoping he'd come around." Jazz said.

"Girl, you couldn't run that boy off with a stick!"

"Y'all know I'm standing right here, right?" I said.

Aunt J came over and hugged me. "Your mother's ring?" I nodded. She patted my chest, "Good boy, she would be proud," she said, wiping the tears from her eyes.

"When is the wedding?"

"We have to wait for Mal and Jade," Jazz said.

"Maybe the other one will take the hint." They both laughed, looking at me.

"What?"

They shook their heads, "Then again, maybe not." They continued laughing and made wedding plans throughout breakfast.

Jazz looked over at me, "Do you have anything to say about any of this?" I took a swallow of my coffee, thinking of the safest answer, "Yes I do."

"What's that dear?"

"I'm glad I'm rich."

They both laughed, "He might be smarter than I thought." Aunt J said.

I was heading out to my office, "You have a message from Commander Jones, they are requesting a meeting with you in the med-bay." *Vee* said.

"Tell them I'm on the way."

"Done."

When I arrived Commander Jones, Doc, and DB were gathered around Cpl. Adam's bed. He'd been injured when assassins tried to kill me and did kill Travis.

"Good morning, gentlemen." They all turned, returning my greeting.

"Sir, I'd like to request the special nanite treatment for Corporal Adams." Commander Jones said. I swung around, looking at Doc and DB and clenching my jaw.

"They broke no confidence, Commodore, they only said it was experimental and may not work." Commander Jones said.

"Sir, I've been in this bed for months. My body has not responded to the normal nanite therapy, so I don't care if it is experimental. I'll take any chance to get out of this bed," the corporal said.

I look back at Doc, "Have you run the compatibility test yet?"

Doc was looking at his feet, "Yes."

"And?"

"All results were positive."

I look back at Adams, "You understand you'll be the first person we tried this on, someone has used it on others, but not us. We think we know what will happen, but we're not 100 percent sure."

Adams was gripping the bedsheet like a drowning man gripping a lifeline. "If it's a chance to get out of this bed, I'll take it, sir."

I nodded, "how soon can you do it Doc?"

"In about an hour."

I nodded, "permission granted."

They put Corporal Adams to sleep and administered the nanites. It was an hour before the Auto-doc stopped infusing any new nanites. He was held, sedated and said it would be 12 hours before it released him.

"Now I guess it's just a matter of wait-and-see." I said.

"Everything looks good according to his readings." Doc said.

"Doc, may I speak to you in your office?"

"Yes, sir."

We stepped into his office, and I closed the door.

"Doc, never do that again. I told you that the nanite technology was top-secret. You were to tell no one."

"It was his last chance," Doc said.

"I understand that, and hopefully it works. You should have come to me before you said anything to anyone. I would have probably agreed to the therapy for him anyway, but you painted me into a corner to get your desired outcome.

"How long do you think it will be before everyone in the Hab knows we have 'miracle working' nanites?"

"I'm sorry, sir. I didn't think of that, I was only thinking of my patient."

"I know, that's why you're a doctor and I'm in charge. I'll see you in 12 hours."

They moved Adams out of the Auto-doc and back into his bed. He was becoming more alert and was starving. We had a cart of food ready for him. Everyone is always hungry when they come out of the anesthesia after a major treatment. Seeing he was all right I told them I would check back with them later.

***

Later, they determined that Adams wasn't completely healed, but his bones were encased in M-carbon-fiber and the underlying tissues were healing.

"That looks like a successful test." I said.

"We think so, too," Doc said. "We're releasing him back to his unit. His cover story is that we used just plain additional nanite treatments. We'll bring him in everyday for checkups and will monitor his progress."

"We found something else, while we were working on Corporal Adams," DB said.

"What's that?" I asked.

"This machine can program the nanite's for more than just bone encasement."

"Like what?"

"Muscle enhancement, tendon and ligament strengthening, reflex enhancement, synaptic nerve enhancement. The notes say not all aspects will take in everyone, but most people respond to the nanite therapies."

"Let's keep an eye on Corporal Adams, mention none of your other findings to anyone." I looked pointedly at them.

"Yes, sir," they responded.

"We'll decide later what our next steps should be. After we see how Corporal Adams does, then I may decide to take more treatment. You keep studying the program, its uses, and side effects." I left them reviewing their notes.

***

The hybrid ships arrived, and we showed the work crews to their quarters and where their families would be living. We planned on doing small refurb and upgrade jobs for local rock wranglers, but nothing big for now. It would just be to keep the men busy and makework to pay the crew's salaries. We still had no word from Admiral Cole, and that was worrisome.

Corporal Adams was in perfect health after a week, so I decided to take the M-nanite therapy. I opted to take the bone encasement nanites only this time, figuring to consider the others later.

Jazz was there when I went to sleep and when I woke up, and, bless her heart, she started feeding me right away. Everything went perfectly, and I was up and around again the next morning.

We decided it was time to get back to *Duty*. Aunt J said she would hold the fort until we returned and brought Mal and Jade back for a double wedding.

I told Commander Jones to keep an eye on Jocko, "I don't think the trouble is over yet."

"I know it's a secret, but would you consider giving the security teams the bone encasement treatment?"

I thought for a moment, "who knows, it may save lives? Let's go see Doc." I said. When we got to med-bay Doc was examining Adams.

"Still a clean bill of health, sir. I want to thank you again for getting me out of that bed."

"I'm glad it worked," I said. He saluted us and left.

"Doc start administering the bone encasement nanites to the security teams, if they want it. Keep a close eye on them and if anything goes wrong, cease operations." I said.

"Thank you, sir," Commander Jones said.

"After a month, if there are no problems, consult with the Commander and start the other enhancement treatments. One at a time if they want it. But do not, I repeat, do not administer the synaptic treatment." They agreed.

Our two cargo ships were due in with their full loads for the two mining colonies. We sent coordinates for them to meet us and decided we would take them to *Duty's* astroid. We left quietly early the next morning. Loki went dark, and we eased out of Conclave-controlled space.

"Sir, we have two watchers, laying doggo at the edge of the rock fields."

"Understood, keep an eye on them."

They gave us no problems. As expected, we arrived at the rendezvous point before the cargo ships, so we sat in the edge of the rock field and waited.

"Commodore we're picking up our two cargo ships inbound, but they're being followed. The followers are at extreme range, and the cargo ships probably don't see her."

"Let's go see who is coming to visit." I said.

"Laser comm our two ships and tell them to hold course and speed for one hour and then cease thrust. We'll go check out the follower."

"Done." Loki said.

We moved out to get a look at the follower. "Anyone behind that one, Loki?"

"Long-range scans are clear, Commodore. The transponder on that ship is different, but other than that, it matches Gunny's cargo ship."

"Interesting. Open a channel."

"Open."

"This is a long way out to be making deliveries." There was no response, so we waited.

"A man's got to make a living." Gunny's image came up on my screen with, "positive ID 97 percent under it."

"That he does, and times are hard. You deliver anything special this run?"

"Yeah, they told me to bring you a cup." Gunny said.

"I thought all those broke."

"Nope, this is the last unbroken one, but it has a crack in it."

"You want to deliver it now or follow us in?"

"We'll follow you in."

"Roger, continue on course until you reached the other cargo ships. Then follow them, ETA to port is two hours."

"Roger, out."

"Channel clear," Loki said.

"Send an encrypted message to Travis and Duty that we are on the way in with three cargo ships. One of them is Gunny and may be carrying Admiral Cole. But cannot confirm."

"Sent. Message acknowledged."

We guided the three ships into Duty's rock. I could tell they had been busy, they had been mining operations going on. I guess it was to keep the supply bunkers full. *Duty* had her sides open in what I assumed was a mining configuration. We held position on *Duty*. All of *Duty's* upgrades appeared completed, and they had her smelter-refiner working.

Gunny landed by *Travis* and the other two cargo ships landed on the other side of *Duty*. I told one of the cargo ships to unload everything into *Duty*, and for the other one to stand by for instructions.

"Let's go see who Gunny's passenger is." I said.

"Commodore, there's something strange going on with *Travis*. No one is talking. They seem to be waiting for something or someone." Loki said.

"Travis, engage intruder protocols but don't alert our guests. Loki, yellow alert, *Duty* are you online?"

"Online Commodore."

"*Vee,* tell the cargo ships, and the cargo ships only, to hold their positions and cease all operations until further notice."

"Done."

"*Duty,* yellow alert, but quietly. Where are Mal and Jade?"

"They are both on the *Travis*."

"*Travis,* once I come on board, jam all internal comms."

"Roger Sir."

"Jazz, you and Buck stay here on *Loki*. Once I'm on board *Travis*, lift off in *LT* and take up high cover over Gunny's ship."

"You want me come with you?" Buck asked.

"No, stay here in case we need to make adjustments on the fly."

"Roger, sir."

I closed my vac suit and headed over to *Travis*, "Let's go see what's going on."

There was no one waiting at the hatch, so I entered and started toward the galley.

"All internal comms jammed." I nodded.

When I got to the galley, I opened my suit and got a cup of coffee like nothing was going on out of the ordinary. I looked at the table, Gunny was there but the admiral was not. Mal and Jade were there, and they did not look happy.

"Why don't you come and join us?" an officer I did not recognize said.

I smiled and walked over. There was a squad of armed Legion Marines lined up along the galley bulkheads.

I took a sip of coffee and looked at Mal, "belted?" They both nodded. "And you are?" I ask, looking at the unknown officer.

"Captain Hollingsworth, the new captain of this vessel," he said, smiling.

"I doubt that."

"Oh, and why is that?"

"Because I didn't hire you and this is my ship."

"I'm sorry, I'm confused. We have your friends here under our guns, we control the ship. Now we have you as well. I think that makes me captain." I felt a cold rage starting to build.

"Some people never learn," I said, setting my cup down on the table. "Isolation protocol." I said. All the doors shut, and the palm pads turned red.

"And you thought I was paranoid." Mal said.

"In hindsight, you were a hundred percent right," I said.

"Release control of the ship or she gets a bullet in the head," Hollingsworth said. My rage went black.

"You shouldn't have said that," Jade said.

"*Travis*, shield Archie and Gunny."

"Acknowledged," *Travis* said.

I looked at Captain Hollingsworth, "you were correct when you said you were confused. I'll give you three seconds for everyone to drop their weapons or I will take them from you in a most painful way."

All the marines chuckled. "At the count of three, shoot her." Hollingsworth said looking at me. I nodded.

"Three, two, one, zero." There was a gunshot.

I was already in motion, I back kicked the marine behind me. The kick crushed his pelvis and spine; he was out and down. More shots were fired. The marine to my left got my extended cyber fingers all the way through his throat and out the back of his neck. I roundhouse kicked the marine to my right, crushing the side of his head. He was dead before his body hit the deck.

All firing stopped. I turned to look at the table, my four had not moved. Captain Hollingsworth was over by the door with his pistol pointed at me. The other four marines had their rifles pointed at me too.

"We can play the numbers game again if you'd like, or you can drop your weapons."

"We have the admiral on our ship, and we'll kill him if you don't surrender," Hollingsworth said.

"There you go again, threatening my friends." I picked up my coffee cup and took a swallow.

"I swear, we'll kill him." He said.

"OK," I nodded, "Go ahead." I took another sip of coffee.

"What?"

"Go ahead, comm your ship and tell them to kill him," I said.

He tried to comm his ship but couldn't get through *Travis'* jamming. "Now put down your weapons and lay face down on the deck," I said. No one moved, "Don't make me have to put my coffee down." The Marines put their weapons on the deck and lay down on the deck beside them.

I look back at Hollingsworth, "you, come sit down." He came over and sat. "Slide your pistol down the table." He did so, leaving his hands flat on the table. I walked down to where the marines were lying, and two finger tapped each one behind the ear. They were out cold. I moved back up to where Hollingsworth was sitting.

I looked at Mal, "Any more on board?"

"Not that I saw." He answered.

"*Travis* any other intruders on board?"

"None, Commodore."

"So, Captain Hollingsworth," I sat down beside him, "You see that young man down at the end of the table?" He nodded. "He loves that woman more than life itself, and you ordered her execution. On top of that they're both my family."

Faster than the eye could follow, I struck his left hand with my cyber hand, flat palmed. It broke every bone in his hand. He screamed and passed out. I held him upright in the chair. His eyes fluttered as he came to, grabbing his broken hand, groaning.

"Hold on, that was only around one. We have more to go yet. Gunny, they've got the admiral over there?"

"Yes," he said, nodding.

"How many more marines do they have?"

"Another squad," He said.

I nodded. I took hold of Hollingsworth's right hand took his pinky finger in my cyber hand. He broke out in a cold sweat.

"Look at me." He did. "We can do this a nice way, where I ask you questions, and you answer them. Or, we can do it the hard way, where I ask questions and you don't answer.

"Then, I break off your finger and ask again. Now you'll notice, and this is an important point, notice I said break your finger "off", not just break your finger. Now part of me really hopes you don't answer the first time because I'm still upset with you about the whole ordering the execution thing.

CHAPTER 4

"Let's begin, shall we?" I asked.

"Who sent you?"

"Johnson."

"Why did you come after us?"

"They want your tech."

"Who is the 'They' who wants our tech?" He swallowed. I raised my eyebrows, smiling coldly.

"The Admiral, the Corporation, and Representative Johnson."

"What were your orders?"

"To secure you and your tech using Admiral Cole as bait, or by any means necessary."

I let go of his hand, "Thank you." I stood.

A knife blade extended from under Hollingsworth's right wrist. Rising, he made to stab at my throat. Before I could react, a gunshot sounded. His brains splattered the bulkhead behind him. He slumped back in his seat with a neat round hole in his forehead.

I looked at the other end of the table, Mal sat there holding his pistol. "Nice shot." I said.

"I've been practicing."

"It shows, appreciate the help."

He nodded, "Family."

I nodded, "Family."

"As I was saying before I was so rudely interrupted, I guess I better go get the admiral."

"How you plan to do that?" Gunny asked.

"I will go over there, knock on the door and asked them to

surrender. Where's the admiral located?"

"Med-bay when we left, he was in the Auto-doc."

"Travis, keep comms jammed, stand down from intruder protocol."

"Yes, Commodore." All the doors opened.

"Y'all tie up our guests here, I'll be back." "*Vee,* message Jazz to maintain over-watch position."

"Sent."

I walked up to the cargo ship's hatch, "*Vee,* can you hack the entry controls?" The palm pad turned green and the airlock hatch opened. I went in and through the airlock chamber.

There was a marine waiting on the other side. Before he asked, "I have a message from Captain Hollingsworth," I said.

"What?"

I grabbed his arm, pulling him toward me, and ear-tapped him out. I opened my vac suit and went over to the control panel. "*Vee,* can you hack the ship system, shut down lights and comms, and keep them down?"

"Yes, Commodore, just a moment ... ready on your 'go,' Commodore."

I shifted my eyes to night vision, "Go!" I said. The lights went out, and the comms went down. That caused chaos on the ship. Everyone was looking everywhere, trying to fix the lights and the comms. I walked through the ship ear-tapping everyone I met. I worked my way through the ship until I was the only one left conscious. I went to med-bay and found the admiral in the Auto-doc.

"Thank you, Vee, that worked nicely. Turn the lights on and bring the comms back online."

The lights came on, "Comms online," *Vee* said. "*Travis?*"

"Yes, Commodore?"

"I have control of the ship. Send Gunny and some of our men over to clean up this mess."

"Yes, sir."

"Jazz?"

"Nic, are you OK?"

"Yeah, I'm fine, you can land now, all boards are green."

"Roger, landing."

"*Vee,* message everyone to resume normal operations."

"Done."

Gunny returned to his ship to get his house in order, Archie was doing the same. *Travis,* being a former Legion ship, had a brig — handy.

I guess you never know when you may need one.

Mal, Jade and I returned to *Loki,* I arrived right after Jazz docked *LT.* I walked in on both girls hugging each other, squealing.

Mal looked at me, "What's going on with them?"

"Why are you asking me? I'm not female and they have their own secret handshake." We stood there watching and waited for them to stop whispering.

"PTSD, you think?" Mal asked. I shrugged my shoulders.

Jade finally turned to Mal holding out Jazz's ring hand, "They're getting married!"

"Uh-oh!" Mal said turning, looking at me.

"Momentary lapse of reason." I said, shrugging.

"Hmmm, I have those from time to time, so I understand. Congratulations." He shook my hand, smiling.

"Thank you," I said. "How are the upgrades going?"

That's when the girls screamed and attacked. I suddenly realized girls don't fight fair. I'm not sure but I think somewhere in the middle of the fight we, Mal and I, agreed to a double wedding.

"Not the most romantic proposal," Jade said, "But whatever works."

"But what a great story for the kids and grandkids." Jazz said, hugging Jade and laughing.

"This will be bad," Mal said.

"What did you say computer boy?!" We both shouted, "I love you," and ran. Laughter followed us all the way to the cargo bay. Buck was standing there looking at us as we ran in.

"You guys aren't too smart, are you?"

"You're fired," I said. We all laughed.

They unloaded the first cargo ship into *Duty*, and half of the second, sending the rest to *Travis*. We started doing upgrades using the new M-components right away. We recycled everything we replaced to make new components.

Jazz and Jade returned to harvesting rock, and I suspect — in between rock crushing — to planning a double wedding. *Duty's* rock was rich in mithrilium, which was probably why they landed here in the first place. We had the smelter-refiners on both ships running 24-7 to keep up with the harvested rock.

Mal and I were in *Duty's* GCD engine room studying its inner workings when the admiral messaged us asking for a meeting on board *Travis*. The meeting was being held at the Captain's table in the galley. Mal and I grabbed coffee and joined the admiral, Archie, and Gunny.

The fleet officer stood and reached across the table, shaking our hands.

"Thank you for saving our bacon," he said.

"Well to be fair, they were trying to steal one, if not all, of my ships and threatened to kill my friends," I said.

"Yes, and that was piracy, for which they have paid."

"I take it plans have changed," I said.

The admiral chuckled. "You could say that. To put it bluntly, I was outmaneuvered, and outplayed. I was playing using kings, queens, and bishops. I never noticed the pawns, knights, and rooks that defeated me.

"They had been placing people loyal to them in secondary positions while I thought having all the primary positions kept me secure. Apparently not.

"What we now have is two-thirds of the ESFL, for all intents and purposes, under the control of Representative Johnson. They also control ESFL's home port and all but one of its capital ships. Unfortunately, they also have Invincible, which throws a lot of extra weight in their favor."

"Not really. They tried to open the ACE computer on Invincible, and it self-destructed, taking our other tech with it,"

I said.

The admiral stared, frowning, at me for a moment, "Good, good!"

"That leaves you how many ships?" Mal asked.

"Twenty-four, but only 16 of those are fighting ships, six are support ships, the other two are troop deployment carriers," The Admiral said.

"Who controls a new SDRV?" Archie asked.

"They do."

"Ah," I said, "So that's why you're here." The Admiral nodded. "You want *Travis* back," I said.

He shook his head, "No not back, but we need your help to have any chance of retaking control of the ESFL."

"Can you legally do that? The civilian government relieved you of command. Technically, they are the proper authorities and can place whoever they want in charge of the ESFL," I said.

"But it wasn't properly done, it was a military coup to take over the ESFL. And in turn, to be controlled by the Corporations, which is against the ESFL charter. There is already a political firestorm burning on Earth and every other governmental body in space. They have ordered all ESFL ships back to home port to await the political outcome. In the meantime, all corporations will protect their own assets."

"In that case admiral, I guess we better get started upgrading your fleet."

"There is a mined out asteroid about two days' distance from us. It had been an early mining Hab but was abandoned years ago after the mithrilium played out. I have had Gunny preparing it as a forward operations base. That's where our fleet will rendezvous and then use it as their home port. You stay here and upgrade the ships as we send them to you. The first ship we need upgraded can be Gunny's cargo ship," The admiral said.

***

Mal, Jade, Jazz, and I stayed on *Loki*. Buck had gone back

over to help on the *Travis* with all the refits. Over dinner I asked, "what do you think of moving over to the *Duty*?"

"You mean moving over there permanently?" Jazz asked.

I nodded. "What about *Loki*?" Mal asked.

"Dock her on *Duty's* spine, in the docking area up there." I answered.

"I guess we have our choice of cabins." Mal said.

"No dear, Jazz and I have already chosen our cabins," Jade said.

"Oh good," Mal said sarcastically, "That saves me from having to worry about it." We all laughed.

"We also need to take *Duty* on a test flight. Once out in open space, we can power up the Cone Drive engines." I said.

"Let's move over tomorrow and get settled in, then we can decide when we want to test fly her." Jazz said.

"We also need to tell Buck, so we can move his stuff over too," Jade said.

We docked *Loki* with *Duty* and moved our things over to the quarters the girls had chosen for us. The original builders had built some penthouse type master suites. The whole top deck, right behind the cone, was taken up by two huge living areas, each with its own galley. Each had a large master bedroom and three smaller bedrooms.

The whole front of the apartment was armor glass that looked out over the cone. The master bedroom's outside bulkhead had armor glass that looked out the side of the cone. There was also a central entertainment area that joined the two apartments together with a formal dining room and its own galley. There was even a maid's and chef's quarters.

It stunned me at how opulent the place was. Mal and Jade found their way into the entertaining suite. Mal seemed as stunned as I was.

"What do you boys think?" Jade asked.

"It's official, you guys do the apartment hunting from now on," I said.

Mal nodded, "I think it will do nicely."

"Yeah, it'll do," I said, laughing.

We took two grav-carts and went down to storage to get supplies for our galleys. We put everything into the entertaining galley because we would probably always be eating together.

We shut down *Duty's* mining operations the next day and had crew stand by each system, hatch, and factory door as a safety precaution. We would run all ops from the bridge to check everything for our first full systems test.

"*Duty*, ship's status?" I asked.

"Environmental online, all boards are green; all shields online, all boards are green; gravitonics online, all boards are green; smelter-refinery off-line, all boards are green; all other systems online, in safety standby, all boards are green," *Duty* replied.

"Close outer factory doors." I said.

"Closing outer factory doors, recommend closing all outer doors." *Duty* said.

"Close all outer doors." I said, smiling.

"All outer doors closed; all boards are green." *Duty* said.

"Ship-wide announcement," I said.

"Ship-wide," *Duty* answered.

"All designated personnel report to their duty stations, all others may disembark. That is all," I announced.

We did a visual inspection of the bridge consoles to ensure all boards were green. Some 30 minutes later, *Duty* announced, "all non-assigned personnel have left the ship. Engineering reports ready, Commodore."

"GCD." I said.

"GCD, Buck here."

"How are we looking, Buck?"

"We're online, in safety standby, all boards are green."

"Roger, bridge out." I took a last look around and satisfied myself that all was well.

"Ladies if you would take the helm and navigation, we'll start the next phase." I said. Mal was monitoring all his readouts and power consumptions.

"*Duty,* bring gravitonics online, lift the ship 1 meter and hold." I said.

"Gravitonics active, lifting ship, 1 meter and holding."

I looked at Mal, "Did we move?"

He nodded, "1 meter and holding."

"Power consumption?"

He grinned, "3 percent"

"No way! Their records said they were using 70 percent power to lift at this weight and gravity." I said.

"Yeah, I know," Mal answered.

I grinned, "What about the shields?"

"That 3 percent is total power usage, including shields," he said, chuckling.

"Good Lord in heaven!"

"*Duty,* lift ship to 100 meters and hold."

"100 meters and holding."

"Readings on boards?"

"All boards are green," *Duty* answered.

"Helm, take us on a circuit of the plains, ahead slow," I said.

"Aye Commodore, ahead slow," Jazz replied. Duty was amazing. There were no vibration, and the only sound was that of the ventilation and recirculation systems.

"Navigation, plot a course to open space."

"Aye, course to open space plotted," Jade answered.

"Helm, take us to open space."

"Aye, on course for open space," Jazz answered.

We were only using our gravitonics to push off asteroids for our forward motion. Power consumption was holding steady at 3 percent.

"Approaching the edge of the rock field," Jade said.

"All stop." I said.

"Answering all stop," Jazz said.

"*Duty,* go dark."

"Dark."

"Anything on long-range scans?" I asked.

"All scans are clear."

"*Duty*, bring main engines online active."

"Main engines online active."

"Helm ahead 10 percent power."

"Ahead 10 percent power Aye."

Mal and I watch the readings and saw that we were up to 5 percent power usage.

"Helm increase thrust to 20 percent."

"20 percent aye."

"Helm increase thrust to 30 percent."

"30 percent aye." Energy readings increased to 15 percent.

"Helm increase thrust to 50 percent."

"50 percent aye."

"*Duty*, status of boards?" I asked.

"All boards are green."

"Helm hold course and speed."

"Holding course and speed, aye."

I looked at Mal, "She's doing great."

"Yeah and I haven't even tweaked her yet," he said smiling.

"Cease forward thrust, let our inertia take us." I said.

"Ceasing forward thrust, aye."

"Ready to bring GCD online active?" I asked.

"We are out for a test flight," Mal said.

"I'm game." Jazz said.

"Me too." Jade nodded.

I nodded, "Buck?"

"Yes, Commodore."

"We are about to take the GCD active, you ready?"

"Yes, sir. Let's fire this baby up."

"*Duty*, you have the helm."

"I have the helm," *Duty* answered.

"*Duty*, bring GCD to active status but do not engage."

"GCD now active."

A gantry slid out of the cone's point, extending about 20 meters in front of the ship.

"*Duty*, engage GCD to the same speed as a normal engine speed would be at 50 percent power."

"GCD engaged at normal engine speed of 50 percent," *Duty* said.

I looked at Mal, he nodded. "*Duty*, status of boards?"

"All boards are green."

"Buck how are we looking down there?"

"All green, the generators aren't even breaking a sweat."

"Understood, let me know if it changes."

"Roger, Sir."

I looked at Mal, "Power usage?"

"5 percent." He said pointing at the screen.

"*Duty*, what was the fastest this ship has ever traveled using the GCD?"

"It never exceeded .378C, because of power requirements."

"*Duty*, increase speed to equal 100 percent of normal engine thrust."

"100 percent."

We look to the power usage. "10 percent." Mal said.

"*Duty*, return us to where we started using the GCD, increase speed so we arrive in half the time."

"Understood, engaging."

The star field swept around, and the power usage went up to 13 percent. "Status of boards?" I asked.

"All boards are green," *Duty* answered.

"Buck, how are we looking?" "No change, Sir."

"Roger, out."

"Designated coordinates reached," *Duty* announced.

"I would say that was a successful test flight," I said.

"That was an amazing test flight," Jazz said.

"*Duty*, test flight results, corporate top-secret close hold," I said.

"Top-secret, close hold," *Duty* said.

"*Duty*, take GCD to safety standby."

We watched the gantry retract.

"*Duty*, take us back to *Duty's* rock."

"Course plotted, engaging."

"Bridge to engineering."

"Engineering."

"How is everything go down there?"

"All green Commodore, you must not have pushed her, you didn't use that much fuel."

Mal and I were smiling, "Well, that was just her first run, we want to take it easy on the old girl. Bridge out."

Duty landed, "Designated coordinates reached, all boards are green."

"*Duty,* conduct post flight checks and go to safety standby."

"Understood, Commodore, all systems to safety standby."

***

Duty resumed smelter-refining operations the next morning. Buck went back to *Travis* to help with the refits. Jazz and Jade resumed their rock harvesting. Mal was working in his shop, and I was working in mine. Gunny was overseeing the upgrades on the ship.

My mind kept going back to the gantry that extended out of the nose cone. Why did they need it? I understood the concept; it kept the gravity wave out in front of the cone-shaped nose. It helped shape the wave, but why didn't they…

"Oh, my Lord, it's because they didn't have OFEs. They couldn't use them to project a bow grav-wave. They had to physically project the bow grav-wave ahead of the ship." I said, shaking my head.

I ran through my figures. They looked right, so I reran them and got the same answer. Using the baseline number, I extrapolated out to a final configuration. I ran the numbers again and got the same results. I fed all my data into the M-Comp and got the same results.

I figured my power usage based on those numbers. They fell right in line with the results we got on our test flight. The perfect configuration number came out to be 5-23-47. I needed to talk to Mal.

I found Mal bent over what looked like a missile housing.

He looked up at me.

"Do I want to know?" I asked.

He shook his head, "Not yet."

"Good, because I want you to look at something."

"OK, what have you got?" He asked.

"You remember when *Duty* told us they could only reach .378C?" I said.

"Yeah, because they didn't have enough power to push beyond that speed."

"Right, and another thing. Why the gantry out in front? That was bothering me. The reason they needed so much power was, they were forcing a bow grav-wave to stay in position. They needed the gantry for a focal point, because they didn't have OFEs to focus the grav-wave without it."

Mal's eyes lost focus, I waited. "Did you run the numbers?"

"Yeah, six times, you will not believe what they came out to be. You remember that emitter, number C-23, that started this whole shield discovery?"

"Yeah."

"According to all the figures the perfect numbers are 5-23-47."

He looked at the numbers for a minute, "5 OFEs to set the base of the cone. 23 segments for the OFEs. And the center focusing emitter is a 47 segment OFE," he said. I nodded. "That could be installed on any ship in no time at all, with little retrofitting."

"It just needs an ACE to control it," I said.

"They're going to kill us again," Mal said, chuckling.

"They'll have to get a line."

"We need to test it on another ship. *Loki*?" He asked.

"That's what I'm thinking, no one will even notice the change, and she's already got more than enough power."

We went down to the M2F 3-D and plugged in the specs for five 23 segmented M-OFEs; one 47 segmented M-OFE; and M-cable to replace the old cable runs. Two hours later we were pulling cable, replacing, and recycling old emitters to make the new ones.

I finished installing the M-OFEs, while Mal worked his computer magic. When I finished, I went inside *Loki,* and made coffee.

"How's it coming?" I asked, as I handed Mal a cup of coffee.

"We're almost there, I had *Duty* download all the GCD info to *Loki*. They're talking about now. We'll need to power everything up to make our last adjustments."

"And tweaks," I said.

He smiled, "and tweaks."

"We are going to comm the girls up for a test flight, right?" Mal asked, smiling.

"Dang right we are, I'm not taking a beating over a test flight," I answered laughing.

"*Loki* open a channel to Jazz."

"Open."

"Jazz, Mal and I are taking *Loki* out on a survey flight, you girls want to come?"

"We'll be there shortly."

CHAPTER 5

We told everyone we were going out on a survey run, and *Loki* lifted off. Buck stayed on the *Travis*. We didn't tell the girls about the GCD we installed.

"Jazz, take us to open space. *Loki,* go dark."

"Dark."

Mal was working at his M-Comp, "I need to upgrade all the sensors to M-tronics," He mused. I brought coffee around to everyone.

"Where you boys taking us?" Jazz asked.

"Consider this a dinner cruise," I said.

"What are you cooking?" Jade asked.

"Soup and sandwiches," I said. We stopped for dinner.

As we ate Jazz asked, "what you guys really up to?"

Mal and I feigned ignorance, "What? We want to spend quality time with our fiancés." Mal said. Jazz and Jade both just gave us "The Look".

"OK, Nic had another epiphany," Mal said.

"And Mal helped me put together," I said.

The girls looked around, "where is it?" Jazz asked.

"It's better if we show you," I said.

We got up and went to the bridge. "*Loki,* bring GCD online active."

"GCD active."

The girls looked at each other, "No way!" Jazz said.

I nodded, "It turned out to be easy."

"They're gonna kill us again," Jazz said. We all laughed.

"*Loki,* take us out into open space," I said.

"Course set for open space, engaging. ETA three minutes."

We sipped our coffee, waiting. "Open space," *Loki* announced.

"*Loki,* zero thrust from main engines and put them in safety standby."

"Zero thrust, safety standby."

"Engage GCD to 50 percent of normal main engine speed."

"GCD at 50 percent NES."

"Condition of boards?"

"All boards are green," *Loki* replied.

Mal was programming his tweaks. I waited. After a few minutes he looked up, "We're good."

"*Loki* increase speed to 100 percent NES," I said.

"100 percent NES, all boards are green." I looked at Mal, raising my eyebrows. He shrugged his shoulders.

"Increase speed to 200 percent NES," I said.

"200 percent NES, all boards are green."

"Unbelievable," Jade said.

"Sweet!" Jazz said.

"*Loki* increase speed to point one C." I said.

"Point one C, all boards are green, sensors are clear."

I looked at Mal, "power usage?"

"4 percent total usage, including Shields." He said, grinning from ear to ear.

"Amazing," I said, "Increase speed to point 3 C."

"Point 3 C, all boards are green, sensors are clear."

"There's another record." Mal said.

"Power usage?" I asked.

"6 percent." He answered.

"*Loki* return to where we started using the GCD and stop."

"Returning to GCD engagement point."

Once we reach the coordinates, Jazz took the helm. "Jazz keep us out in open space and practice maneuvering using the GCD. I suspect it will be the same as with the normal engines, but I'm not sure, you never know," I said.

"Let's see how she does." Jazz said.

"I think you're right, and if so, we'll be able to operate on

100th of the fuel usage." Mal said.

Jazz and Jade did their pilot thing, twisting, turning, and rolling. I didn't see the difference, but I'd wait for Jazz to tell us. After an hour, Jazz said, "that was so sweet, she's more responsive."

"So let's try using the GCD all the time unless we need the other engines. We will also change *Duty's* GCD gantry to use our segmented OFEs. We'll use the same formula except we'll use a seven OFE base instead of five." I said.

Mal nodded, "No one will see us engage GCD, it won't react any differently."

I nodded, "That's what I'm thinking too. Jazz take us back to *Duty's* rock please."

***

The next day we got Buck to help us install the new GCD-OFEs on *Duty*. "You're kidding, it was that simple?" Buck asked.

"Well, they did all the hard work, they just didn't have segmented M-OFEs," I said.

"So, we're just going to mount the focusing emitter on the end of the gantry." Buck said.

"Yes," I nodded. "But we won't have to extend the gantry to get the GCD to create the bow grav-wave."

"On it." Buck said. Buck and I finished the GCD-OFE install, Mal was working on calibrating them.

"How's she looking?" I asked.

"We are dialed in," Mal said.

"I've been thinking." Buck said.

"Uh-oh," Mal said smiling, "Every time one of us says that, it causes trouble." We both chuckled.

Buck smiled, "I don't think it's 'That kind' of thinking. It's about the 2 million creds I will get from *Duty*."

"What about it?" I asked.

"I would like to take stock in HMS instead of the creds." He said.

I thought for a moment, I looked over at Mal. He shrugged

his shoulders, "Sounds reasonable, but the board would have to approve it."

"And it so happens there is a board meeting tonight," I said.

Buck nodded, "I appreciate the consideration."

After dinner, over coffee, we open the board meeting. Buck is not present because we would talk about him buying into the company.

"Buck wants shares instead of creds?" Jazz asked.

Mal and I nodded. "That would be easier, and we wouldn't lose 2 million creds of operating capital," Jade said.

"That's what I was thinking, and that's a big incentive on our part to do it." I said.

"Non-voting member?" Mal said.

"Correct," I said, nodding.

"He does know a lot of our secrets, and if he owns part of the company, that will keep him with us," Jade said.

"There is that," I said.

"I think we should sweeten the deal to keep him 'all in' with us," Jazz said.

"What did you have in mind?" Mal asked.

"Let's offer him, I don't know, say 2.25 million creds worth of HMS stock for his share," she said.

"That will keep his attention on HMS' doing well and staying with us," Jade said.

I nodded, "Any objections?" Everyone shook their heads. "OK, the deal is approved." I said.

"Now on to more important decisions, that being the GCD. So far we're the only ones who know about it. Once again, we find ourselves in need of some covering story. Not as complete as before, but we'll still need some. As soon as the corporations find out about it, they will pull out all the stops. They'll send their ESFL after us and ours." I said.

"By the way Mal, Aunt J got your parents to move into A14." Jazz said.

"How'd she manage that?" Mal asked.

"I don't know, she went out, they came back with her." Jazz

said.

"Was she carrying a gun?" He asked chuckling.

"Not that I could see," she said, smiling.

"So do we sell or give GCD to the loyal part of the Legion, or do we keep it to ourselves?" I asked.

"The shields and the ACE comps already have them head and shoulders above everyone else." Jade said.

"And no one else is even close to our tech." Jazz said.

"OK, so we hold on to the GCD for the time being. What about equipping our ships with GCD?" I asked.

"The more ships we put them on, the more chance there is of the secret getting out." Mal said.

"That's true, but the simple fact is that eventually the tech will get out. We'll just have to be ready for it, and ready to react to it." I said.

"Do we register the patent?" Jazz asked.

"That's a double-edged sword. If we do the rumors will start. If we don't, we can't sell it in the open. Let's wait and see for now, we'll revisit it next meeting." I said.

The next day Jazz and Jade went back to harvesting rock. I messaged Buck and told him he now owned 2.25 million creds worth of HMS. He was ecstatic and appreciative of the deal we made him. Mal went back into his mad scientist lab.

Meanwhile I upgraded my baton with M-components, which doubled its power and battery life without changing the size.

Our first cargo ship, *Cargo One*, was out of refit. We loaded her with refined metals. We were sending her to Titan to sell our product and bring back supplies.
We sent the crews that had been working on her over to help finish Gunny's ship.

Once Gunny's ship was completed, we loaded it with refined metals, so they could sell it and have operating creds. We met with Gunny and the admiral before they left.

"We will sell the metals — thank you for that — and buy supplies for the fleet. We have sent the two Marine deployment carriers to the operations base. If you could send a supply ship to them, that would be a great help," the admiral said.

"We can cover that. When should we expect the first ship for refit?"

"I'm not sure yet. We're pulling all our ships back to the New Legion base. We'll let you know when they arrive."

"In that case we'll load up on product and head back to Conclave Station to give the crews some time off. We'll be waiting for your message," I said.

We sent our second cargo ship, *Cargo Two*, to Titan to buy supplies for the base, then harvested rock and fed the smelter-refiners on both *Travis* and *Duty*, until all our storage bunkers and cargo bays were full.

"*Duty* to *Travis*, we are ready to lift for home." I said.

"Roger *Duty*, right behind you."

"Roger *Travis*, *Duty* has the lead. *Duty*, take us to open space using GCD at normal engine thrust only."

"Once we reached open space, set a course for home base, A14. Use an elongated course, approaching from deep space. Send *Travis* the adjusted course."

"Adjusted course sent."

"Increase speed to 50 percent."

"50 percent."

***

The two weeks we took to get back to A14 passed quickly. Every day we explored *Duty* learning more of its abilities and design.

"We are clear all the way in to A14," *Duty* announced.

"Very well, send an encrypted message to Aunt J that we are on the way in."

"Encrypted message sent."

Both ships landed in A14's parking yard. We set security protocols in place, set port watches, and released everyone for shore leave. All the crews were paid, including bonuses, and given two weeks leave.

Aunt J was in the hanger to meet us. The ladies had their heads together, and I heard, "Double wedding." They all giggled.

Aunt J hugged Mal and I. "How long are you in for?" She asked.

"At least two weeks, that's the amount of leave we gave all the work crews." I answered. We stepped over, so Aunt J could look through the hanger door enviro-field to see the *Duty*.

"Wow, she is huge."

"That she is, and she special too." I said.

Suddenly, there was a blinding light, but our contacts blacked out, saving our eyes. *Major* blacked out the hanger door as his shields slammed in the place.

Red emergency lights flashed. "Medical emergency on the parking yard, medical emergency on the parking yard. This is not a drill, this is not a drill," *Major* announced over the loudspeaker system.

Major's shields became transparent again, "Major, report."

"One of the tugs that was awaiting refit engine's core went critical and exploded."

"Accident?" I asked.

"Negative, that was deliberate. All power to the tug was shut down."

"Collect all info on the tug and anyone who has touched it in the last month. Go to red alert, message security teams to be prepared for attempts to attack all assets."

"Done."

"There is a large group of people gathering at the end of Alpha spoke, and it appears to be the same group that tried to attack us before," *Major* said.

"Increase grav outside our hatches to 3g."

"Done."

Security teams and medical teams arrived to help the injured. Aunt J directed traffic. They left the dead lying and concentrated on the living.

"Commodore we have two corporate ships approaching at attack speeds and vectors. *Vanguard* has launched from A12 at full power, weapons hot."

"*Vanguard*, if they fire on you or us, smoke'em! If they try to get past you to us, smoke'em! I have your back."

"Never doubted it, Commodore," Captain Smythe said.

"Commander Jones, deploy shielded grav-cars to support Jocko, I think he's gonna need it. This thing just went hot."

"Roger, Commodore, deploying."

"*Vanguard* is warning off the corporate ships, but they are ignoring the warning." *Major* said.

"Target them with the Hab rail guns," I ordered.

"Targets acquired. The enemy ships have fired on *Vanguard* … no damage reported. *Vanguard* has destroyed the first corporate ship. The second ship is inbound and has fired missiles. Hab rail guns are engaging missiles… all missiles destroyed… enemy ship has launched a second salvo. *Vanguard* has engaged and destroyed the second ship. Hab rail guns engaging incoming missiles… all missiles destroyed. *Vanguard* is taking up a high cover position. No damage sustained, all boards are green."

"Understood," I said.

"Commodore, there is a heavy weapons grav-vehicle in route to a Jocko's headquarters. It will arrive just after our shielded grav-cars." *Major* reported.

"Have them evacuate Jocko and all teams through the Van Dams' Shipyard. *Vanguard* to provide cover and extract," I said.

"*Vanguard* copies, en route to Van Dam for fire support and extraction."

I comm'ed Doc, "Do you need anything?" I asked.

"We're handling it, but some of these people are bad shape. Some have most of the bones in their body broken. It would help if we could use the special nanites."

"Do whatever you have to do to save our people. If you need anything, let me know."

"Roger, out."

"*Vanguard* holding station at the Van Dam's yards," *Major* said. I re-focused on my surroundings, to find that Mal, Jazz, and

Jade had formed a circle around me, directing people away while I dealt with bigger issues.

"Jocko's team is evac'ed and is en route to Van Dam's yards. We are being fired on, but no damage reported to shielded grav-cars, collateral damage to the corridor," a team leader reported.

"Understood." I answered.

"Jocko's g-car has entered Van Dam's yard, but an enemy heavy weapons vehicle is pursuing…

"*Vanguard* engaging…

"Heavy weapons vehicle destroyed," *Major* said.

"Commodore, all security teams and principal are safely aboard, extraction complete, no casualties." *Vanguard* reported.

"Very well, deliver Jocko to A12, then return to high cover," I said.

"Roger Commodore … A12, then returning to high cover."

"*Major*, anything new on the group in Alpha spoke?" I asked.

"One person approached but as soon as he felt the grav change he turned back. There's been no further movement."

"Monitor and record all comms."

"In process."

I refocused and saw that four fully armed security guards had replaced my three friends. "*Major*, location of Mal, Jazz, and Jade?"

"All three are assisting in med-bay."

They had set up a temporary morgue in the far corner of the hanger, with curtains set up around it. I went over and entered the area; the guards stepped aside for me. They had laid our dead out in neat rows covered with white shrouds.

My people. I stopped each one and looked upon their faces, so I would never forget. Eighteen… they had killed 18 of my people. For what? Tech? Greed? Lust for power?

I don't know how long I stood there, letting my black rage wash over me and become cold hatred. If there was ever any mercy in my heart for the corporations and their lackeys, it was now gone.

I realize my hand was hurting, and saw that I had had my fist clenched so hard, for so long, it was aching. I relaxed it.

Lost in thought, I stood silent vigil over my people. The security company had set an honor guard in full dress uniforms at the entrance and the four corners, heads bowed. I was vaguely aware of people filing through to pay their respects.

Families mourned, but no one approached me, and I stood my vigil alone. At some point the honor guard was silently changed. Somewhere in the night I said my goodbyes.

"I'm sorry I didn't do a better job protecting you," I whispered. "But I promise you, I will find out who was responsible for this and repay them with interest. We've been saying that business is war. Now they have killed those under my protection.

"Now it's just war. As a reminder and a warning to all those who see me and hear about me, my eyes will remain the color of my rage — black.

"Father God give them grace, peace, and grant them entrance into your Kingdom, Amen"

I stopped by the med-bay to check on our wounded. "You need anything, Doc?"

"No," said Doc, pausing briefly as he took in my solid black eyes. "We've got everyone taken care of, as soon as an Auto-doc comes open we put another patient in. Everyone is stable."

I nodded and walked around the med-bay, looking in on every patient. 20 of them — 20 people in enormous pain, for greed.

I stopped by the galley. I wasn't hungry, but I knew I needed to eat something. As always, there was soup and sandwiches, and I ate but tasted none of it. I went up to our apartment and took a long hot shower. Jazz was asleep. I went out into the observation dome and stared at the heavens until I dozed off.

I didn't feel like eating when I woke up, so I went straight to my office and had coffee. "*Major* do you have what I ask for?"

"Yes, Commodore."

The screen came on showing two men meeting: "All you

have to do is plug this device into the engine control console's wiring harness," said one of them. "Take the tug in for service and repair, we'll take care of the rest."

"If I do that, you will pay me 10K creds?" asked the other.

"Yes, 10,000 creds, as agreed."

The internal security cams on the tug showed him installing the device, and several other cam views showed him flying the tug to A14.

"*Major*, saturate the net with this and a vid of the explosion, but not of our rescue operation."

"Done."

"Pull up all the video on every councilman's meeting until you find out who has been bought, blackmailed, or threatened into the Corporation's pockets. Post those to the net.

"Whatever system tries to take them down, crash it."

"Done."

"Search the asteroid mining charts and find the biggest abandoned asteroid Habs and their locations." The screens went live with four locations.

"Show me selection number three." It had a population of 6,000 when it closed, and looked like a helmet sitting on the plank. That was an option, I thought.

There was a knock on my door, and Jazz stuck her head in. "Can I come in?"

"Of course, you can come in!" I said.

She came around my desk and rested her hip on it. "You OK?"

"As OK as I can be at the moment," I said.

"Are you up to having a meeting? A few, actually."

"Where is your meeting?" I asked.

"Boardroom, with all the command staff."

"Sounds like a good start."

CHAPTER 6

We entered the boardroom where all the command and management level staff were waiting. "Please, everyone take your seats."

I remained standing. "First, I'd like to thank everyone for all the help they gave us yesterday. I thought I had already seen the worst day of my life, but I was wrong. If there were any doubts that the corporation was at war with us, yesterday removed it.

"Until yesterday they were at war with us, and we were on the defensive. Today I'm at war with them. Not everyone will agree with me and want no part of this — and that is perfectly understandable. Anyone who wants to resign and go work somewhere else is free to do so, with no hard feelings and full pay for your time worked and bonuses.

"Before you decide, I want you to know that we are leaving. If we stay here too many innocent bystanders will be hurt. Where we are going, I can control the where and when of the battle space. My ship outside can house 1,000 people and is a factory smelter-refining mining ship. We have provisioned her, and she is ready to go.

"We also have two cargo ships, three haulers, two hybrid haulers, an SDRV, and an armed exploration ship.

"I'm sure you've heard rumors of a split in the ESFL ... that's not a rumor, it's a fact. If you go with us, you'll be working on upgrading what they are calling the New Legion's ships.

"The New Legion is under the command of Admiral Cole, the Admiral of the Legion who was ousted by a military coup, orchestrated by Representative Johnson and the Corporation. They have pulled all other Legion ships back to Earth. This gives the corporation's ships free rein out here.

"As part of your pay, I will house you, feed you, and also pay a wage.

"If you are a surviving family member of those killed in our service, you have a guaranteed berth, if you want it. No one will discuss our destination, but once there we will have plenty of work and better protection than here.

"That's all for now; we'll meet again tomorrow at 1300. Go spread the word. I'd like security personnel and captains to stay behind, please, but everyone else is free to go."

Once everyone but those asked to stay had gone, I started again. "Gentlemen, you are under a different contract, but most of you didn't sign on for a war. If you want to leave, no hard feelings, but I need to know now." I looked at each one. No one moved. When I looked at Reggie, he smiled and said, "We're still riding for the brand, Commodore." I nodded.

"Commander Jones, our agreement is of a different sort, but going up against heavy weapons and Legion Marines wasn't part of our deal. No hard feelings if you want to opt out," I said.

"Commodore, I think me and mine still owe some on the equipment you've given and loaned us. We'll," he looked at Reggie, "stay with the brand."

"Jocko you're welcome to come along for the ride, I will need someone to help manage all this, especially when we set up a Hab somewhere."

"You got room for my boys too?"

I nodded, "and their families. The way I figure it, if every one of my employees comes with their families, we are still under 500 people. There will be a need for support people, and miners," I said.

"When do you plan on leaving?" Jocko asked.

"Four days at the latest. Send everyone you have coming with us ASAP, so we can get a headcount."

He nodded, "We'll be here."

"If there is nothing else, let's go spread the word, and get packing."

The family stayed. "What are you planning, Nic?" Aunt J asked.

"Pretty much what I laid out. We're going back out there to refit ships for the NL, and rain fire and brimstone down on any corporate ship that even looks our way."

"You're not going out looking for a fight, are you?"

I shook my head, "no, if they don't come after us, I will not go after them. But based on past behavior, I think I can count on them to be stupid… they'll come after us."

"And if they come?"

"It will get expensive for them," I said.

"Do you ever plan on coming back?"

"Yes! My family helped start Conclave. We own all that we live in, and they can't have that. *Major* will keep watch for us, keep everything secure and pass on Intel about our enemies."

***

Bob and his crews inspected all the ships that were within the blast radius of the tug bomb. They all had shields up per SOP, so there was no damage to them.

We started loading operations that afternoon, making sure all the ships' tankage was full. Once we left, *Major* would put the facilities into hibernation until we returned.

We left everything viable, so that whoever came back, whenever they came back, would be able to walk into a fully functional, fully stocked, and fully equipped facility. We were also leaving a small M2F3D printer, and all our plans and inventions locked under cyber code in *Major*'s database.

Mal was working in his shop when I found him, tweaking the missile I had seen him working on before. I leaned against the door frame, and waited. He finally looked up at me.

"Do I want to know?"

"You do now," he said.

I nodded, "OK, what have you been working on?"

"You know that ear tap thing you do?"

"Yeah, the mag pulse that knocks people out."

He nodded, "I was thinking, what if we up the power? Would it knock out a crowd of people?"

I looked at the compact device, "or a whole ship full of people?" I asked. He nodded. "Interesting theory ... have you tested it?"

"Kinda."

"Kinda?" I asked.

"You remember those Marines that tried to kill Jade?"

"Oh yeah, I *remember* them."

"I shot them with it, and they dropped like a bag of rocks."

I busted out laughing, "you didn't!"

"I did. Twice actually, once through the bulkhead to see if it would work."

"I take it, it did work?"

"Like a charm."

"Any side effects?"

"Not that I could tell, but I didn't really care."

"I see your point, OK, back to the missile. Did the mag pulse affect any of the electronics, like an EMP pulse?"

"Nope, this operates at a different mag wave frequency. So I was thinking, what if we could do the same to a whole ship, knock them all out and take the ship?"

"I hear a 'but' in there."

He nodded his head, "If the power level is high enough to ensure full coverage it may knock them out permanently," He said.

I shrugged my shoulders, "I can live with that. If they fire on us, that's piracy, and that's an automatic death sentence. They haven't had a problem spilling our blood, I'm not going to be squeamish about spilling theirs."

"I feel the same way ... they killed our people, so it's an eye for an eye time."

"How many missiles are you going to build?" "Two for now, in case we have to send one missile to each end of a ship to ensure coverage."

"What ship were you planning to launch them from?" I asked.

"I was thinking *Loki*."

***

We departed on Day Four after the attack on A14, and the final headcount leaving with us was 653. No one opted to stay behind. Our two hybrid haulers and *Loki* were docked on *Duty* while their crews were housed in *Duty's* quarters. When we sailed, *Duty* took the lead, *Travis* followed, and *Vanguard* had rearguard.

We followed the same course we came in on to make it harder for them to follow us. When we were two days out, *Vanguard* called us.

"We seem to have a follower, Commodore."

"How far back?"

"We caught her on long-range scan, and she's a big one. At least frigate-sized."

"ESFL?"

"I don't think so. She's probably corporate, aince she's acting too brazen to be Legion, even with a stupid skipper."

"Keep an eye on her."

"Roger, Commodore."

"You girls have the helm, Mal and I need to take care of something."

"Don't get into trouble," Jazz said.

"We'll be good."

"Yeah right!"

We launched out on *Loki*. "Let's go see what she wants." I said. "*Vanguard,* hold course unless we comm you back."

"Roger *Loki*."

"She's a big one all right, and squawking corporate hull numbers." Mal said. "*Loki,* close to 10 klicks, then hold relative position."

"Roger, 10 klicks and holding relative position."

"Corporate ship, this is the mining ship *Duty*'s Pinnacle, state your reason for following our convoy."

"Pinnacle, this is the corporate long-range frigate *Aspire*, this is free space, we go where we please."

"That looks like a fancy new ship, bet she's fast."

"She's the newest in the fleet, not the 'has beens' you've been going up against."

"Maybe, but we still won!"

I muted the mic: "Load your missiles, ready to fire, one to the bow, the other to the stern." Mal nodded and I unmuted. "I'll admit you're the biggest one we've seen so far." I said.

"There's a new theory," the enemy captain said.

"And that is?" I asked.

"That your ships have to be big and overpowered to run your shields, and that you can't hold out long."

"Interesting theory, have you tested it yet?"

"I'm about to," and he fired his missiles.

"Fire missiles," I said. At only 10 klicks range their missiles hit us in three seconds but our shields just shrugged off their detonations. Ours hit them at the same time. "*Aspire*, want to try Round Two? *Aspire* respond, are you quitting already? It looks like your missiles worked." I said. "Let's go check out our new ship."

"Are you going to comm *Vanguard* back?"

"Not until we take possession of her. Besides we're wearing our shields."

"OK, let's go get our new ship," Mal said.

"*Loki,* go dark, and dock with the corporate ship."

"Roger."

Loki landed us in *Aspire's* landing deck beside two Marine attack landing craft. *Aspire* and the shuttles were painted with black non-reflective paint, probably radar absorbing. Each looked big enough to carry a platoon of Marines and their equipment, and the ships were armored and armed for close support.

"These guys must be part of the enforcement branch." I

said.

"Hopefully, they are all knocked out," Mal said.

"I'm sure we would have known by now if they weren't," I said.

"*Vee,* unlock the hatch."

"Stand by, there is an intruder program running at the airlocks... disabled." The palm pad turned green. We went through the airlock and into the ship. Bodies lay where they had dropped, knocked out... permanently. A fact that made our job easier.

"Maybe two missiles were overkill," Mal said

"There's no such thing as overkill, where the corporation is concerned. Let's get to the bridge and make sure we have total control." I said.

Mal followed me toward the bridge. We looked in hatches as we went, making sure there were no survivors.

"He wasn't lying when he said this was a new ship, the paint still smells fresh," Mal said.

"We should send the corporation a thank you note for donating it," I said, and we chuckled. I wondered at the morbid sense of humor we had developed, but I guessed the human mind does what it has to, to remain sane.

The bridge crew were slumped over their consoles, all of them dead.

"I believe you're in my seat." I said, as I pushed the captain out of the command chair onto the floor. Mal did the same to the body at the engineering console, plugged his M-comp in and went to work.

"*Vee*, send a message to *Duty* to remain on course ... we are green here. Also send a message to *Vanguard* to drop back and provide high cover for us and our new ship, *Aspire*."

"Sent."

Vanguard was on station within five minutes. Mal turned to me, "we have control of the ship, all of their command codes have been replaced with ours and all self-destruct programs have been canceled and removed."

"Outstanding! Can you install your ACE program while everything is operating?"

"I don't see why not, I'll just have to add a few lines of code to take that into consideration. I can install it on their system now and upgrade it to an M-comp when we get to *Duty's* Rock."

"Let's do it, then. We have plenty of time while en route, and who knows? We may need her."

"OK, but I'm renaming her."

"Oh? Do you have a name picked out?" He nodded, smiling. "*Black Ice*."

"Well, she is black."

Mal shook his head, "That's not it. That's what you have become known as, Commodore — Black Ice."

"How did I get that name?"

"It started out as 'Black Eyes', and just morphed into Black Ice."

"Then *Black Ice* it is. *Vee,* send a message to *Vanguard* to dock with us. I'll meet a team at the lock. All secure, we have the ship. All boards are green."

"Sent."

***

I met the security team at the hatch. They were fully armed and armored, just in case. "Gentlemen, welcome aboard HMS' newest ship, *Black Ice*." The team came in and spread out, upon seeing the bodies they relaxed.

"Team leader to *Vanguard*, all boards are green, we are with the Commodore."

"Roger team lead, *Vanguard* out."

"Corporal, send two of your men to the bridge to guard Mal." He signaled two of his men, and they left for the bridge. "You may want to send for more men, we have a lot of trash to take out."

Commander Jones came over with the rest of the security platoon. "Nice ship, Commodore."

"Thank you, the Corporation donated it to the cause." I said. "We need to search these bodies for Intel, strip them out of their uniforms, and space the bodies."

"Roger sir, we'll take care of it."

"Once that is done, we can start doing an inventory. I'll be doing a survey of the ship."

"Understood."

I checked engineering, moving the bodies out of the way of operating equipment and machinery when necessary. All the engineering boards were green. I walked toward the armory, in what was referred to as "Marine country".

The armory was fully equipped with weapons and ammo. Along the back of the armory wall was a platoon's worth of power armor. It wasn't second rate equipment either, it was top-of-the-line. The Marine's open berthing area was just down the corridor.

Commander Jones was there looking around, "They were set up for a heavy company of Marines, and all their support staff. Have you been to the cargo bay yet?"

"No, anything special there?" I asked.

"Two heavy weapons g-vehicles, two medium APCs, and two light APCs. Enough to deploy a whole company of Marines, less the power-armor squad, who can deploy themselves. I think I'm in love," everyone laughed.

"I think it's time we upgraded our security platoon to a security company," I said.

"I like the way you think, Commodore."

"Mal says he's done installing the ACE program," *Vee* said.

"On the way," I answered.

The security guards were posted at the bridge hatch. "We good?" I asked Mal.

"Yep, fully integrated."

"I think it's time to catch up with our convoy."

"Yeah, the girls are probably getting curious about what we're doing," Mal said.

"*Ice,* increase speed to catch up with *Duty.*"

"Increasing speed," Ice replied.

"*Ice*, send an encrypted message to the convoy that we are closing up with the convoy on our newest ship, all secured, all boards are green," I said.

"Sent."

"Send message to *Vanguard*, ask Captain Smythe to come over, please."

"Sent."

"Are you thinking of pulling Captain Smythe from *Vanguard* to take command of *Black Ice*?" Mal asked.

"He's our most experienced battle captain." I said.

"True," He answered.

"Besides, I think it's time we upgraded our security forces."

Reggie joined us a short time later. "What're the payments on something like this?" Reggie said, as he entered the bridge.

"Not bad, but the fuel cost is where they get you," I said smiling.

"They didn't spare any expense on her," he said.

"How would you feel about moving up?" I asked.

He turned to look at me, frowning, "seriously?" I nodded.

"Who will take the *Vanguard*?"

"I'd like your suggestions on who to move in which positions. You'll need a first officer here, too. So you tell me." I said.

"Since this little fracas has gone hot, I'd take my crew off *Vanguard* and move Captain Williams and his crew over to take our place. We can find a cargo ship's captain and crews almost anywhere — or train one," he said.

"Sounds reasonable," I said.

"What about Commander Jones and his security platoon?" He asked.

"He'll be moving over here to become commander of a security company, as soon as we hire some more people," I said.

He chuckled, "he must have found some new toys."

"Oh, you've met him," I said, laughing.

"Convoy joined," *Ice* announced.

"Very well," I answered. "Why don't you go take a tour of your new ship, I'm sure you'll run into Jim down there somewhere drooling over his new toys."

"I think I will."

"You find anything interesting in those logs and files?" I asked Mal.

"The usual corporate crap. You know, take over the solar system, rule the world. However, *Aspire* was sent specifically to locate and engage us."

"Then we can expect more to come looking for us. Let's go check out the med-bay... we'll probably be putting it to work." Like everything else on the ship, med-bay was state-of-the-art and fully equipped.

"Nic, look at this." Mal said.

"What did you find?" I said, walking over to him. He chin pointed to a line of auto-docs along the wall. "Cool, we've got plenty of auto-docs." I said.

Mal shook his head, "they're M-auto-docs, for augmentations," He said. I looked closer. He was right.

"Check and see if they are the same type as we have," I said.

Mal pulled up the command screen, "the same."

"Well, at least they're no better," I said.

"Commander Jones," I commed.

"Yes, Commodore?"

"Do you still have any of the bodies on board?"

"All of them, we are gathering them in the cargo bay."

"Have a medic cut one open to see if he's augmented."

"Stand by."

"Roger."

"We opened a Marine's arm, and he was augmented."

"Check them all, see who is and who isn't augmented. While they are doing that, come to med-bay. Is Reggie there with you?"

"He is."

"Bring him along."

"On the way."

Jim and Reggie came in to the med-bay; "all of their personnel were augmented." Jim said.

"Augmented, how?" Reggie asked.

"We have an auto-doc that administers mithrilium nanites that augment people. We don't know who has access to the technology. As far as we know the ESFL does not have it.

"We got it when we captured *Loki* from the assassin. We think it was part of his pay for working for the corporation. We started using it on the seriously wounded, then on the whole security team to give them an advantage on the battlefield. Now it seems the Corporation gives it to all of their thugs."

"What does it augment?" Reggie asked.

"It encases bones in M-carbon fiber, increases muscle and tendon strength, reaction times, you know the usual sci-fi movie things," I said, smiling.

"Commodore, you have an encrypted message from *Major*," *Vee* said in my ear. I blinked up the message on my HUD. "Nero," was all it said.

"Well, Reggie, we'll let you and Jim get everything transferred over from *Vanguard*. We've got to get back to *Duty*."

"We'll get started right away, sir," Reggie answered.

"*Vee,* have *Loki* ready to depart upon our arrival."

"She'll be ready," *Vee* answered.

"*Loki,* take us to *Duty*." I said as soon as we were on board.

"Enroute to *Duty*."

CHAPTER 7

"It must be bad if *Major* sent a "Nero" message," Mal said.

"But how bad, is the question." We arrived at *Loki*'s bridge, "*Loki* play *Major's* "Nero" message."

The message started, "Commodore, as instructed I have been monitoring and gathering Intel from all sources, including our ACE network. I now have proof that Representative Johnson, the Corporation, and Admiral Cole have colluded to subvert the ESFL and manipulate HMS — and specifically, you, Commodore — into upgrading ESFL ships.

"Once all upgrades are complete, they plan on turning over all intellectual properties to the Corporation. Please observe the following surreptitious video of a meeting between Admiral Cole, corporate representatives, Representative Johnson, and CEO Baker, via video comm."

The video showed the Admiral, Gunny, some corporate suits, and the Admiral's Marine guards. "Freeze picture," I said. "Zoom in on the faces of the Marine guards, one at a time," I said.

"Those are the same Marines that were with Hollingsworth," Mal said.

"And the ones on Gunny's ship," I agreed.

"I think we're being played," Mal said, and I nodded, reluctantly.

"Pull out from zoom and resume play," I said.

"You said you could deliver the tech, Admiral," Baker said.

"Losing the *Invincible* was a minor setback. I had everything under control until you attacked his Hab and killed his people," the admiral said.

"As you say, a minor setback. That was done by an

overzealous manager, that has been corrected," Baker said.

"Is the ESFL split story still viable?" Johnson asked.

"Yes, it's still in play. I'm on the way to home port to gather my "New Legion" ships to take to him to have them upgraded. I'm also sending two Marine deployment ships to an abandoned asteroid mine under the guise of using it as a New Legion's home port. The two battalions of Marines will guard all HMS employees until he hands over the tech."

"And if he won't?" Baker asked.

"Then it turns into a prison until he does, and accidents happen on mining operations all the time. He'll turn it over. His people are more important to him than his tech."

"And the ESFL?" Johnson asked.

"I have recalled all ESFL ships to the home port for a maintenance stand-down, together with 'top-secret strategy' meetings. I have selected ships and commanders in position to continue the cover story. We'll get as many upgrades as possible done before we are forced to redeploy the ESFL to normal patrols."

"I have everything under control. Once he calms down from the attack on his people, I'll be able to maneuver him where we want him to go," the admiral said.

"We won't wait forever... you better produce results, and soon!" Baker threatened. The screen went blank.

"The Admiral is in route to the ESFL home port at the present time. I'll send updates as Intel dictates or as previously scheduled. *Major* out."

The rage I felt before was a hot rage that wanted to burn those who had hurt mine — but this rage was a cold, dark abyss. We had been used, betrayed, our people murdered, and they were laying plans to use our people as hostages.

All for the greed of money and power. A quick death would be too easy for these people. I was going to bleed them until they were bone white, then maybe I'd let them die.

"We no longer wait to be fired on, this war just got hotter. We take everything we can from these people. First the Corporation, then the Admiral. Then we'll see where the ESFL comes down in this." Mal just nodded. "*Vee*, signal the fleet to coast and await further orders."

"Sent."

We had docked with *Duty* while we were watching the video of the Admiral. "*Vee,* message the board we need to meet in the entertainment galley."

"Sent."

Jazz, Jade, and Aunt J were already there when we arrived. As soon as Jazz saw me, she said, "what's wrong, what's happened?"

"It's better that you see for yourselves," I said. Everyone took a seat. "*Vee,* replay *Major's* message in its entirety." As they watch the video, I looked for other bits of Intel I could discover. When the video ended, I waited for reactions.

"I recognized two of the Marine guards that were going to kill us," Jade said.

"What!?" Aunt J said. "When did this happen?"

"Sorry Aunt J, so much as happened, it kinda dropped through the cracks," I said. We told Aunt J about the attempted piracy and the ensuing fight to free our people and to retake Gunny's ship to free the Admiral ... which apparently was an elaborate con job.

"And those were the same guards, the ones the Admiral supposedly executed for piracy?" We all nodded. "That evil, conniving, backstabbing, traitorous..."

"So, they set us up for betrayal from the beginning?" Jazz asked.

"Maybe not from the very beginning, but from shortly thereafter," I said.

"What are we going to do?" Aunt J asked.

"We know who our enemies are now. But they don't know that we know. I plan to keep it that way for as long as I can. The longer we can string them along, the longer we have to prepare and build up our forces.

"First, we tell all our ships that have either delivered or have bought cargo to go radio silent and dark, boost straight to us. We will put *Black Ice* in for upgrades immediately, and wait for everyone to arrive. If the admiral messages us we'll acknowledge his orders to keep him thinking we are still heading for the meeting place. When he contacts us again, we'll tell him we're being pursued and are trying to break contact, and will let him know when we lose our attackers.

"After that, we'll play it by ear. The bigger problem is who we can trust among our former Legion personnel, and how do we find out who is working against us," I said.

"That's a good question," Aunt J said.

"My gut tells me those who have shed blood with us can be trusted. But I was taken in by the admiral, too. So, I don't know whether to trust my gut or not," I said.

"Let's get Jocko in here and see what he says," Aunt J said.

"*Vee*, message Jocko and have him join us, please."

"Sent."

Jocko joined us, and we played the video for him, then told him about the supposed pirate takeover attempt where I killed three of the Admiral's guards.

"How do you plan to handle this?" he asked. After I told him our plans, he nodded slowly, weighing my answer. "And you're wondering who you can trust, of the people who are with you?"

I nodded, "Primarily former Legion members."

"Oh, those you can trust. I had them all checked out before they started working with my security.

"Captains Smythe and Gallant have no love for Admiral Cole. As for the Legionnaires as a whole, once they see this video, they'll be ready to gut the admiral. He's not only betrayed them, he's betrayed The Legion, and that they will not forgive.

"Everyone else, and I include myself in this, should be vetted and watched. We think we know who we have with us, but a threat to one's family member is a powerful motivator," Jocko said.

"The next thing I would do is show this video to your former Legion crewmen. Those men have a great respect for you, since you have bled with and for them. That kind of loyalty you can't buy."

"Thank you for your advice, Jocko, I appreciate it."

"Any time my friend, any time."

"*Vee*, send a message to our haulers and hybrids to complete current contracts. Once unloaded, go radio silent, then move away from all shipping traffic and go dark. Meet us at this location. To the cargo ships, once they have purchased supplies, go radio silent, then move away from all shipping traffic and go dark. Meet us at this location."

"Messages sent."

"*Vee*, set up a video conference with Captain Gallant, Captain Smythe, and Commander Jones for 30 minutes from now."

"Message sent and acknowledged."

With everyone present on screen, I started the meeting. "Gentlemen, I will not waste time or pull any punches. We have been betrayed. Before you start asking questions, watch this video. *Vee,* play video." The video started, and I watch their reactions: intense concentration, shock, disbelief, anger, and then back to concentration — on me.

Once it was over, Archie asked, "Are you sure of this video's authenticity?"

"It was taken by our ACE program on Gunny's ship, so there is no doubt it's real."

"Did you notice the Marine guards?" Archie asked.

"We did, and yes those are the survivors of the attempt to take the *Travis*."

"I thought so," he said, nodding.

"I knew he was an ambushing cutthroat, but I never thought he would stoop this low," Archie said.

"He doesn't see it as stooping low," Reggie said. "He's playing his grand chess game and we are all merely pieces on the board to be moved or sacrificed as need be for him to win the game."

"Well, he'll soon learn that these chess pieces aren't his to play God with." I said.

"Now you have to wonder who he may have placed in your camp." Archie said. Jim and Reggie looked thoughtful and nodded.

"The thought crossed my mind," I said. "But I remember that we fought and bled with, and for, one another. Reggie and his crew dove headlong in to the fight and placed himself, his crew, and his ship between me and the enemy, destroying two corporate ships. Jim and his men dragged me out of the rubble to get me back to Doc, saving my life. Archie was in the room held hostage as bait, ready to be sacrificed for the admiral's chess game.

"No, gentleman, you are trusted until you prove otherwise. To prove that point. Reggie, move *Ice* over to *Travis* to begin immediate upgrades. Jim, you will be doing the same to all your new gear and new vehicles. The rest of our fleet is on the way here to meet us.

"Reggie, have *Vanguard* ready to react to any visitors we may get. Once we have those plans started we'll meet again, and I'll brief you on future plans. Questions?" I asked.

"Commodore, I'd like to show our men the video," Jim said.

"I'd like for you to do exactly that, but I wanted you to see it first, so you weren't blindsided," I said.

"I appreciate that, and I appreciate your trust. We will not let you down."

"You never have, Jim. Carry on, *Duty* out."

***

Within the hour *Ice* was docked with *Travis* for work to begin on her upgrades. I looked at our board members, my family, "I guess we need to make a video for our people explaining what is going on. Then show them the video of the Admiral's betrayal." They all nodded.

We made and showed the videos that afternoon. I expected people to be mad and confused, but what they were was pissed off, and they wanted blood. The amazing thing to me, was that no one ever doubted that our security forces, although former Legion, were ever suspected of being the enemy or even helping the enemy.

We ate with the crew and our people that night. We wanted to show everyone we were all in this together. Chef had set aside a table for the family, but as always we all ate the same food.

Over coffee I said, "It will take time for our fleet to get here and to get *Black Ice* upgraded."

"Who named the ship *Black Ice*?" Jazz asked.

I smiled, and chin pointed at Mal. "And there I go, right under the bus," Mal said, laughing. Jazz looked at him questioningly.

"It's because that's what everyone has started calling Nic, Commodore Black Ice," Mal said.

"I see," Jade said, "Black eyes, black ice."

"Anyway," I said, "we start upgrades on Commander Jones's equipment and vehicles tomorrow. We also need more of your special missiles." I said, looking at Mal. He nodded. "If you ladies will keep everything else running and the good will flowing, it will be a great help. Also, start thinking about where we should go for our new home, and what we should do.

"I'm sure our people have some ideas that they'll be glad to share with you once they see you."

***

Mal, Buck, and I went over to the *Black Ice* the next morning to help with the security platoon's upgrades. When we arrived, they escorted us down to the cargo bay. When we entered the bay, the security platoon was in formation, wearing the all black uniforms they had liberated from the corporate troops.

"Platoon!" The platoon leader shouted, "ATTEN-tion!" The platoon snapped to attention. Commander Jones took me to the front of the formation.

"Commodore, we have all seen the video, and to a man

agree that the admiral has broken faith with us and is a traitor to the Legion and what the Legion stands for.

"You have not broken faith with us and even though you never served on active duty in the Legion, you have upheld the values of the Legion. It would be an honor if you would take the rank of commodore of our newly formed 'Black Ice Legion'."

They presented me with a black uniform, black uniform jacket with the rank insignia of commodore on the epaulets. I was stunned. I took the jacket and put it on, buttoning it closed.

"It would be my great honor to serve as your commodore." I said.

"PRE-sent!," the platoon leader shouted, "ARMS!" Everyone saluted me. I returned their salute. "OR-der! ARMS!"

"Admiral Cole and his ilk have betrayed us, but I never doubted that when the situation went sideways, and things got hot, that you had my back. I swear that I will always have your backs."

The platoon leader yelled, "BLACK!"
The platoon responded "ICE!"
"BLACK!"
"ICE!"
"BLACK!"
"ICE-ICE-ICE!" They shouted.
I raised my fist and yelled, "To the Black Ice Legion!"
"Oorah!" They shouted.

Once everyone went back to work, Commander Jones brought me a complete uniform including a pair of black knee-high armored combat boots.

"Mal, do you want uniform?" I asked, smiling.

"Not on a bet, you're the fighter, I just fix computers." He said, laughing. I noticed the patch on the shoulder, a Legion eagle with black eyes, and "B.I.L." over the top. I looked around. Everyone was wearing the same patch.

Captain Smythe approached us, "Commodore."

"Captain," I answered.

"I'd like to request that myself and my crew be given the

same M-nanite treatments as the Marines."

I nodded, "I see by your uniform and the patch on your shoulder that you're part of the Black Ice Legion."

"We all are, Sir."

"I think the M-nanite treatment should be standard issue for the BIL."

"An excellent idea, Sir," He said, smiling.

"Let Doc know that he can start administering the treatment right away."

Commander Jones joined us, "Commodore, would you be interested in increasing our ranks to build a complete, fully manned company?"

"Can we get them quietly?"

He smiled, "with one message, we could fill out the rest of the company."

"You think we need more men?" I asked.

"Better to have and not need, then to need and not have."

I nodded, "send your message, but remember, this is top-secret. We'll send *Vanguard* to pick them up."

"Yes, sir."

"And Captain Smythe, we may want to find another ship's crew, I think we're going to need them. I'd be willing to bet good money that the corporation is going to donate more ships. Since we are all standing here, let me share what my, or the beginnings of my strategy is for our next moves."

※※※

It was two weeks before our first ship arrived, one of our haulers, which had just dropped its load when the recall was issued. Two weeks after that, the other three haulers came in. Within the next week the two hybrid haulers and the two cargo ships arrived.

We finished the upgrades on the Marines' equipment and vehicles using M-components, which increased their performance dramatically. We upgraded all the power armor with M-components and added shields to them. Everything that got shields got an ACE, which included all the vehicles. All BI Legion personnel got the M-nanite treatments, including the ships' crews, and I opted to get the rest of the M-nanites myself.

True to his promise, Commander Jones found enough men to fill out three platoons to give us a full company of Marines. One of our cargo ships was sent to pick them up and would be back in about a week.

We needed to get our miners people back to work ... they were helping where they could, but we needed to get them mining.

Jazz messaged me asking to meet her in the galley. I got there before her, got a cup of coffee and waited.

When she arrived, there was an older gentleman named David with her. "David has an interesting story to share with you, Commodore."

"Oh? What's that?"

"I was telling Jazz," he said, "that my great uncle mined out on the rim of one of these rings. But it was too far out to make it pay for itself."

"OK, what's so special about this specific strike?"

"Well, it was a shape of the asteroid itself. It was shaped like a cone and had a depression in the fat and. He always said it looked like God had eaten the ice cream and left the cone."

"Did he say how big the cone was?" I asked. He thought a moment, "Between three and five klicks long and between one and two across the bottom."

"Do you know the location?"

"I know about where it is, but I've never been there myself."

"If you'll give Jazz the location, we may go look at her," I said.

"I sure will, thank you Commodore."

"No, thank you David, we need to get these people to work and this may be what we're looking for." I said. David and Jazz left, and I went to find my ship-building engineers.

***

I found them working on improving a superstructure on *Black Ice*. "Gentlemen, I have a challenging task for you. You tell me if I'm crazy or if we need to adjust our way of thinking."

"Oh, we're pretty sure you're crazy," they laughed.

"Point taken!"

"What are you thinking about building this time?"

"We're going to build a ship out of an asteroid. Using the rock as the superstructure and walls. We'll cut away what we don't need and leave voids where we need them. We'll run all our piping and cabling like normal. What you think?" I asked.

"That's been talked about for years, but nobody wanted to actually build it once they mined the rock out it was cheaper to just move to the next rock. How big are we talking about?" He asked.

"Three to 5 km long, cone shaped, a couple of km across to the bottom." I said. One of them whistled.

"The power to run it would be monstrous, and the engines to push it haven't been built yet, unless you use a lot of them."

"I'm working on that. What I need from you is a list of what we would need for infrastructure, environmental, etc., for a city factory ship. I'm working on the engines and power plants. We need to have plans to hollow out the asteroid, then build it into a city-ship."

"We'll get started right away," one said.

"I'll get with Mal to get you a dedicated computer for the project." I said.

"That would speed up the project."

CHAPTER 8

Jade had gotten the approximate coordinates for what we were calling "Cone Rock" and we took *Loki* to check it out. It had become standard practice, once away from Habs or stations, to go dark. With *Loki*'s speed we were at its location in an hour.

"*Loki,* do a scan survey of the highlighted asteroid. I want as much info as possible on dimensions, structures, and composition. You have the helm."

"I have the helm," Loki replied. Jazz and I made small talk over coffee as *Loki* glided over and around Cone Rock.

"Survey complete," *Loki* said.

"Rock's content?" I asked.

"Iron 47 percent, mithrilium 18 percent, 35 percent is a mixture of other metals and rock," *Loki* said.

"Any major fracture faults?"

"None detected."

"I think this will do nicely, and it will keep our people busy for quite a while. *Loki,* take us back to the fleet." I said.

"Course laid in, engaging."

Mal had set the design engineers up with a new dedicated M-Comp. *Loki* fed the data about Cone Rock to them, and they got to work filling in requirements.

Commander Jones arrived with the three platoons of former Legion Marines to fill out our Marine company. Along with the Marines they brought a replacement ship crew, all former Legion. With the fleet all present, we started back toward Cone Rock.

Black Ice was still docked with *Travis,* but we could still make way, as long as we attempted no hard maneuvers. It would take us about two weeks to get there and by that time *Black Ice* should be out of space dock.

I found Mal, as usual, in his workshop. "I have an idea." I said.

"Is it going to get us killed?" He asked without looking up.

I chuckled, "This one shouldn't, but who knows."

"In that case it will probably be boring to work on."

"Maybe," I answered. "You remember those mining bots or drones we had somewhere around here?"

"The one we took apart to look at for the crusher program?"

"Yeah that one. What I want to do is make mining bots, or upgrade what we have to follow a designated mining and tunneling plan."

"How complicated?"

"It could be pretty complicated. It has to follow the designs the ship design engineers lay out, for the city-ship we will make Cone Rock into."

"OK, so we may have to install an ACE in them. Let me get with Earl and his team and see what we can come up with." I went to my shop and worked on how big a cone drive would have to be to handle a 6.5 km ship and how much bigger a reactor it would take to power it. I already had the formula for the GCD itself, I needed to account for some variables. Then I could run the numbers for power usage.

***

The work crews completed *Black Ice* and pulled her out of *Travis*, and she went out on her shakedown cruise. There were only a few minor corrections that had to be made, and once they were completed, she moved to our rearguard position.

We sent the four haulers back to hauling rock in from the mining Habs. That would generate income, and when we had a load, they hauled it in for us. OEM would process our rock and keep it quiet.

The ship design engineers wanted to meet with me to discuss issues, so Mal and I went down to their offices.

"What we need to know is, what engines we'll be using and how much room to allow for them ... and for the fusion reactors," the lead engineer asked.

I pursed my lips, thinking. "There will be no conventional engines inside the ship," I said.

"So we'll be placing the engines outside the ship?"

"For your planning purposes, yes." I said.

"And the fusion reactors?"

"I'm still working on the design for those."

"A new design?"

"Yes, a smaller, more powerful design." I said. "What I'd like for you to plan for now is, us hollowing out the base with a hole in the center like a doughnut, deep enough for our ships to go inside.

"That will be our ship's maintenance and docking area. Next will be the smelter-refinery area or level. We will load rock in from the side of the ship via grav-channels, process it into metals and store it in warehousing areas.

"The next area will be the power generation areas, then Hab areas, then engineering, then command and control, and finally reactors and engine area. But let's start with the maintenance and docking area.

"We have to mine all that out. Then we can work through the other areas. As soon as I have a final design, I'll get you the info." I said.

"We were hoping for more data, but we can start with this," he said.

***

There was a celebration the day we arrived at Cone Rock and people were ready to get to work. All our ships docked on the big rock, since it had just enough gravity to hold us in place.

Duty and *Travis* would process rock and locate all the metals in a laydown yard. We fed the specs from the ship designer's M-Comp into the computers on the tugs and we started hollowing out the base of our new habitat.

Mal and Earl had a prototype mining bot out doing test runs to see how much they could use of the old ones, to see if we needed a whole new generation of bots. I suited up and went out to see Mal and his new toys.

"How's it working?" I asked.

"We used the old bots as a test-bed for some of our new tech, and I think we've got some workable ideas. You want a bot that is basically set it and forget it, right?"

"Yep, let it mine out the design. Then our miners come in and scoop out the gravel. The bots can work 24/7. We'll probably need to come up with some kind of machine that collects the gravel that the miners can operate." I said.

"We already have them, they are being made right now," Mal said. "We should have our first new mining bot by tomorrow. The design engineers also want to add a grav-compression feature to add strength on the final pass made by the bots.

"As it finishes an area, it will run a grav-compression pass over everything it leaves. That will make it as hard as steel. Once finished, the rock ship will be as strong or stronger than any ship built," he said.

"That's what we want," I said. "When you get a chance come by my shop, I want to bounce an idea off of you."

"It will be a while, but I'll swing by."

It's funny how thoughts will just pop into your head, creating one of those "oh crap!" moments. "*Vee*, message Buck, have him make and install a M2F3D on *Black Ice*."

"Sent."

I was looking over my figures in my workshop for the OFEs to cover Cone Rock. There was a lot of area to cover — after all, it was 6.5 km long and 2.5 km across to the base. Then there were the GCD emitters that would interact with the shield emitters to propel this monster of a ship.

I was checking the figures I had run and crosschecked them again with the M-Comp. I had the grid laid out that I needed to give the data to the engineers.

"So, this is where you been hiding," Jazz said.

"Yep, you've caught me. I'm a theoretical math-acholic."

"That's why I'm a pilot, I jump in and take off. It's more fun."

"Am I interrupting?" Mal asked, sticking his head in the doorway.

"Did you bring coffee?"

"No."

"Then you're interrupting, but since you're here, let me show you this so you can crosscheck me."

"Fine, show me."

"For full coverage outside the cone ship it will take 1,123 OFEs. Each one of those will be a 23."

"I like it so far. That'll give us heavier shields."

"To feed them and the GCD we'll have five sets around the ship, five rings feeding the GCD, starting at 23s at the base and increasing as we move toward the focusing emitter. The five feeder rings will be 23s, 43s, 53s, 73s, 83s, and the focusing emitter will be a 97."

Mal's eyes lost focus, as he processed all the info I just threw at him. "Wow, that will take a lot of power!"

"Yep, and a lot of redundancy. Jazz will work on the fusion reactor plans," I said.

"Oh, thank God," Mal said, "I thought for a moment you might try to do it."

"You two should take that act on the road," She stuck her tongue out at us. We laughed.

"Those numbers look good. What are you thinking of using to power these babies?" Mal said.

"Something you said gave me an idea, and before you ask if it works, yes it could get us killed. You said you were working with grav-compression." He nodded. "Part of the problem with fusion reaction is containment, and the concentration of fuel you can introduce into the containment area."

"Yeah, I'm with you," he said.

"What if instead of using an hourglass configuration, we used a double globe configuration, with grav-compression as the containment field a super compressed M-uranium fuel pellet, disc, or ball, whatever works best, as the fuel source?"

Mal held his finger up, eyes unfocused.

"Oh crap!" Jazz said, "He's gone, I'll see y'all at dinner," and she left.

"If this works, they will definitely kill us. Using what you described it will reduce the amount of rads. This is a whole new generation of containment. By compressing the fuel and using an M-mixture we will be able to miniaturize the reactor and literally put it in almost anything.

"From g-cars, to toasters, almost anything," Mal said.

I laughed. "OK, maybe not toasters, but definitely g-cars and bigger."

"OK, let me draw up some specs and see what we have. Do we have a fusion reactor engineer with us?"

Mal smiled, "when I tell you, you'll think I'm lying."

"Who?"

"Jocko."

"No way!"

"I told you."

"He was a rockhound."

"Yeah, after he got tired of babysitting reactors."

"No way!"

"Ask Aunt J."

***

"Yep, he sure was, and a good one too." Aunt J said.

"Jocko, our Jocko?" She nodded, laughing. "Well, I guess I judged a book by its cover. I'll see what he thinks of my idea."

I took a good part of the next day to draw up my plans and add some minimal data. I had the plans up on the wall screen when Jocko showed up for our meeting.

"Thanks for coming, Jocko," I said.

He was already looking at the plans. "Julie said you were working on something special and needed another set of eyes."

"Exactly right. What I need is someone with more practical experience on reactors than I have."

He was following my drawings and schematics, reading my data. "Double globe containment?" I nodded. "Using the same design as your shield emitters?"

"Yeah," I said, nodding.

"Fuel source?"

"Compressed mithrilium-infused uranium."

He turned to look at me, frowning. "What kind of output increase have you figured that would give you?"

"Based on past percentages, maybe twice as much."

Jocko shook his head, "More like four times as much if you compress it. They tried something similar to this some years back. They used M-uranium, but it wasn't compressed and the containment field didn't hold, so they scrapped the idea. Of course they didn't have your emitter tech.

"That, I think, is the key ingredient. If you can keep the power contained and controlled. That is the million cred question, isn't it? What shape are you going to compress the M/U into?"

"I'm thinking a ball or more likely a marble, that will make it the same shape as the double globe containment field and will aid in field strength." He nodded his head and went back to studying the plans.

"May I?" he said, pointing at the plans. "By all means, please." He started adding a few lines here and there. "We're going to need a bypass line here for stabilization, and if we move this to here..."

I questioned some of his moves, and he showed me why, adding the practical view as well as the theoretical. I showed him some places where our tech would do the job of a whole section of valves and relays. Several hours later we were standing back admiring our work.

"Now that is a thing of beauty!" he said.

"Wait until Mal puts his M-tronics and M-Comp into the mix. He will double the speed and output and make it half the size," I said. "Which reminds me, we need to talk about upgrading your cyber-legs. Mal has mine packed with tech.

"So, who will build it?" I asked. "You drew half of the new plans."

"I'd love to."

"We'll need to build an M/U compressor to make the fuel, first," I said.

"You said it was kind of like the grav-compressor they use on the mining machines to cut passages in mines?"

"Yeah, it compresses the walls to make them smooth and hard."

He nodded, "that's what has made you guys rich, you look at old tech with new eyes, and no preconceived notions."

I nodded, "Yeah, but we still need the grounding of practical experience to fill in the gaps in our knowledge

***

I gave the design engineers the layout specs for the OFEs, so they could map them and cut all the channels for the cabling and equipment. They also got the layout specs for the GCD, assuming it was for just more shield emitters.

Jocko and I started making our prototype M-fusion reactor. The first would be about the size of the tool chest. We wired in all our testing diagnostic equipment, so we can see exactly what was going on, and to make sure we were safe and not overloading anything.

The mining on the base doughnut hole was moving along at a good pace, and we were getting good materials from the rock.

"Commodore, Admiral Cole has sent a message that the Marine deployment ships are on their way to the NL base, ETA 30 days." *Vee* said. "Understood, send an acknowledgement. Also, send a message to Red Johnson asking how many tugs he has that he guarantees are in working condition and to give us a bulk price for all of them."

"Sent."

"Send a message to the cargo ship's Captains to prepare for departure to Titan to sell a load of metals. *Vanguard* will act as escort; Captain Williams will be commanding *Vanguard's* deployment, which will include a platoon of Marines, with full load out. It will leave no later than three days from today."

"Sent."

"And send a message to the next hauler that delivers a load to OEM, to pick up the tugs from Red Johnson. Once they pick them up, to return to the mines via normal routes. We'll send more info when he gets close."

"Sent."

***

Mal and Earl had a working prototype mining bot, and they were putting it through its paces. They said everything looked good so far.

"Red Johnson says he has six good-quality 50 KLT tugs." *Vee* said.

"We'll take them, tell him I'll have them picked up. Pay for them, and tell our hauler we'll pick them up."

"Sent. Our cargo ships with *Vanguard* as escort has left."

"Understood."

"Commander Jones request permission for a field training exercise on the surface of Cone Rock." *Vee* said.

"Granted." I answered.

We needed to find high-grade uranium, since Jocko and I were almost ready to try our M/U compressor. We tried regular metals and rock to see how the prototype worked. After Mal's tweaks, it worked like a charm.

"*Vee,* message *LT* that we need at least two ounces of high-grade uranium."

"Buck has acknowledged."

***

Humpty was a week out of Conclave when he messaged. "*Humpty* reports they have a follower since they left Conclave with the tug shipment. The follower has stayed at the edge of long-range scans."

"Understood, tell them to stay on course... we will intercept them."

"Sent."

"Send *Black Ice* the coordinates to intercept *Humpty* and to investigate the follower. Orders are to capture or destroy it, if it is a corporate ship."

"Sent."

"Have Jazz meet me on *Loki* to assume high cover mission."

"Sent and acknowledged."

We boarded *Loki* and took off for an area sweep. Rather than spend all the time on *Loki* on standby, we located sensors at a one hour distance from Cone Rock. I don't know why we didn't do it before. We set six sensors and returned to Cone Rock. Now anytime a sensor was activated by an incoming ship, we would know it and have an hour to be ready.

"*Black Ice* reports warning off the ship following *Humpty*. The corporate ship immediately fired on *Humpty*. *Black Ice* returned fire, launching two of the hammerhead missiles. They have taken possession of an armored corporate cargo ship. There were no survivors. They are on their way home. All boards are green." *Vee* reported.

"Acknowledge."

CHAPTER 9

A week later, *Humpty*, *Black Ice* and our new cargo ship arrived. The crew of *Humpty* took a few days off to visit family. *Black Ice* stood down for a few days' rest and our new cargo ship, which we named *Cargo Three*, went into refit.

Cargo Three was full of supplies. She must have been enroute to the NL base on a resupply run. I'm guessing they were making sure NL base was resupplied and not depending solely on us. No new Intel came out of *Cargo Three*, but she was a good ship, and we'd put her to good use.

We put the six 50 KLT tugs in for refit, noting that they had priority over *Cargo Three*. Mal's mining bots were working great and were cutting in foundations for all the OEF's and GCD-OEFs. They had now made more bots to prepare for the next phase of hollowing out our asteroid ship. As the new tugs came out of refit, we loaded the ship's designs into their M-Comps and put them to work.

Buck on *LT* had found and harvested a good amount of high-grade uranium. He set it aside out of the way until we were ready for it.

"What percentage of mithrilium to uranium you plan on using?" Jocko asked.

"Everything I've read and have been taught says 20 percent M is the max that can be added to anything and have it affect a change. We've used from 2 percent to 20 percent on our projects, depending on what they were. We used 2 percent in our electronics, so let's start with 5 percent M to U and see what we get. Once we see our results, we can raise the percentage in 5 percent increments until we get what we want or until the whole thing gets unstable," I answered.

"OK, 5 percent will do for a starting place."

We made the U/M marbles with 5 percent, 10 percent, 15 percent, 20 percent, and tested each one for stability and output. 5 percent gave us four times the power of pure uranium. 10 percent gave us six times the power but lost some of its stability. 15 percent gave us eight times the power, but we lost a little more stability. 20 percent gave us 10 times the power, but we were on the edge of a problem.

"Know any more tricks to stabilize it?" I asked.

"No, and we are in uncharted space here. I'm impressed that we got past 10 percent and could stabilize it," Jocko answered.

"Well, that shows a 20 percent rule in action," I said.

Something was tickling my brain. 20 percent rule? I wonder how far beyond 20 percent they went.

"I wonder ..." I said.

"You have a thought?" Jocko asked.

"More of a gut feeling."

"Follow it, those are the best kind."

"OK, let's do a 23 percent mix, and see what we get."

"Why 23?"

"The universe's idea of a joke?"

"OK, 23 percent it is."

We made a 23 percent M/U mixture and compressed it.

From the start it looked different, smoother, shinier. We loaded the new marble into the test reactor and started our readings.

"Oh, my Lord, would you look at that. 10 times the power, rock-solid stability, but look at the rads. Almost zero. Almost the same as the universe's background noise," Jocko said, staring at the readings.

"A joke from the Universe," I said.

"With a marble this size and this powerful we could run Conclave at 100 percent power for 10 years before having to replace it. This is incredible," he said.

"Now we need to build a prototype full-size model." I said.

He nodded, "and we need to get Mal in here to tweak the M-Comp control."

It took us a week to make a full-size reactor. We made a 23 percent M/U golf ball. With Mal's M-Comp to add timing to our stability mix, she'd run forever as long as you loaded more fuel. We made the design to sync with the GCD emitter network. Five M/U reactors to interlocked with five feeder lines in the pentagon configuration and one reactor in the center for the focus OFE.

The center reactor we made bigger, with the M/U ball about the size of a cue ball. We could also place smaller reactors at strategic locations if we needed or wanted to. The ship designers didn't think the area I wanted for the M/U reactors was enough, but they followed my spec requirements. They proceeded with the ship prints. We made parts for the M/U reactors, using the printers.

"Commodore, there is a message from *Vanguard*: 'Convoy enroute returning to home base. They were being followed at the edge of their sensor range. They dropped back to investigate contact and found a corporate frigate. "They also detected a second contact at the extreme range of their sensors, following the first frigate. Upon investigating second contact, they found a corporate battleship.

"Tactical suggests first contact to be bait ship for the second to observe our tactics and then engage them. They are letting the cargo ships travel in the open, lights on, drawing the enemy farther from prying eyes." *Vee* finished the report.

"Understood, continue on course, we're dispatching *Black Ice* for reinforcement to take on the battleship, while *Vanguard* takes the frigate at the same time. Execute plan well away from prying eyes."

"Sent."

"Notify *Black Ice* of mission include *Vanguard*'s message and my reply. Leave ASAP."

"Sent, *Black Ice* acknowledges."

Black Ice left within the hour.

With all nine of our tug's mining away at the insides of Cone Rock, we were making good progress on the ship maintenance and docking area. Now that the designers had all the specifications, we could finish the preliminary designs.

"How many people did you want the ship to house?" The head design engineer asked.

"How many can the ship and Hab space safely support without crowding us, with plenty of safety margins on environmental and for emergency overcrowding?" I asked.

"We have designed the ship like a leveled space station. If you stood the ship on end with the base as the bottom, and per your requirements, we could easily house 20,000 people."

"What will the consumption level on environmental be?"

"At normal use about 70 percent."

"Increase environmental areas to bring that number down to 50 percent, also each level would need a park and promenade area for shops and restaurants. Each level will also have its own M/U reactor, a small one, ensuring that power usage will not be an issue." They were nodding and taking notes.

"Set up a meeting with Jazz, Jade, and Aunt Jay to go over the housing requirements. I don't want to get beat up over apartment sizes." We all laughed.

Earl's team had built 25 mining bots. We loaded the areas the bots were to work in into their ACE, and it put them to work. We also had 25 gravel-removing machines that were operated by miners to put more people to work. We ran three shifts a day to keep up with the mining bots.

Cargo Three was now in refit, but with everyone working to mine out the ship, work seemed to slow. I went down to the assembly area where they were working on assembling our new M/U reactors and I found Jocko elbow deep in a reactor.

"I thought you were in management, not labor," I said, smiling.

"I am, but I don't micromanage," he said, smiling back.

"Am I correct in remembering that Conclave has a high percentage of unemployment?" I asked.

"You are. Last I heard, it was almost 20 percent. Why? Are you thinking of bringing in more people?"

"I am. Work is slowing because we are trying to do everything at once. We need more manpower."

He said wiping his hands, nodding, "how many do you think we need?"

"250-300 of the right mix. We need the right people in the right jobs. They will probably want to bring their families. Bringing families will make them more loyal to HMS."

He pursed his lips, nodding his head, thinking. "Let's say 200 families of the right mix, when do you want them?"

"As soon as we can get them. I'm sure the admiral and the Corporation will only wait so long before turning up the heat."

"Do we have secure comms I can use?"

"Yeah, we feed everything through A14's comms."

"Let me make some calls, give me a list of the trade skills we need, and I'll see what I can do. If we put Conclave people to work, all the better."

"I agree but keep the who and whereas quiet as possible."

"Grandmother and eggs, as my Dad used to say."

I laughed, "Yes sir."

Vee spoke into my ear, "Message from *Black Ice*, Commodore. Mission complete. *Vanguard* docked with a frigate. *Black Ice* docked with a battleship. No casualties. Enroute home, ETA one week."

"Acknowledge, well done."

"Sent."

***

The mining of the maintenance and docking area was complete. Jazz and Jade flew *Taurus* to other local rocks, bringing in more materials to the refineries. *LT* docked with *Loki* and Buck went back to helping with the refits. We pulled five of the tugs out of the maintenance and docking, what we now called the MD area, and put them to helping *Taurus* mine local rocks. The last two tugs we kept to load out what the miners were removing after the bots carved out the Rock Ship's interior.

Black Ice's convoy arrived and parked our new ships inside the MD area of the Rock Ship, in preparation for refit. The battleship was massive, four times the size of *Black Ice*.

The upgrades I had in mind would take a while, but shielding her came first. The same went for the new black frigate — shields first, then we work on everything else. Now that *Black Ice* and *Vanguard* were back, I pulled Buck back to *Loki*.

"It's time for *Loki* to get a few upgrades," I said.

"Cool! What are we adding?"

"First, we are removing all the M-gens and replacing them with two small M/U reactors. That will give us twice as much power and will only use the M/U marbles, so we won't have to refuel for years. Once we see how the system works on *Loki*, we will upgrade the rest of the fleet to M/U reactors rather than M-gens."

"That will give us more room for other improvements." He said.

I nodded, "plug us into shore power and we'll get started."

Pulling the M-gens took no time at all. All that was needed was to unplug, unbolt, and unload them. Installing the M/U reactors took a little longer. Mal had to do some calibrating and tweaking to get everything "Dialed-in". She was purring like a kitten when we finished.

Vee spoke into my ear, "Message from the admiral, Commodore. ETA of supply cargo ships to NL base?"

I smiled, "reply, 'two cargo ships missing and presumed lost. Enemy ships in pursuit, trying to break contact.' "

"Sent."

"Send a message to Red Johnson. We need a passenger liner that will hold at least 600 people for trips between Conclave and Titan. One that he and his family would fly on. Let me know what you hear."

"Sent."

"Message the hybrid haulers to take a load to OEM, and

to leave as soon as they are loaded and ready. *Vee*, how much processing power are you using controlling my cyber augmentations, shields, and being my assistant?"

"The most you have ever used was 8 percent, and that was during combat."

"How much of your storage capacity have we used?"

"2 percent."

"Can you run the ship design and engineering programs?"

"Easily."

I smiled, "Load ship design and engineering program and any other engineering programs we have into your database. Add our own discoveries to our new engineering database. Catalog all engineering knowledge and experiments to our new engineering database. Load backup copies to *Duty* under my encryption codes."

"Done."

"Also update the ship's design and database with all discoveries, tests, and findings made by our design team."

"Done. Message from Red Johnson: 'I'm guessing used? Any requirements as to age, or amenities? Budget?'"

"Reply, yes, used, but a good solid ship. Plan to refit within six months but she needs to make some runs to Titan. Get the best deal for the money, and don't break the bank. You'll make your usual profit margins, plus 2 percent. Send it."

"Sent. Hybrids have left for OEM." I nodded my head and got a green light on my HUD and recognition of my head nodding answer.

"Message from Red, he's found two ships. One is still in service, but the company wants to retire it. It carries 600 passengers, and it's good for another six or eight runs to Titan and back. The other is a 3,000 passenger luxury liner. No engines, no generators, but the rest is complete. Living areas in good condition, all other systems check good on shore power. Same company, owns both. I may be able to work a package deal."

"Reply, go ahead and work a deal. We'll pick up the liner with the 200 KTL tug, that you will sell me. The liner will be chartered as soon as the sale is complete. Send."

"Sent."

***

At breakfast we were catching up on things, as we all had been busy. "We met with the ship designers yesterday and told them what we wanted for apartments, and for our family areas," Jazz said.

"Who is 'we'?" I asked.

"Jade, Aunt J, and me," she answered.

"Good, that way I won't get beat up for leaving anyone out," I said, smiling. "They will install the infrastructure metalwork today ... you want to go see them?" I asked.

"Yeah! Jade and I moved a lot of rock out of there, we want to see how it turned out."

We took *Taurus*, and even Aunt J came along. "You really don't get the feel of how cavernous the MD space is until you a fly ship into it." Jazz said.

"My lord," Aunt J said, "You could park a fleet of ships in here."

"That's the idea," I said. "We wanted enough room to load them, unload them, fix them, build them, transport them, whatever we needed."

"This is mind-boggling." Aunt J said.

We watched awhile as the shipwright mechanics hung metal girders. "We should build a bot to do that, as well as outside ship maintenance." I said. Mal smiled and nodded his head.

Jazz and Jade looked at each other, "They're at it again." Jade said, they laughed.

It had taken a week, but Red messaged me with a quote for the two passenger liners and the 200 KLT tugs. The price was not as bad as I had expected, but not as good as I'd hoped.

"*Vee*, message Red to go ahead with the deal through Aaron Stein. Also hire the crew to go with the 600 passenger ship. Send

Aaron all the details of the deal and account info."

"Sent."

"Comm Jocko."

"What'cha need, Nic?"

"HMS just bought a luxury liner and four 200 KLT tugs. We need four pilots or families for the four tugs that can tow the liner out here."

"How soon do you need them?"

"Within the week."

"I think I can get four."

"I'd prefer families."

"OK, I'll make some calls."

"Where do we stand on the 200 new hires and families?" I asked.

"When will you be ready transport?"

"Within the week if all goes well."

"I'll send the word for them to be ready to leave in a week."

"We'll have an HMS charter waiting for them." I said.

Aaron was his usual highly efficient self, and they did the deal by the third day. Four families signed on with HMS and occupied our four new 200 KLT tugs. We dispatched *Vanguard* for overwatch of both the liners. Jocko had filled 568 slots of our 600 seat passenger liner. Our convoy left Conclave with no problems and no followers.

"*Vee*, show me the ship blueprints for the 3,000-guest luxury liner." The plans flashed up on my HUD.

"Remove all generators. Place M/U reactors here and here." I pointed. "Make this area into storage and tankage. Expand this area for more crew quarters. Using our standard formula, install OFE 7s for the shields, and the same GCD configuration as *Loki*. Add power runs to feed all the new additions."

As I made changes, the plans on the wall would change to reflect my updates. Out of curiosity, I asked, "Suggested changes, *Vee*, based on our database?"

"Add one additional M/U reactor here." The plans highlighted the area *Vee* referred to, "This would give us an independent power source for shields and GCD."

I looked it over, "Good idea, but make it two smaller M/U-Rs for redundancy." The changes appeared on the updated plans. "Send that to the ship design engineers to verify the changes and make recommendations."

"Sent."

"Bring up the 600 passenger liner plans. Based on the changes we made to the luxury liner, make recommendations for changes to be made to the passenger liner to increase seating capacity using the standard already used on the liner."

"Will the main engines be remaining or be removed?"

"Removed, we will use GCD as propulsion."

We updated the plans with *Vee's* recommendations. "Using our new specifications those changes will increase seating to 750 passengers while adjusting environmental issues with the increase in passengers." *Vee* had added more restrooms, galley spaces, and storage.

"Replace all gens with M/U-Rs and add redundancies. Good. Send that to the design team to evaluate and recommend changes."

"Sent."

CHAPTER 10

Cargo Three was now out of refit and ready to be crewed. We shifted the crew from *Cargo Two* over to send *Cargo Three* out on a shakedown run. She returned with all green boards. We loaded her with metals and sent her to Mars Station to sell the cargo, buy supplies, and return.

The liner convoy arrived with no problems. Everyone pitched in and got our 568 new hires and families settled into *Duty*'s housing. I met with the crew from the passenger liner. It turned out to be two extended families that flew and serviced the passengers on the liner.

"We were concerned that we would lose our jobs or would at the least be split up between three or four other liners," the captain said.

"So, you'd all be willing to take a full-time position with HMS?"

"Could we move here?" his wife, the copilot, asked."

"We'd recommend it, actually. We've had trouble with the corporations. You would be safer here."

They all looked at each other, nodding. "Yes, we would be interested in becoming HMS employees," the Captain said.

I held up my hand, "welcome to the HMS family." We all shook hands, "let's get you guys into housing." I had a sudden thought, "Have you ever considered living aboard the passenger liner? I mean with its own self-contained living quarters?"

"We have, but those ships are just too expensive to own and operate," the Captain said.

"I'll pay for the operating cost. You just crew it. I'll tell you what, we're going to put the passenger ship in for a refit anyway.

You guys get some paid vacations here with us. I'll get some plans together for you to look over, then we'll talk turkey, as my grandfather used to say." They all agreed and were shown to housing.

It was Ol' Home Week at dinner. Everyone was welcoming the new arrivals and catching up on the news from Conclave. I told the family about the offer to make the passenger liner a family live aboard ship for the crew. They loved the idea.

We went into the conference room and *Duty* displayed blueprints of passenger ships of our size that had family quarters on them.

There were several viable options to choose from. Since we would remove the engines and install faux engines to make it look like they still had normal engines, while using the GCD propulsion. Once we removed the engines from the plans, we superimposed different versions of living quarters on to the plans until we came up with a version that met all our specs.

The next day we met with the passenger liner family. "Everyone come in." I said. I made introductions around the table. "I'm sure you've been between Titan and Conclave enough to have heard about our troubles with the corporations." They all nodded.

"What it all boils down to is, we have some new tech, and they want it. They don't want to buy it, they want to steal it. You've probably heard rumors about our shield tech around the docks. It's not a rumor. That's one piece of our tech they want. We've also made improvements in other areas too, some of which will go into the passenger liner during the refit."

"Display the up-dated plans for the P600." It displayed the plans on the wall. Everyone got up and looked at the plans, especially those of the family living area: bedrooms, bathrooms, common areas and galley.

"There are no engines or fuel tanks," someone of them finally noticed."

"One of our newer pieces of tech is a propulsion system that uses gravity. We'll leave the shell of the old engines on the outside for public consumption, but you'll have a whole new generation propulsion system. It handles and acts better than conventional engines. You will have shields on her as well."

"How is she powered?" the captain asked.

"Small fusion reactors, which are perfectly safe and give off no radiation." I answered.

"More of your new tech, I suppose?"

"It's all sealed so no one can tamper with it."

"No wonder they want to take your tech ... no one else has anything like it." We all nodded. "We have a ship that has been fitted with the tech, captain so you and your copilot can fly her and see how she handles. If you don't agree it's as good or better, we'll leave the P600 as is, and you can live here on *Duty* with everyone else."

"That sounds more than fair," the captain said.

Jazz and Jade took them out onto *Loki* with the secrets covered. They were back three hours later.

"You said nothing about the ACE comp," he said, smiling.

"Icing on the cake," I said, returning their smiles. They signed the contracts, and the NDAs on the spot. The P600 went into refit that afternoon. It would come out as a "P550-plus Hab".

The big liner was connected to shore power, so M/U-Rs could be installed and we could power up the shields. There was a whole list of things to be installed as workers became available.

"Commodore you have a message from *Major*," *Vee* said.

"Standby, have Mal meet me in my office, tell him we have a message from *Major*."

When Mal arrived, "have you played it yet?"

"No... *Ve,e* play message."

"Commodore, Admiral Cole has moved two ships out to the New Legion base, and has moved two additional tending ships to support it. *Gunny's* ACE was successful in integrating itself into the ESFL Comp Core."

Mal punched his fist in the air, "YES!" I looked at him.

"What?"

"It must be the company you keep, you're getting sneaky

and underhanded."

"I'm just returning the favor."

"Well done, my fiendish friend," I said.

"Resume message."

"The Admiral made the following conference call, to CEO Baker and Rep. Johnson."

"You were supposed to leave them alone," the admiral said.

"And you were supposed to get me that tech," Baker retorted.

"How bad is it?" asked Johnson.

"His last message said he had lost three or four ships, and was being pursued, trying to break contact," the admiral said.

"Good, that only leaves him with two or three ships, he must give up soon."

"Idiot," the admiral said. "How many ships have you lost?"

"We can afford to trade him ship for ship," Baker said.

"What happens when you destroyed the ship he's on?" Johnson asked shaking his head, "I'll tell you what, no more golden eggs."

"Then we'll go back to business as usual." Baker said.

"What about our deal?" the admiral asked.

"No tech, no deal," Baker said, "I suggest, if you want your precious spending bills passed you better get your Legion ships out there and find him and bring me my tech."

"How much time do you need?"

"A few months without interference, six months at the most. We'll have his people and he'll give us everything to free them."

"Baker?" Johnson asked.

"Six months, after that all deals are off and I'll take the muzzles off my dogs," Baker replied. The conference comm ended.

"We also planted Comp Integration seeds on CEO Baker's comp and Representative Johnson's comp. Those seeds should bear fruit in a week or 10 days.

"The news avatar is now complete, and our first

'Unreported News' broadcast will begin tomorrow night. We'll be listing all the council members who have taken bribes, along with the videos of those meetings. I will keep you updated on activities as they develop. *Major* out."

"You and *Major* have been busy." I said.

"Just trying to do my part. I'm just proud to be part of the team," he said, laughing.

"Couldn't hold a straight face, could you?"

"No, I'll have to work on that."

"You know those guys can't see the forest for the trees." I said.

"They know they have lost ships. They've heard we've lost ships. But they haven't put together that we are lying about the ships we've lost, or the strength of our shields."

"I think it's arrogance, they have been top dog for so long it's impossible for them to believe someone else can beat them. They can accept taking ship losses as long as they are destroying the other side's ships. They can't accept a totally one-sided defeat." Mal said.

"According to that message, we have six months before it gets crazy — well crazier. In the meantime we need to look at arming Cone Rock with battleship size rail guns and lasers." I said.

"Yeah, in our spare time," Mal said, chuckling.

***

The maintenance area behind the docking area had now been mined out and infrastructure was being installed there. Mining bots were now starting on the factory area, which also held the Smelter-Refinery.

"We will need smaller mining bots to get around in tight areas, and the number of habs they need to dig will slow us down," I said.

Mal looked at me, "what was it Jocko said? Something about grandmothers and eggs?"

"He's old enough to pull that saying off, you will need to wait a few more years before you use it again."

"Yeah, yeah, yeah ... whatever. The point is, we've got this."

I held my hands up in surrender, "If you say so, I believe you."

The P550 was nearing completion, and we'd made a few changes to her. We removed the forward flight deck and made a bridge as part of the living quarters, and put internal shields to divide the living area from the passenger area. She would be complete in about two weeks.

"Jocko, we need another 200 people, but including families we can't bring more than 550 passengers," I messaged him.

"Send me the list of trades we need. And I'll have them ready in two weeks," he answered.

The big PL3000 was ready for occupation, with shore power and shields. We continued to work on her while she was being occupied. The two hybrid haulers were back from their run and, together with *Cargo Three*, had brought in supplies. With these in hand, the PL3000 could be fully stocked.

Earl and his crew had made 25 new smaller mining bots and had turned them loose to mine out the Hab areas. The P550 came out of refit and passed its shakedown cruise. The pilot, crew, and family moved aboard and tested everything in the family area. They left for Conclave Station a week later to pick up our new hires and families.

Major's "Unreported News" broadcast was having the desired effect. Three council members had resigned, and two others were under investigation. It was all being called political mudslinging by the opposition, but the voters were not convinced. It was making things harder for the corporation to operate in their normal underhanded ways. Politicians were not taking bribes as readily.

Our new frigate, which we had named "*Black Blade*", was getting the now standard refit of shields. We loaded *Cargo One*, *Two*, and *Three* with metals and loaded the two hybrid ships with gravel and sent them all to OEM. Once *Black Blade's* refit was complete, Captain Williams would move up from *Vanguard* and two platoons of Marines would move over from *Black Ice*. "Vee, message Commander Jones that we need another company of Marines to fill out our frigates." "Sent and acknowledged."

***

"Trade me," Mal said, holding out an M-baton.

"New model?"

"Yep, we added a "Hammerhead" stun gun to it. Earl and his crew are making the new ones and trading them out with all of our issued ones. We've also added a hammerhead crowd control setting on all of our vehicles."

"Good idea, I'd rather not kill anyone I don't have to. On another subject, I'd like you to consider taking the M-nanite treatment too. Better to have it and not need it," I said.

"Than to need it and not have it," he finished.

I nodded, "the girls, too, for the same reason."

"I'll think about it."

"Let's go take a tour of the battleship." I said.

"Oh, yeah, let me grab an M-Comp. We might as well install an ACE while we are there."

She was a serious-looking warship. I'd seen pictures of the old bluewater Navy Battleship "USS Mighty Mo," that's what this reminded me of, except where that ship had three 16" barrels per turret this ship only had one. You only needed one barrel, since the round coming off each railgun could weigh a ton and travel at a tenth of the speed of light. If that hits a target, you didn't have to worry about a second round. She also had missile tubes for ship to ship missiles, missile defense systems, lasers, planetary missiles, ECM pods, and other weapons even I didn't recognize.

"We will remove the engines, right?" Mal asked.

"Yeah, but I'm not sure what to use the extra room for."

"Attack drones, that can fly both close air support, for Marines? Or fighter cover for the battleship, or attack ships against enemy ships." Mal said.

I thought a moment, "How many do you think we could fit in that area?" "12 to 15, with a maintenance bay."

"ACE controlled?" Mal nodded.

"This is probably a stupid question, but propulsion and power source?"

"Yeah, stupid." He chuckled.

"Miniaturized GCD, and M/U-Rs?" He nodded.

"You've already been working on it, haven't you?"

Mal shrugged, "I may have jotted down a few notes, and sketched on a napkin or something."

"*Vee*, is there a new plan in our database for attack drones?"

"Yes, Commodore."

"Display it please." It was sleek, and since it was unmanned, there was more room for weapons and ammo. "Nice napkin sketch."

"I try."

"I like it, I'll look at the battleship plans and see how many we can support." We walked toward the bridge, looking around as we made our way. "We will need more Legionnaires." I said. Mal nodded. On the Bridge, Mal started installing the M-Comp and the ACE program.

"Have you thought of a name for her yet?" Mal asked.

"*Black Anvil.*"

"And we could call the new attack drones *Hammers*." Mal said.

I nodded, "I like it."

"*Vee*, bring up the battleship's plans." The plans appeared on my HUD wall. "Remove engines." They disappeared from the plans. "Remove all generators, install OFE 11's for shields and the same GCD as we used on *Duty*. Install M/U-Rs, here, here, and here. Open the flight bay all the way back to empty engine compartments. That will now be the hanger and maintenance bay. Based on the size of the *Hammer* attack drones, how many can we store along the outside of the *Anvil*, in covert slots, if we start here and here down both sides?"

"Using a wasp cone hexagon pattern, we could carry and support 30 Hammers." Answered *Vee*.

"Show me the layout, and the placement you recommend on the plans." The plans changed, showing the new layout. "Reroute all plumbing and M-cabling to support the changes. Upgrade all electronics to M-tronics and M-cabling. Add an M-printer to engineering support. I looked the plans over again, "Any additional suggestions, *Vee*?"

"Remove rear dorsal fin, and mount railgun turrets here, here, and here." The plans changed as *Vee* made suggestions.

I nodded, "send the plans to the ship design engineers for eval and suggestions."

"Sent."

Anvil's ACE was installed and integrated in less than three hours. We moved *Anvil* to *Travis* the next day to start refit.

Buck's crew worked on assembling the *Hammers* as the parts came out of the M-printer. Once Buck saw all the *Hammer* hanger plans for *Black Anvil* he said, "We should pull all the engines and put *Hammers* on all of our warships. Including *Loki* ... she could hold three easily."

I nodded, "Good idea, have them do *Loki* next."

***

The P550 arrived with our new workers and families and we got them settled in to the PL3000. We gave them a few days off and then put them to work.

The P550 left for Titan to pick up a load of new hires we contracted for through a hiring service. We allowed the P550 ACE to take the ship up to 200 percent of normal engine speed. We need to speed things along, but they refrained from engaging 200 percent until they were away from traffic and dark.

"Message from cargo ships convoy," *Vee* said, "They have picked up two followers."

"Acknowledged, sending escort, continue on course and speed, stay in the open, don't go dark."

"Sent."

"Alert *Ice* and *Vanguard*, to leave ASAP. If corporate ships fire on our ships, use hammerheads. Other than that, use your own discretion."

"Sent."

Vanguard and *Ice* deployed within the hour.

The MD area was now complete and the Factory-Smelter-Refiner area was well underway with infrastructure installations. The new area could be online in a month. All the Cone Ship emitter foundations had been cut in, and the installation of the OFEs had started. They had assembled all the M/U-Rs, and they were ready to install.

Mal, Jade and Jazz finally got the M-nanite treatments and took a few days off to recover.

"I think we're in trouble," Mal said.

"Why, what's happened?" I asked.

"It's the girls."

"What about them?"

"They have been getting together with five or six other women and Aunt J, like some kind of sewing club."

"So?"

"They don't sew."

"Maybe they will start," I said, smiling.

"I overheard the word 'chapel' from one of them."

"Uh-oh."

"Yeah, Uh-oh."

"Do you think it's too late for us to get away?" I said, smiling.

"That ship has sailed," he said, laughing.

"I guess we better man-up and go hide in our shops like every other man has done since the beginning of time," we laughed.

CHAPTER 11

The smaller liner arrived with another batch of workers, and since most of this group were engineers, we put them to work refitting our ships.

"Commodore, we are picking up an unauthorized transmitter activation," *Vee* reported. "Per SOP we have jammed and blocked transmission, and have isolated the transmission to Berth Delta 373 on the PL 3000.".

"Seal the berth and notify security, confiscate the transmitter and take that person into custody. Search him or her and scan for augmentations ... take no chances.

We went down to detention to see our detainee. "He's augmented and has internal comms, but we're keeping his equipment jammed. His tech is nowhere close to ours," *Vee* reported.

"Any clue as to who he works for?"

"A corporation, or well-funded independent organization," Mal said.

"Well, let's go see what he's willing to tell us." I said. Mal stayed at the observation window.

I went into the holding cell; he was handcuffed to the table. I sat down across from him. "Why are you holding me, since I have done nothing wrong? If this is the way you treat employees, I quit! Just pay me for my time and send me home," he said.

"Do all you guys get the same manual to learn lines from if caught? That is almost word for word what the last guy said. Next you will tell me it was not smart to come in here with you alone. And because they have augmented you, you could snap those cuffs and come across this table and kill me. I've seen that movie before. He didn't like the way it ended. I'd like to keep this conversation civil, so please do nothing that will turn out badly."

"My guess is you're a corporate spy, or a spy hired by the Corporation. You were to infiltrate us, find our location and see if you could get our tech. Well, two out of three, as they say. When you report back to your employer's, tell them to leave us alone. All we want is to be left alone. You'll be held here until the next ship to Titan, which should only be a few days."

I stood up to leave. "Will you sell it?" he asked.

I turned back, "We tried that first. We sold them a shield installation for a tug. The first thing they did was to take it back to their engineers and take it apart. When they did that, it self-destructed. They sued for replacement and lost.

"Ever since then they have been trying to steal it. They have killed my people over tech they could have bought. So, the answer to your question is no. I will not sell it to them. I may someday sell it to the public again, but I'm not even sure about that."

"They will not stop, you know, you have challenged the status quo, and they can't allow that to stand. If they do, their kingdoms will crumble."

"I figured as much. We've lost ships to them, but it took multiple ships with overwhelming firepower. I have decided that when I die, my secrets die with me. Safe travels." I left the room and stopped outside the door. "*Vee*, can you wipe his recording augmentation?"

"Yes, Commodore."

"Do so."

I stepped into observation where Mal had been watching and listening. "Hammerhead him and have Doc tranq him until he is well on the way to Titan."

"Good idea." Our guest left us the next day, unconscious.

Black Ice messaged that they had taken two more ships — two destroyers with new weapons on board. ETA six hours.

The new weapons turned out to be ship-sized rail guns. Each vessel had a rail gun running down the full-length of each of its sides.

"It looks like we've got our rail guns for Cone Rock, courtesy of the corporation." Mal said.

I nodded, "Yes, it does. This is also an opportunity to sow contention and confusion to the enemy," I said.

"How's that?" Mal asked.

"The corporation has a new weapon that just destroyed the *Travis* and *Vanguard*. We can't stand against that kind of firepower. We quit, and we're going into hiding," I said.

"Too bad about all those ships and crews," Mal said, smiling.

"*Vee*, recall all ships except P550. Radio silence and go dark as soon as they get away from traffic. Return to Cone Rock."

"Sent."

"Send a message to Admiral Cole. The Corporation has a new weapon that can penetrate shields. The *Travis* and *Vanguard* have been destroyed. This is a hopeless fight. I'm quitting while my friend and I are still alive, she's all I have left."

"Sent."

"That should spin them up." Mal said.

I nodded, "It should indeed. We need to go to Titan: we have business to attend to." I said.

"Vee, message Buck to get a team together and pull the engines out of *Loki* and install three *Hammers*. Highest priority. Plans to follow, attach the plans and send."

"Sent."

"We need some things loaded on to *Loki*. I need to go and talk to Jocko," I said.

"What can I do?"

"Get this list of supplies and equipment loaded onto *Loki*, and tell the girls we are leaving, and they can't come."

"You have lost your mind! Just shoot me … it would be a mercy killing," Mal said, shaking his head, hands in the air.

"Coward!"

"You're dang right."

"All right, we'll tell them together."

"Why don't we take them with us?"

"Sissy."

***

We found Doc in the med-bay, "Doc, I need you to make me a face prosthesis."

"What? Why?"

"Part of a disguise."

"OK, that's easy ... the M-nanites can do it, or I think they can. Let me check."

"So how does this work?" I asked.

"We found subsections in the M-nanite programs. One of them was a section on spec op-counterintelligence. I noticed a part about facial recognition, voice prints, all kinds of stuff," He said.

"I guess I should read more of the program." I said. He opened the code and scrolled down through the sections.

"OK, good news, bad news. Bad news is you have to take another treatment, good news is I'll have you out of surgery in less than six hours."

"Surgery?"

"For this program, *Vee* can control and operate it, but you have to have implants. We'll put them behind your shoulder blades. Once that is done the M nanites will come out through your pores forming a metal prosthesis and will reabsorb when you don't need it."

"*Vee*, download the program specs and see how involved this is, and if it will do what I want."

"Minor surgery for implants, it will do what you want and more, I will have full control."

"OK, Doc let's get this done, I got things to do." Seven hours later I was walking out of med-bay fully healed, going to find Jocko.

"*Vee,* apply the nerve block before releasing the nanites through my pores next time."

"Yes, sir."

"On the plus side, I don't need my contacts anymore ... the M-nanites are in my eyes."

"Yes sir, if we have a retina pattern of someone, the M-nanite's can duplicate it to pass a retina scan, fingerprints too."

"Don't tell me they can reshape my face to look like anyone."

"No, sir."

"Aw-man!"

"But they can make you not look like you, to full facial recognition scan."

"I guess it's better than nothing."

"Yes, sir."

I found Jocko in the galley having a cup of coffee. I pulled a cup of coffee for myself and join him.

"Mal said you were looking for me," Jocko said.

I nodded, taking a sip of hot coffee. "You have any contacts on Titan?"

"Some, what do you need?"

"I have need of a special contact, who has no love for the corporation, but who will not cut my throat when my back is turned."

He looked at me for a moment, taking a swallow of his coffee. "I'm going to need more information before I decide who, if anyone, I should send you to."

I told him of the message to the admiral, and that I needed to sell off HMS, on paper and give the appearance of disappearing. We would form a new corporation to transfer or sell all my assets to, so we could keep doing business.

Some of them would be off the books, and I needed to move among the shadows. All our ships would be re-flagged under the new corporation. We also need a small hanger and a presence there in a shady part of town.

"OK, that will throw their camp into disarray. I know someone who fits the bill, I'll introduce you."

"I mean no offense, but how far do you trust him?"

"With my life, he's my brother. He's a thief and a rogue,

but he believes in honor among thieves. You treat him honorably and he'll do the same. We'll meet. You decide."

"Fair enough. We'll be leaving in a day or two."

He nodded, "I'll be ready."

***

"Commodore, you have a message from *Major*."

"Locate Mal."

"He is in his shop."

"Tell him to stay there … I'm on the way." When I got to Mal's shop I went inside and closed and locked the door. He looked at me with raised eyebrows.

"Message from *Major*," I said. "*Vee,* play message."

"Commodore, the following is the latest conference comm between Admiral Cole, CEO Baker, and Representative Johnson."

The wall screen came on, "Have you lost your mind? You couldn't wait, you childish idiot!" Admiral Cole said.

"What are you babbling about?" Baker said.

"What's happened, Admiral?" Representative Johnson asked.

"I got a message that the HMS fleet was engaged and destroyed by corporate warships. They destroyed his fleet, killed his friends, and sent him into hiding, God only knows where. He has no capacity to refit our ships even if he wanted to, now."

"Is this true, Baker?"

"Possibly, I don't have the full report yet, but apparently his shield tech was not as strong as he believed," Baker said.

"That was very shortsighted of you Baker," Representative Johnson said.

"Even if the shields weren't perfect, they were generations ahead of where we are," Admiral Cole said.

"Now we can get back to business." Baker said complacently.

"What a waste! All that time, creds, and energy." Admiral Cole said.

"I'll make sure they cover your budget," Representative Johnson said.

"Look on the bright side, Admiral, at least now you don't have to execute any civilians to get your tech or your budget for your precious Legion." Baker said.

"Those people are meaningless, I'd have sacrificed them all and executed the two battalions of Marines for atrocities if it would've gotten me that tech and all my appropriations. This would have guaranteed the ESFL for generations to come. I would have gladly killed the lot of them," Admiral Cole declared. The display ended.

"Shortly after that, Admiral Cole recalled the ships from the NL base and dispatched the ESFL back to normal patrols."

"The Unreported News has become the most watched news blog," said *Major*.

"We have exposed corrupt security force members and their leaders. We have exposed strong-arm tactics by corrupt union members and union bosses. We have exposed the mob connections within and support of union and corporate enterprises.

"We now have ACE integration and CEO Baker's organization and corporate headquarters. We have ACE integration in Representative Johnson's offices, headquarters, and the United Nations Space Agencies, UNSA. More will follow as they become accessible," *Major* out."

"The Admiral just shot himself in the foot and blew his leg off." Mal said.

I nodded, "it gives us more time, but we can't assume we are free and clear. *Vee*, locate Gunny's ship."

"She's returning from the NL base. She was recalled before she arrived. She is 20 hours away from our present location."

"Message to *Vanguard*, send them location of the ship, with orders to hammerhead it, seize and return with it to base. Go dark all the way."

"Sent."

"Now they'll have no shielded ships, and we will make it

look like the corporation destroyed her with a fake last gasp comm from Gunny," I said with satisfaction.

"He's getting off easy for what they did." Mal said.

"Vee, message *Vanguard* ACE, when they get to Gunny's location send a voice-only message using Gunny's voice, to Admiral Cole. Say corporate ships are attacking, then cut it off as if they destroyed the ship in mid-sentence."

"Sent and acknowledged."

Mal nodded, "Confusion to the enemy!"

"*Vee*, message *Gunny* ACE let her know we are coming to bring her home, and not to reveal our intentions or presence."

"Sent."

***

The smaller liner, P550, arrived with another load of new hires and their families. That would be the last of our fresh personnel until we concluded working on Titan to create a new corporation.

"*Vee,* message Commander Jones. I'm going to need four people for a mission. They must be able to install surveillance gear as well as other equipment — leaving within a day, two at the most."

"Sent and acknowledged." *Loki*'s refit was nearing completion and should be ready in time for our departure.

***

When *Loki* was ready for departure. We loaded all our equipment and supplies. Our crew, including Jocko, was present and ready for departure.

"Message from *Vanguard*," Vee said, "Mission successful, distressed message sent. Enroute home, dark."

"Acknowledge."

We left Cone Rock for Conclave that afternoon. *Loki* went dark and sped toward Conclave, and at .3 C. we would arrive in less than an hour.

When we approached, we held our position just outside Conclave space. *"Loki,* comm Aaron Stein."

"Commodore it's good to hear from you. What can I do for you?" I explained to him what we needed and what we were trying to do, and why.

"Basically, HMS will be sold off and dissolved," he repeated. "A new corporation will buy HMS out, but it can't appear that you are just changing names."

"Correct. I will need info for five board members."

"What about your holdings in OEM?"

"The board member info will be sent to you, with the CEO's name and info. I'll get back to you on the OEM matter in an hour."

"I'll be waiting, so I'll go in and get the easy stuff started."

"Commodore, out."

"Call BB at OEM."

"Good to hear from you," BB said.

"You too, sir."

"All is well, I hope."

"Life has gotten complicated. Which is the reason I'm calling."

"What do you need?"

"I need to make it look like I'm having a fire sale. I'd like you to buy me out at 50 percent of face value. We're sure our enemies are watching you, and this will help sell my story."

"OK, what do you want done with the other 50 percent?"

"I can't take it, and you can't take it out of your accounts. They'll be watching for that."

"OK, I can see that. On paper, I'll buy you out at 50 percent of face value. But between you and me, this is a loan, since you still own 10 percent of OEM. That's only fair for what you've done for us."

"OK, but if you get pressured to sell out, or even want to sell out, do it. We'll settle up someday."

"Done, stay safe."

"*Major,* I need five fictitious identities for myself, Mal, Jazz, Jade and Aunt J that will stand up to background checks. They will be board members for a new corporation we are creating through Aaron Stein. I also need a new identity under the name James Hermes, so I can be the CEO of our new corporation and be seen in public. Work with *Vee* on what my M-nanites can do for facial recognition, retinal scans, and fingerprints. All the identities need full workups, the works."

"Understood. Mr. Stein will have all the info within the hour."

"Commodore out."

"Commodore you have a message from *Vanguard*. Closer inspection of Gunny turned up multiple kilotons of gold. They apparently didn't trust banks to hold their ill-gotten gains."

"Acknowledge. We need to take a detour before we go to Titan, since *Gunny* has contributed to the cause." I said.

Aaron called back, "I have all the info I need except the name of the new corporation."

"Hermes," I said, "with James Hermes as CEO and majority owner."

"That's everything I need, we'll get it transmitted to Titan, but give it a few days before using it."

"Got it, we'll be in touch." "*Loki* take us back to *Duty*."

"Roger, enroute."

"It looks like we'll be going home for a few days, then we'll be heading to Titan."

When we docked with *Duty*, I called Buck, Mal, Jade, and Jazz to move to *Loki*. "*Loki,* take us to dock with *Gunny.*"

"Enroute."

We docked with *Gunny*, and used *Loki*'s two vehicles to load crates of gold, as much as *Loki* could carry. The amount wasn't limited by the weight but by the room in *Loki*'s cargo bay. Once we were finished we returned to *Duty*.

***

We had gathered in *Duty*'s family galley for a meeting about the counterintelligence upgrades to everyone's nanites.

"No, it's not the only way, but it's the easiest way. That is if you ever want to be seen in public while you're still young." I said.

They all just looked at me. "You have *Vee* in your cyber legs, how are we supposed to control ours?" Jazz asked.

"It's all part of the implants and I'm sure Mal can tweak that to boost the power and capabilities," I said. Mal nodded.

They all finally agreed to get the upgrade. Mal upgraded them with M-Comps. Doc made the reservoir look like a bone, in case someone scanned them, just as he had done with mine. Luckily, there were no complications, and everyone was fine the next day.

"We might want to take a medic with us in case something happens," Jazz said.

"OK, good idea. Let's take the medic who's been working with Doc," I said.

We waited three days to make sure everyone was comfortable with their upgrades, trying out our new faces in private. It was strange looking at everyone in their new identity, and looking in the mirror was even stranger.

Once comfortable, we left *Duty* and headed for Titan. "*Loki*, take us out and around and come in from the Sun side. Once on that side, we'll approach Titan in the open. Also arrange for an armored vehicle to meet us at the port for the gold transfer to the bank and Hermes' corporate accounts. Charge all fees to the Hermes Corporation."

"Roger."

"*Loki*, change your transponder codes to *Raven*. *Vee*, prepare an ID for "Captain Roger Glass", captain of the cargo ship *Raven*."

"Done, all information transmitted."

It felt strange having the M-nites make a metal face, or rather partial metal face, on my head. Captain Glass, however, liked the look. We landed at the spaceport on Titan and found our armored vehicles waiting. I signed the paperwork and they left for our bank.

That part of the mission completed, we left the port and headed back in-Sun. Once we were away from Titan, we went dark. *Loki* monitored the gold transfer into Hermes' corporate accounts. The Hermes Corporation now had creds to work with.

CHAPTER 12

Jocko messaged his brother and arranged for us to meet. *Loki* landed at the designated hanger, and we were met there by William, or as his friends called him "Wild Bill."

The brothers greeted each other with what seemed to be a heartfelt hug. As soon as it ended, Wild Bill turned and looked at me.

"Is this him?" Jocko nodded. Wild Bill laughed and reached out his hand toward me, "I want to shake the hand of the man who taped a plate to my brother's butt. When I saw that on the net, I laughed till I cried."

"It wasn't that funny," Jocko said.

"You know it was!" Bill said.

"OK, it was funny the first 10 times, after that, not so much," everyone laughed.

Wild Bill led us into his office. "My brother tells me you are an honorable man. I've had you checked out, and all I have found says that is true. He also tells me you have helped him frequently as well as saving his life.

"Thank you for that, I only have one brother and I like him. Most of the time, anyway. How can I help you?"

"I'll speak plainly. Your brother says you are an honorable man as long as you are treated honorably. He also says I can trust you. I trust your brother with my life, I trust his judgment.

"The wealthy and powerful people who tried to kill us are still trying. We've had to make changes and we are moving some of our operations to Titan. I need someone I can trust on Titan who knows how the local games are played, to tell me who deals straight and who doesn't.

"I need to buy a hanger for my operations, but not just

any hanger will do. We have some specific requirements. I don't want trouble with the local bosses, and I don't want to waste time with a salesman trying to sell me a property he will make the most profit from. Can you help me with all that?"

"You spoke plainly, so I will. I can offer advice on properties and local customs. Who is friendly and who is not. But I need to know how dirty my hands will get."

I nodded, "99 percent of what we do is aboveboard, unless someone hurts me or mine. That they will not walk away from. And if it comes to that, I'll do the wet work myself, so you won't have to.

"I know everyone has to make a living, so I'll pay for services rendered."

"I can work with that," he said, "what are the requirements for your business?"

"I don't want to be near a lot of traffic. Not in the nicest areas, but not in the worst of slums. A good sized hanger, but not anything I could fit a super carrier in, and with a decent size Hab.

"It should be on the main power grid, as well as the main comms trunk line." I said.

"Commodore, there are two vehicles approaching this building fast, a potential threat," *Vee* said suddenly in my ear.

"Are you expecting trouble?" I asked.

"Always." Bill said, looking at his man who was listening to his com.

He answered the unasked question, "It's Randy, there was an explosion at the club in your office. They're bringing in Riley, and they say it's bad."

"Why didn't they take him to the med center?" Wild Bill asked.

"Someone had set up an ambush and were waiting for them. It looks like they were after you again."

"I've got an Auto-doc on my ship, bring them in," I said.

Bill nodded, "take him into the hangar bay."

"*Loki,* prep med-bay for incoming casualties."

"Roger, Commodore, standing by."

They took Riley straight to med-bay, and our medic put him in the Auto-doc.

"Sir, he's bad, he'll need more than the standard treatment. If he doesn't get it, he will die," the medic said.

I nodded, "whatever it takes, save him if you can."

"Yes, sir."

The medic started the M-nite treatment on Riley. He only had to give him the Level One treatment, which included the M-carbon fiber bone casings. After an hour the medic said, "he'll make it, sir."

I nodded, "Keep me informed."

Bill had been there the whole time, watching. "He wasn't going to make it, but you gave him something extra, something special," he said.

I nodded, "military grade nanites."

He nodded, "thank you," and left the ship.

"That's his son-in-law," Jocko said behind me. "Bill reacts to anyone hurting his family like you do. Someone will pay for this."

An hour later, Riley's wife Mandy came to the ship with Jocko asking to see Riley.

"Of course," I said, "Jazz take her to the Med-bay please." Jazz and Jade did so, then fixed her a place so she could stay the night with her husband.

Bill and Jocko came in to check on Riley the next morning. All was going well. The Auto-doc said it needed another 24 hours.

"What do we owe you for this?"

"We don't charge for saving a life if we have the means. There may come a day when me, or mine, will need help. You can repay us then. But I pray that day never comes," I said.

"Amen," Bill said.

We were having lunch in *Loki*'s galley, "Interesting ship," Bill said.

"That she is. The assassins that killed my friend and almost got me didn't need her any longer," I said.

"Business is war," Bill said.

"Sometimes it's just war," I answered.

"I think I found a property that may fit your needs, but it's not exactly what you asked for," Bill said.

"What are we talking about?" I asked.

"There is a medium-sized smelter-refinery that closed about a year ago. The owners fell on hard times and couldn't keep it open. Truth be told, the Corporation undercut their prices and drove them out of business.

"It has a good size hanger and Hab, is on the main power and comms trunk. You could buy it for creds on the K-cred. The bank has been begging for an investor to take it over and put people back to work.

"I didn't know whether you would want to get involved with something like that. On the upside, it sits out on its own. As far as local bosses interfering, it was neutral territory, because all the people that worked there from all the local Habs."

"Let's go look at it," I said.

We took a ride over to see the property and spent a couple hours checking everything out.

"It meets all our specs," Mal said, "The equipment is a little out of date but not bad for a medium-size smelter-refiner. Good bones, good foundation, and it has its own fusion reactor power plant."

That sold it. "We can upgrade all of this in plain sight. It's a great place to launder gold and extra rock. This will cover us nicely," I said. Everyone agreed.

"Now we have to negotiate and buy it."

"That I can help with ... what if I could get the bank to sell it to you for a cred per K-cred, and finance 100 percent of it?" Bill asked.

"Who do I have to kill?" I asked, everyone laughed.

"I own the bank that owns the property, so you'd be doing me another favor," Bill said.

"We'll take it. Draw up the paperwork for Hermes Corporation to buy it," I said and we shook hands on the deal.

Riley got out of the Auto-doc the next day. "They tell me I have you to thank for saving me," He said.

"Nah, I just helped stuff you in the Auto-doc," I said smiling.

"Nevertheless, thank you, sir."

"I'm just glad it all worked out."

"Mr. Bill told me you had to give me special nanites to save me."

I nodded, "mil-spec nanites, they make your body's healing systems work better when you are hurt. They also harden your bones and make them harder to break."

"I hope I never have to test that bone-breaking part," he said, smiling.

"Maybe you could go back to your old job," Bill said.

"Yeah, if they'd reopen the smelter-refinery."

"What did you do there?" I asked.

"I was the assistant plant manager."

"Young for that position, aren't you?"

He shrugged, "Yeah, I guess, but I had a knack for it."

"Mr. Mallory liked me and helped me along, teaching me the business."

I looked at Bill. "Mallory still around?" Bill nodded. "Do you think he'd come back?"

"Probably." Bill said.

I looked at Riley, "Want your old job back?"

"Yes, he does," Mandy quickly answered for him, and everyone laughed.

"Well, that settles that. Contact Mr. Mallory and tell him we are reopening the plant, and say I'd like to talk to him about managing it for me," I said.

"I'd like my old job back too, sir." His wife said. "I was head of HR, that's how Riley and I met."

"You're hired, and you are about to become very busy. We have a lot to do and you will both need to sign NDA's."

"Yes sir, that's kind of standard here on Titan," Mandy said.

"Good to know, we will meet after the paperwork to buy

the plant has been completed. I will have a list of people and trades I need to hire. Riley, I need to talk to you and Mr. Mallory about specific people."

"Yes sir," Riley answered.

***

I sent the contracts over to our new lawyer's office to make sure we had covered everything. It was the same lawyer Aaron used to route all of our paperwork through. He also happened to be Aaron's brother, Joshua Stein, who said everything was in order.

We met at Bill's bank and signed all the paperwork. We also opened another account with them and moved half of our creds to that institution.

We moved *Loki* over to our new hanger, and Mal got started installing our M-Comp's while our security detail installed their equipment. We met with Mr. Mallory, Riley and Mandy the next morning. Over coffee in *Loki*'s galley we got down to business.

"I want to hire as many of the laid-off plant workers back as we can." I said. "However, I also want to take this opportunity to get rid of any deadwood and troublemakers. If they were trouble in the past, or nonproductive, I don't want them." They nodded as Mandy took notes.

"Will you be wanting engineers and maintenance trades?" Riley asked.

"I want them first."

He nodded, "my brother, Braden, was one of the lead engineering maintenance men. After the layoff he tried to start his own business, but it's been slow for him."

"Do you think he'd come back?"

"I'm sure he would."

"Does he also have 'the knack'?" I said, smiling.

"In fact, he does," he said chuckling.

"Bring him on board then."

"He'll want to bring his crew with him," Mandy said.

"Hire them, too," I said.

"Mr. Mallory, you'll run the day-to-day operations? I don't have time so I'll stay out of your way. But if anything comes up that you need help with, I'm always available. The first thing we will do is to upgrade the smelter-refinery and reactor," I said.

"I need to see Braden as soon as possible."

"This afternoon?" Riley asked.

"That works." I answered.

We met with Braden that afternoon and went over all we wanted changed and upgraded. "That's a lot of work, Mr. Hermes, what's our timeline for finishing?"

"The faster the better. We'll be bringing in parts, and you'll be working with myself, Buck and Jocko. You hire all the temp engineers you need, but only ones you trust to do the work right, and not talk about our work here."

"All right sir, when do we start?"

"Right now, get your guys in here and start pulling parts to be refurbished or replaced. Go through management to get them hired in."

"Yes, sir."

"Let's take a walkthrough of the offices," I said. It didn't take long. "We will have to upgrade this. Jazz, you and Jade go through Joshua and get a prefab construction company to expand the Hab office complex. It will, after all, be our corporate headquarters. Build us something nice, but also fairly fast. We need to be up and running soon."

We started hiring the next day putting them to work. We were assembling a list of parts we needed from *Duty*, and we knew we would have to make a run back in a few days, anyway.

Then Security commed, "Commodore, we have trouble outside."

"On the way."

Security was already moving in that direction. I saw the issue right away. A huge man was standing leaning over the in-processing table yelling at Mandy, Jazz, and Jade.

"Excuse me, sir," I said.

He turned to look at me, "What you want, little man?" I suppose when you're 6 foot nine almost everyone is little.

I smiled, "it's not so much what I want, as it is what I need."

"And what would that be, boy?"

"An ambulance, if you don't back away from the table and show some courtesy," I said.

He laughed, "Well, I'm here to be hired back to my old job."

"Were you called for an interview?"

"No, that's why I'm here, I don't have time to wait to be called I need to get these men back to work. These stupid women are holding me up."

"You don't have to worry about that, you're not being hired, and if you are on the list to be hired you aren't anymore."

"You can't run these crews without me," he shouted.

"I'll risk it."

"I'll break you in half, little man."

"Before you do, I'll need your name for the ambulance driver."

He laughed, "Robert Smythe, they call me Big Rob."

"Any relation to Captain Reggie Smythe," I asked.

"Never heard of him."

"Good. I'd hate to hurt Reggie's feelings," I smiled. "This is your last chance to leave uninjured," I said.

He lunged at me, trying for a bear hug. I went under his lunge and gave him a palm strike to the ribs, breaking at least four.

"Are you going or staying?" I asked. He came at me again, and I wasted no more time, using an uppercut to his diaphragm, which stunned him. He swung at my head and I went under it. I broke both of his shoulder blades. He dropped to his knees, and I stomped on one of his legs, breaking it.

I took him by the hair and turned his head, so he could see the ladies. "And if you are ever rude to those ladies again, I will not be so nice." I ear tapped him and let him face plant into the floor. "Load him into the ambulance and get him to the Med Center."

"He's always been a bully," Mandy said.

Jazz came over and kissed me on the cheek. "Thank you, dear."

"I was saving his life, if he'd made you mad you might've killed him," I said.

"Yeah, but I would have just shot him." Jazz said.

"If Dad had been here, that's what he would've done."

"OK folks, show's over, let's get back to work — I've always wanted to say that." Everyone laughed, and that broke the tension.

We transmitted the list of parts we needed to *Loki*, and they started them running through the M-printer. Mal was upgrading what he could with what we had on hand. We named the corporate ACE *"Herm"* and integrated him with the plant and the comm system. He was already receiving encrypted updates from *Major* and it wouldn't be long before he was integrated into other systems across Titan.

Our security team had all our equipment installed, and *Herm* had taken control of it. Jazz, Jade, and Buck made a fast run to *Duty* to pick up parts, a 12-man security team and as much gold as they could fit in *Loki*.

When they got back, I messaged Bill to see if he could come pick up another deposit for his bank.

"How big a deposit?" he asked.

"Several tons, I'd guess."

"I'm on the way!"

We unloaded the parts and Braden got his team to work installing the emitters in the smelter to make smaller gravel. We moved the M/U-R into position to prepare for installation. Meanwhile the crew moved the old fusion reactor out of the way and installed the new one.

The week had gone fast, and we made a lot of progress while the prefab building company was on-site erecting the building Jazz and Jade had ordered.

Mal and Jocko said they were ready to bring the new reactor online. At the moment we were only using two percent of our available power. We figured with the plant running at full capacity we might hit 30 percent, so we planned to sell some of our excess power to the Titan power grid, but keep to about the same amount that the plant had sold them in the past. No use in causing anyone to question where all the extra power was coming from.

Bill picked up the gold and deposited it into our accounts. We figured it would be another week before the plant was up and running.

"*Vee*, message the hybrid ships to bring us a load, heavy on mithrilium. Make sure all our ships, when traveling in the clear, are squawking the new Hermes Corporation registrations," I said.

"Sent."

My plan was to have the two hybrids work locally for a while to build up metal stock before starting to sell it.

"Commodore, Robert Smythe is at the personnel hatch requesting entry."

"Is he armed?"

"No, sir."

"Go ahead and let him in, this should be interesting." Security was close, should they be needed.

"Mr. Hermes, Mr. Smythe asks if he may have a moment of your time?"

"I'll be right there."

"Round two?" Mal asked.

"I don't think so."

I walked into the hiring office, Big Rob was standing by the wall. "Come on in Mr. Smythe," I said. I went to my office and he followed. "Have a seat." I went around the desk and sat. "How can I help you?"

"First, I'd like to apologize for my actions the other day, I was totally 100 percent in the wrong. I deserved the beating you gave me.

"And, upon reflection, I appreciate your restraint."

I nodded, "Apology accepted, Mr. Smythe."

"Second, I'd like to ask for a job, any job. I'll start at the bottom and work my way up.

"I really need this job, Mr. Hermes. To be honest, I had to explain to my wife how I not only didn't get a job, but how I wound up in the Auto-doc. To put it mildly, she was not happy."

"I can only imagine."

"No sir, I don't think you can. I'd rather take another beating than go back home without a job."

I nodded, "your old job is no longer available."

"I understand sir, like I said, I'll start at the bottom."

"What did you do before you made foreman?"

"I worked the smelter floor."

"If I hire you, this is your second chance, there will not be a third."

"I understand, sir."

"I want to be perfectly clear, you will bully no one. You are not in charge of anyone, you work your shift and be helpful. If you don't, you'll have to face your wife with no excuse."

"I understand, sir, you'll have no problems for me."

"Why didn't you approach me like this other day?" He looked at the floor.

"When you're as big as I am you get used to being top dog. It made me arrogant, thinking I could demand and get anything I wanted. I didn't care about how I treated other people.

"The Auto-doc gave me time to think, that and sitting at the house listening to my wife tear me a new one. It was a hard lesson, but one I'll take to heart."

"Mandy," I called.

"Yes, sir?" She said when she reached the door.

"Add Mr. Smythe to the smelter floor crew, whatever position and shift we have available."

She looked at him, "Rob, does Cindy still work the night shift?"

"Yes ma'am, Miss, uh, Mandy, she does."

"Would you rather have a night shift too?"

"Yes, ma'am, if it's available." Mandy looked at me.

"Works for me," I said.

She nodded, "come on Rob, let's get you checked in."

She led him out the door, but he stopped and turned back to me, "Few men would give me a second chance, thinking I'd be looking to get even."

"I'm not worried about that Rob, if you were going to come at me, you're man enough to face me to do it."

"Thank you, sir. You won't regret this, and you may have saved my life. My wife would've killed me if I came home without a job." We both laughed.

CHAPTER 13

The plant was ready to be fired up when the two hybrid ships arrived later that week. Mr. Mallory and Riley brought the machinery online and the ships unloaded.

"You said your new systems were efficient, but this is significantly better than efficient."

I nodded, "You have account creds available to those who want to be paid on the spot."

He nodded, "Some do, the other refineries charge them a two percent service fee for doing it that way."

"Do they now? Well, we won't, so that should bring us some business. If you get outside pressure and I'm not around, let Wild Bill know, we'll deal with it." We had messaged the two hybrid's to work around Titan until further notice and keep our smelter-refiner full.

Before we left, we took the girls shopping. But we got blindsided. We never saw it coming. They bought wedding dresses, bridesmaids' dresses, and tuxedos. I must admit they looked beautiful in those dresses.

Jocko and Bill laughed so hard they cried. "It wasn't that funny!" I said. That made them laugh all the more.

The Hermes Corporation was up and running. Everything was in place and financed. It was time to get back to *Duty*, but I wanted an update from *Major* before we left the area. We left the security team in place for the moment. I'd have to talk to Commander Jones about rotation or hiring a security company on Titan.

We took off from the big moon and went dark as soon as we were away from traffic, leaving Saturn and its magnificent rings behind. "*Major,* give us an update on the admiral, and the

Unreported News."

"Yes Commodore: the admiral suspects Baker of destroying Gunny's ship, and possibly taking the gold. He has stopped all comms with Baker and will only talk to Rep. Johnson.

"He has re-tasked all ESFL ships to shadow corporate ships, making it hard for them to operate in the gray areas of the law. The tension level between the two is rising. Johnson is trying to keep the peace, but leans more toward Baker and his dealings.

"Our ACE network recorded the admiral talking to himself, saying it was too bad Gunny's ship was destroyed before he could make deposit the gold at the New Legion base. Evidence points to the base as a hiding place for their ill-gotten gains.

"The Unreported News is still the most watched news blog on Conclave. We have exposed every corrupt official, union boss, union tough, and crooked security officer of all ranks.

"Anytime the Corporation tries to start something new, we expose it. There is now a 100K-cred reward being offered by the Corporation for anyone who can shut down the Unreported News blog."

"Sounds great! Keep up the good work, and hold the fort," I said.

"Aye-aye, sir."

"Anyone up for a field trip to the New Legion base?" I asked the crew.

"Sounds like fun," Jazz said.

"We'll make it a quick trip," I said. *"Loki,* take us to NL base, fastest route."

"Roger." An hour later, we were approaching the NL base. "Is there anyone at the base?"

"A scan shows minimal power usage, and no ships on or around the base." *Loki* responded.

"Take us in closer and scan with Tri-dar for minerals."

"Yes, sir."

"Most of the material deposits have been mined out. However, I am reading a large concentration of gold, inside the inner level of the Hab area."

"That snake! He's been skimming off every deal he's ever been part of," Jocko said.

"It would seem so," I said. I looked at Mal, "Can you hack the base from here?"

He gave me "The look." "Seriously?"

I smiled, "I'm sorry, forgot again."

Some 30 minutes later we were landing, and the base was ours. "You better go in by yourself first. I have control of all the comps and electronics, but not of any physical safeguards or traps. You remember how this ship was when we first got it." Mal said.

"Yeah, and if I was the admiral, I'd definitely have my loot protected."

I headed to the complex's main door, which was open, thanks to Mal. *Vee* mapped my way to where the gold is stored via a route map on my HUD. When I arrived at my destination, deep in the complex, I found that the admiral had converted the Arms Bay into his private bank vault. The doors were heavily reinforced, and it would take some serious effort to open them.

"*Vee*, pull up the plans for the base, showing the Arms Bay and modifications." The plan showed up on the HUD wall. I looked at them for a moment, then laughed.

"What's so funny?" Mal said in my ear.

"The Admiral was so focused on the front door he failed to realize there was potentially a back door. The wall in the back of the Arms Bay is another corridor, and the wall there is only two feet thick. Send me a mining bot, and we'll go in the back way."

The mining bot met me in the corridor and I programmed it to give me an 8' x 8' door. Less than three minutes later I had my door. The bot was backing out of the way to let me pass when it exploded, and armor-piercing rounds screamed through the opening, pulverizing the opposite corridor wall.

"Combat Mech," *Vee* said. My shields shrugged off the explosion and the shrapnel from the rounds. I looked into the Arms Bay and saw the Mech. It engaged me as soon as I looked in.

"Can you hack it?"

"Working on it." Mal said.

The Mech was moving toward the new door we just created. It fired an RPG, which detonated on my shields. I stepped back behind the wall again.

"Got it." Mal said.

I waited a moment, until all was quiet. I looked through the hole and the Mech was just standing there.

"About time!" I said.

"Everyone's a critic," Mal said.

"You OK, Nic?" Jazz asked.

"Fine, but the bot didn't make it," I said, laughing. I walked into the Arms Bay, to find there were five more Combat Mechs along the wall.

"That's one way to guard your creds," I said. The only other thing in the bay were crates stacked from floor to ceiling. "*Vee*, confirm the contents of those crates." The answer came back almost immediately.

"Gold ... 99.8 percent purity."

"This will hurt him more than any beating I could give him." There were 10 times more crates in here than *Loki* could carry. "*Vee*, is *Anvil* out of refit yet?"

"Yes sir, refit was completed two days ago, she is out for her shakedown cruise now."

"Comm them."

"Commodore, good to hear from you."

"You as well, Reggie, how's the shakedown going?"

"No problems, we came out fully crewed to give her a full test, and we're green across the board."

"Good. There are a few things about the ship I have not briefed you on, but I have a mission for you. So, you'll get it on the fly."

"All right sir, what do you need."

"*Black Anvil*'s propulsion systems are next generation, as I'm sure you've guessed. I'm sending you coordinates, and please order Anvil's ACE to bring you here best speed. When you arrive, we'll talk."

"Coordinates sent, ETA 30 minutes," *Vee* said, in my ear.

"See you in 30 minutes," I said.

"Roger, sir."

I looked around the rest of the bay for any more surprises and found none.

"Mal I'm sure you've already done it, so I don't have to look … can these Mechs act as loaders?"

"Oh yeah, they'll do all kinds of things."

"Good, would you get them started moving these crates out to the landing pad?"

"Can do," he said cheerfully.

By the time the Mechs had started moving the crates, *Black Anvil* was on station. I returned to *Loki*, and we docked with *Anvil*. We went over to see Reggie.

I put on my uniform since we were going on our battleship.

Reggie met us on the hanger deck and piped us aboard, which was a new experience for me.

"This is one awesome ship, Commodore."

"We try," I said smiling.

"You said next generation, but this is way beyond that."

"That's why we need to keep it secret for as long as we can."

"Understood sir, what's our mission?"

"We're going to strip that base of everything we can and then nuke it," I said.

"OhhhhKaaaay! Timeline?"

"ASAP," I said, "you'll also find some new toys in there. Six Combat Mechs, courtesy of the Admiral."

"I'll be sure to send him a card," Reggie said. We all laughed.

"I think we cleared all the booby-traps, but I'm not a hundred percent sure I have them all, so be careful."

"Yes sir, we'll get started right away, carefully."

We took two days to load out all we wanted from the base. The loot packed both of our ships to the bulkheads. We cleaned out everything that wasn't welded down. Weapons, ammo, parts, supplies, food, comps and comm gear.

Once that was complete, we backed off, and *Anvil* fired

a nuke tipped missile deep into the base's Hab. There wasn't much left after that. The asteroid didn't disintegrate, but was in several chunks. We headed for home base.

Our people have been busy while we were gone. Smelter-Refinery-Factory level was complete and the M/U-Rs had been installed. They had run all checks to prepare for startup.

The Hab areas were almost completely mined out as well as the reactor level and the operations area.

We unloaded the gold from *Loki* and *Anvil* into Gunny's ship, which we had renamed *Cargo Four*. The rest was unloaded into *Cargo Three*, and all the arms and ammo were distributed between our combat ships. I divided the six Mechs between the battleship and the two frigates. Our last frigate, *Black Blade*, was almost out of refit.

I had gotten tired of calling our asteroid ship, "Rock Ship", "Cone Rock", and everything else, so I officially named her *Hermes* and made her The Hermes Corporation flagship.

They had installed all the OFEs and GCD emitters and the cables run to them. We were just waiting for the MFR level to be completed.

The girls had unloaded their booty from Titan and had sequestered themselves in the entertainment area of the master level. Apparently no men were invited. That made Mal and me nervous.

***

We brought the SRF online without a hitch. The only problem we were having was with the factory-sized M-printer. We had built it based on the design of the small and medium M-printers. The problem was the main joints needed to be welded and sealed solidly. But so far nothing was working because normal welds would not hold to pass a self-diagnostic test in the program for integrity.

We climbed all over the huge thing, double checking everything. It came down to weld integrity. I was talking to the welder, looking at his welds.

"They look perfect." I said.

"They're as close as we can get to perfect," he said.

"How does their factory do it?"

"I don't have a clue, probably some high tech," he said.

"So it's not the weld and it's not the material, what are we missing?" I mused. "Are you using mithrilium welding rods?"

"Yep. The only thing I can think of is they might weld it under pressure."

"OK, hold off for now, and let me chew on it for a while."

"Yes, sir."

I stood there staring at the weld. "You figured it out yet?" Mal ask.

I shook my head, "there is something tickling the back of my brain,but I can't grab it." I said.

"It will percolate up, just give it some time." I held up my finger. "And there it comes," Mal said, chuckling.

"Grav-plates, magna-flux resonance." Mal looked at me, waiting. "In school, while learning welding, my grav-plates cracked at the welds. It was because the welds could not stand up to the mag-flux-resonance. Every time we turned on the gravity to the plates, they cracked the welds."

"How did you fix it?"

"I actually never did. But I think I know how to," I said. "Now we know about "Odd-numbered Force Emitter's" so we can make an OEF mag welding machine."

It took Mal and I almost a week to build a working prototype. Our welder came over to check it out and try it, and made some suggestions and adjustments; which made it more efficient. Once everyone was satisfied we tried it on the factory M-printer.

The weld looked perfect. When the factory M-printer ran its self-diagnostics it passed the first time, all boards green. The factory level was now 100 percent operational, and we put it to work.

We shut down *Travis'* and *Duty*'s smelters and moved

everyone who was working those jobs over to *Hermes'* operation. This allowed us to run three shifts if we needed to. We programmed the factory M-printer, and the SRF did the rest. Parts rolled off the production line.

Blade was now out of refit, and *Black Ice* went back in as well as *Cargo One*. We moved all ships inside *Hermes,* using the maintenance and docking area. We loaded *Cargo Two* with rock and sent her to Titan.

"*Vee*, message Jocko that we are ready for 200 more workers. Crosscheck your list of trades we need."

"Done."

The MFR areas were complete, and we started installations. "What do we have planned for the ACE comp on Hermes?" I asked.

"I've already installed them, each level will have its own dedicated M-Comp, but all will be linked as part of the whole. As we bring another level online, I'll add an M-Comp and components."

"That should make for one heck of an ACE," I said.

"By far the biggest I've ever made," he agreed, "and most powerful."

Cargo One was an easy refit. We pulled her engines, added MFRs and the GCD emitters. Of course, it's always easier to say than to do.

P550 left for Titan to pick up another load of new hires and their families. We told the Captain of the P550 about his special engines, but not to use the extra speed with passengers on board unless I told him to, or if it was a matter of life or death.

Once *Cargo One* was out of refit and had passed her shakedown cruise, we loaded her with rock and sent her to Titan. We told the captain he could use his new engine speed once he was dark and outside normal traffic lanes. *Vanguard* was the next ship for refit.

"What do you think about rotating a platoon of our security forces through Hermes headquarters on Titan?" I asked Commander Jones.

"I actually think it's a good idea, it will give them some time to blow off steam," he said.

"OK, set up a rotation, they can go in and out on the P550. Include yourself in the rotation at least until we get some of the promenades up and running," I said. But emphasize the need for security."

"You don't have to twist my arm," he answered.

***

"Aunt J we need to think about businesses for the Promenade and how to get them to open shops, stores, and restaurants on Hermes."

"Probably the easiest way would be to offer them free-rent for six months or a year," she said.

"Good idea, you got any contacts who would consider coming on board?"

"No one off the top of my head, but I could check."

"Please do. It will take a while to get everything set up, but I don't want to wait until the last minute to try to find people to open businesses."

"Will do."

We took the ship-sized rail guns off the corporate ships and mounted them at the four corners of the base on Hermes. From there they could cover most areas of the ship and aim down to be within the cone of the GCD. We removed all the tankage and supplies from those ships and fed them into the smelter.

The MFR installations were complete, and our emitters now had power which gave us shields. The P550 arrived with the new hires and their families, and we got everyone checked in to the PL3000. Hermes now had power and was sealed. Environmental started their O^2 soup to make air. When she was aired up, we could get the people working on the Habs and Promenades.

Vee spoke into my ear, "Commodore, you have a message

from Bill ... there is trouble starting at Hermes headquarters."

"Understood. Prep *Loki* for departure and comm Commander Jones."

"Line open."

"Commander Jones."

"Yes, Commodore."

"We have trouble at Hermes headquarters ... send a squad with full kit to *Loki*, ...we'll be departing soonest."

"Yes, sir."

"Jazz, I have to make a run to Hermes headquarters. I'll be back as soon as I find out what's going on."

"OK, be careful."

"Mal, I have to make a run to Hermes headquarters, Bill messaged and said trouble was brewing."

"Want me to come?"

"I don't think it's that big of a problem, so you stay here and keep everything moving."

"Alright, Stay safe."

Loki left with the squad, with Sergeant Adams as their squad leader. As we approached Titan, I said, "*Vee*, have *Herm* give us a sitrep."

"All operations normal, no threats noted," *Herm* said.

"*Vee*, comm Bill."

"Nic, it's good you got here so fast, you have some strong-arming about to take place at the plant."

"Roger, we'll be there in 10 minutes."

We parked *Loki* at the Hermes headquarters hangar. All the security teams met to make sure they covered everything. At shift change our problem showed up, pushing our workers around.

I walked out to where they had gathered. "It seems we have a problem," I said. My security team was mixed in with everyone, but close by.

"We sure do. You haven't paid your union dues and you haven't hired union workers. We're shutting you down," their leader said.

I nodded, "I'll need two names," I said.

"Two names of what?" The leader asked.

"Your name for the ambulance driver, and the name of your boss so I can go talk to him."

I heard somebody behind me laugh. The leader looked at the person laughing, "That you big Rob?"

"Yep."

"This guy for real?"

"Oh, he's for real. He asked me for my name, I laughed at him and gave it to him. I spent six days in an Auto-doc. He's for real, and you do not want to push him," Rob said.

"He's alone, we can take him."

Rob shook his head, "he's never alone, and even if he was, the 10 of you couldn't take him."

"You've gone soft, Rob."

"OK, just remember, when you wake up in the Auto-doc, I tried to warn you."

"Whatever."

"OK, playtime is over, either get gone or get to it," I said. They pulled their batons out. "All right. baton practice," I said, drawing mine. Four of my security guys stepped forward, extending their batons. They weren't expecting that. "Last chance to walk away from this unassisted." I said.

Their leader attacked. He made a straight thrust at my throat; I stepped outside of its arc and broke his elbow. *Vee* warned me of an attack coming in high from my right. I went low and left, and broke his kneecap, arm, collarbone and ear tapped him, he was down and out.

"Their leader just pulled a gun." *Vee* said. I spun, grabbing his gun hand, forcing his arm into him. The gun barrel was pointing up under his chin. All the rest of his men were down or out.

"I don't think you want to do that. I took his gun and did a leg sweep, breaking both of his legs.

"Rob, do you know who he works for?"

"Whoever pays most." I slapped his cheek a few times to

wake him. He came to groaning, gritting his teeth.

"I'm gonna kill…" I broke his hand. He passed out and I slapped his cheek again, he came to.

"Before you start threaten me, I should warn you."

"I'm gonna kill…" I broke one of his fingers and he screamed.

"I will ask you questions and you will answer, or I will break things. Who do you work for?"

"I'll tell you, because they will kill you. Wayne Hall, Union President." I broke his other arm, and ear tapped him.

"Rob get these guys into the ambulances, please."

"Yes sir, Mr. Hermes."

"Mr. Adams, get us some transportation, we're going to join the union. Well, sort of."

CHAPTER 14

The union hall was easy to find. We walked in. "Can we help you?" A man behind the desk asked.

"Some of your men said we needed to join the union and said to speak to Wayne Hall."

"Mr. Hall's busy, I'll take care of you."

"No, we need to see Mr. Hall."

"Look you," he said standing pointing his finger in my face. I grabbed it and broke it.

"I'll kill you..." these guys were reading from a script. I broke his arm, and ear tapped him.

I walked past the front desk, and down the hall to the door marked "President" and walked in. They were four goons in suits in the office.

"Mr. Hall?" I asked.

"Who wants to know?"

"Oh good, I have the right place." I turned to Sergeant Adams, "You guys wait out here, so no one disturbs us." He nodded and closed the door as he left.

"I said, who wants to know?"

"James Hermes, Mr. Hall, pleased to meet you. I'm afraid there's been a misunderstanding."

He smiled, "I see you got my message."

"Yes sir, I did. I thought I'd bring you my answer in person, since your men are unable to do so."

He lost his smile, "What do you mean, unable?"

"Well, they are all at the Med-Center being put into Auto-Docs about now I would imagine."

"So that's how it's gonna be?"

"It doesn't have to be, you can stop this before any more of your men get hurt, or you yourself winds up in a ward." They all laughed.

"Boys, make an example out of him!" They all came at me. The first one swung a haymaker at where I used to be. I broke his arm, ruptured his diaphragm, and ear tapped. I broke the second man's leg, shoulder, and ear tapped. The third one pulled a knife and stabbed at my face. I let it slip past, stomping his foot, crushing it. I took his knife and pinned his hand to the table with it.

Hall reached into his desk drawer, so I kicked the desk while his hand was still in the drawer, pinning him between his desk and the wall.

"As I was saying, there has been a misunderstanding, and please don't threaten to kill me."

"You don't know who you're messing with."

"Please, tell me, so I can get this straightened out."

"This goes all the way to the Earth union."

"Well, they aren't here, and you are.

"Here's what's going to happen. If I see a union sign at my plant, if I hear the word 'union' around my plant, if I read an article with the word union and Hermes in the same sentence, I'm coming back to see you. And next time, I will not be so nice."

"You can't threaten me!"

"Why? You do it to others. You see, that's the problem. You think you are untouchable because you're connected. Well, I don't play by those rules. I play by yours. You mess with my business, I mess with yours. You hurt my people, I put yours in the hospital."

"I'm protected, you can't touch me."

"Your protection doesn't seem to be working today."

"I make one comm," he blustered, "and you disappear."

I moved his comm over to him, "Make the comm."

"You're crazy!"

"You just realized that? I don't care who's protecting you, you are the one I'm coming after. Or your replacement."

He got a hard look in his eyes, "I'm gonna..." I broke his

arm, he passed out and I walked out of his office.

"How'd the negotiations go?" Sergeant Adams asked, smiling.

"They are at a standstill at the moment, because everyone's unconscious." He chuckled.

We headed back to Hermes headquarters, "*Herm,* monitor all comms from Hall, and the union building. Build a dossier on him and those he associates with. Find out who he works for and assemble financials on everyone associated with him."

"Yes, sir."

"Change of plans ... I need to talk to Bill, so please take me to his office." We arrived at Bill's office, and they showed me in.

"How's business?" Bill asked.

"Not bad, minor problems, but we worked it out."

He chuckled, "So I heard."

"Tell me about Wayne Hall."

"Smalltime enforcer uses the union as a cover and an excuse for extortion. Usually hires muscle to do his dirty work."

"Who's he work for?"

"A relatively new player on Titan, Wilbur Bryant. He's got big creds backing him. Came in about a year ago, and brings in muscle from outside when creds can't get the job done. The bombing at my club that almost killed Riley was some of his work."

"I guess he tried to buy you out, and you said no."

Bill nodded, "he only offers 30 percent of what anything is worth, intimidates the rest from you."

"Do you happen to know where Mr. Bryant's office is?"

"I do indeed." He said chuckling.

***

"Take us back to *Loki,* I need to change clothes for my next meeting."

"Yes, Sir."

I changed into the tactical suit "The Tailor" had made for

me. "*Vee,* I will need another persona. Black hair, close trimmed black beard. Scar through my right eye but leave the eye untouched. Hair pulled back into a short ponytail."

I watched in the mirror as the changes were made... weird.

"Yes, that will do nicely, I also need all the IDs for Mr...." I thought for a moment, "Mr. Jay Wright," I said. "Change me back to Hermes, before the team sees me and shoots me," I said.

The team had rented an executive protection armored G-limo. "Nice ride," I said, "Buy it, we'll need it."

"Yes, sir," Adams said.

"I'm going to change into my new persona now." The team nodded. I had *Vee* change my appearance to Jay Wright.

We arrived at Wilbur Bryant's office and went inside. The man at the reception desk looked at me, "May I help you?"

"Mr. Wright to see Mr. Bryant."

"Do you have an appointment?"

"Mr. Hall recommended I come to see him on a business matter."

"Just a moment, please." He commed someone and listened. He ended the comm, "Mr. Hall's never heard of you."

I looked hard at him, "I find it hard to believe you spoke to Mr. Hall because the last time anyone saw him they were putting him into an Auto-doc. And unless you want to join him, I suggest you announce me to Mr. Bryant and let him decide if he wants to see me or not."

He looked at the security team and then back at me. He commed again and listened. He ended the comm, "Someone will be with you shortly."

"Thank you." I looked at the art on the wall while *Vee* hacked all the electronics in the building.

A man in an expensive suit approached us from down the hall. "Mr. Bryant will see you now, but only you, your security stays out here."

I looked at Adams, "If you have to come in, try not to kill everyone." Adam's eyes were hard. He nodded once.

I followed the suit down the hall. "We are being scanned,

I'm rerouting it to scan the escort," *Vee* said.

We entered a room where four men waited. "Mr. Bryant decided he didn't have time for you and told us to take care of you." They laughed.

"How unfortunate for you."

I didn't wait for them to make the first move. I back-kicked the doorman and sent him through the sheetrock wall. I snap kicked the one in front of me and ruptured his diaphragm. The left side man pulled a gun, so I grabbed it and crushed it around his hand. He screamed, dropped to his knees, I held on to him. The right-side man stepped into a sidekick that sent him through the other door.

I pulled the gunman to his feet, "Why don't you announce me to Mr. Bryant?"

He nodded his head weakly, stepped up to the door, and wheezed, "Mr. Wright to see you, sir."

"You'll need to have that looked at," I said, as I passed him.

"Mr. Wright, won't you come in."

"Thank you for seeing me, I realize I don't have an appointment."

"No trouble at all. How can I help you? Please take a seat."

"There's grav-plating under the seat, I've disabled it," *Vee* said. I took the offered seat. He flipped the switch and smiled evilly.

"You think you can come in here and bust up my boys and walk away?"

"In my defense, they did start it," I said, smiling.

"Before I have your body rolled up in that rug, was there a message you were to deliver?"

"There is, Mr. Hermes says to tell you that you have interfered in his business and it's costing him money. But he's not an unreasonable man, he knows business is business, not personal. He's willing to buy you out at a profit, so you don't lose money. You paid 30 percent of the value of everything you've gotten. He'll pay you 2 percent over what you paid."

Bryant chuckled, "Was there anything else?"

"Yes, this is a onetime offer, take it or leave it. If you take it, I pay you on the spot."

"And if I leave it?" he said, laughing. I reached across the desk, grabbed him by the throat and pulled him back across the desk.

"Then that body in the rug is still an option." I said.

In a few minutes, Bryant signed over everything for 2 percent over cost. "Mr. Hermes has reserved a first-class ticket for you, he suggests you take a vacation, so you won't be tempted to do anything stupid," I said, and left his office.

On the way back to Bill's office, I began looking over all my new acquisitions: a bank, a casino and hotel, some bars, a restaurant, a space dock with hangers and warehousing, other properties, a medium-sized closed shipyard, and a closed factory. All the things you need to be a smuggler and mob boss.

I took a closer look at the properties. They were all located around my smelter, including the shipyard, factory, space dock, hangers and warehouses. That was why Bryant wanted Wild Bill out of the way —. he was building his own little kingdom, and if he took over Bill's businesses he'd have it all in one spot.

***

"You did what?" Bill asked me.

"I bought him out," I said.

"Is he still alive?" he asked, laughing.

"He was when I left him, and he was catching a ship headed back to Earth," I said.

"Did you notice the addresses of those properties?"

"I did, and saw why he was after you so hot and heavy."

He nodded, "I was the only thing keeping him from turning this whole area into a slum. The casino, hotel, and restaurant are nice though. The bank will need an infusion of capital. Bryant was skimming all the profits off it, as well as those of the casino." Bill said.

"How illegal are these places?"

"Not bad, since he hadn't had them long enough to change all the management and put his people in place."

"Good, I need to get Joshua Stein to look over all this and make sure nothing is about to blow up in my face."

"Joshua is a good man ... I do business with him too. Would you be interested in selling any of those properties?"

"Which ones would you be interested in?"

"The bars."

"Yeah, I'm no bar owner, I'd have to hire managers."

"Well, I'm no banker, I'll trade you a bank for the bars."

"Sold." I said.

We went to see Joshua, to make sure everything was done legally. Bill and I traded the bars for the bank, and I changed its name to Hermes corporate bank. I closed my accounts at the other Titan bank and moved everything over to my new bank, thereby providing the needed capital influx.

"If you gentlemen will excuse me, I have businesses to run," Bill said as he left.

"What else can I do for you, Mr. Hermes?" said Joshua.

"I need someone to manage all my assets, and I'd like to start — or buy — an investment firm. I'd like you to consider taking the job. I'll raise your salary 15 percent and give you 5 percent of the profits on the businesses you run."

"17 percent salary raise, and 7 percent on the profits."

"20 percent salary raise and 10 percent on the profits," I countered.

"You know you went up, right?"

"Yep, I figured I'd save and creds by having a lawyer and manager." He laughed.

"I'll take it, I was getting bored anyway. I know of an investment firm we can buy. At the moment, the price is right."

"Why is this 'the moment'?"

"They took a major hit on an investment that didn't pan out. But they have a good track record. This is their first major loss in over 20 years, and I invest with them."

I smiled, "any relation to you?"

He smiled, "as a matter of fact, yes. My father, uncle, and cousins."

"How much do they want to sell?"

"How much control do you want?"

"51 percent, with a track record like that over 20 years, I'll be willing to pay for their expertise."

"They'll deal hard," he said.

"That's why I'm hiring you," I said, laughing.

"I'll see what kind of arrangement we can come to."

"Tell them I'll be hands off the business, but I will request certain investments I'm looking for. Other than that, they run the show."

"That puts you ahead of the other offers already," he said.

"I'll also need corporate lawyers, do you think you could talk to your brother Aaron into coming over with you?"

He smiled, "I'll see what I can do."

***

Joshua made the deal for 51 percent. It wasn't cheap, but I needed to invest our profits and gold. The two banks would help cover a lot, but we needed our creds earning creds. We visited the casino, and I approached a floor manager.

"I'd like to see the manager please."

"Is there something I can help you with, sir?"

"I'm the new owner and I like to meet the manager."

"One moment, sir."

Shortly, a fit-looking man in his 50s approached us. "I'm Steven Street, the casino manager," he said, smiling.

I shook his hand, "James Hermes, the new owner. All documentation of my ownership should be in your email by now."

"It is, Mr. Hermes, I was reading through it when I was called to meet you. Would you care for a tour?"

"A short one, as I'm sure you are a busy man." The casino was very nice, and they impressed me with the shows and talent they were able to get.

"The only change I'd like made, for now, is to lower the house take from 25 percent to 20 percent. Word travels fast when people win at the tables and slots."

"I'll see to it right away." We toured the hotel — it was nice, but we could make it nicer. We went to the restaurant for lunch and the food was excellent.

I introduced myself to the restaurant manager, "Everything was perfect, and we want to keep it that way. If there is anything you need to improve the operation, let me know."

"I will, sir, and thank you for buying Mr. Bryant out, he was a nasty character. I don't know how long we would have stayed in business if he had stayed."

"The restaurant would be here, but you probably would not."

"I'm sure of that. Now that I think of it, there is something that comes to mind. Since you are a shipping corporation, you can probably get our supplies brought in cheaper than we can buy them, and probably get higher quality product."

"Consider it done."

***

We hired a company to clean and repair the Hermes space dock, hangers, and warehouses and also wired them into our power grid and security systems.

"Mandy, start hiring people to put those businesses back into operation, and give yourself a 10 percent raise, you'll earn it."

She laughed, "I'll do that, sir, thank you." We opened the businesses and put them to work. This gave us a way to buy in bulk and ship out supplies to the *Hermes*.

The same company cleaned and repaired the shipyard, and the parts factory, wiring them into our power and security grid. We pulled in more security people from Commander Jones to cover all the new properties. We left the remaining properties alone for now.

I asked Braden if he would rather run a shipyard or work in the smelter. He jumped at the chance to run the shipyard.

"We need to find some ore haulers that need their engines overhauled, or don't have engines at all. The hulls need to be in good shape. We will refit them with a new type of engine and reactors," I said.

"What K-ton range are you looking for?"

"The bigger the better."

He nodded, "I think I know where some might be. They were talking about scrapping them because they use so much fuel to operate. We may be able to get them at scrap prices."

"That sounds like what I'm looking for, let's go see them."

Braden flew us over to a huge ship boneyard and introduced me to Mr. Hughes, the elderly owner of the yard.

"Long time, no see, Braden."

"Yes, sir, we've been busy getting the smelter back online."

"That brother of yours ever marry that smart little thing of Wild Bill's?"

"Yes sir, I don't know why she'd have them, but they got hitched." The old man laughed.

Shaking my hand, he said "Mr. Hermes, I've been hearing good things about you."

"We try to do right by people, Mr. Hughes."

"What can I do for you? You looking for scrap, hulls, parts?"

"All the above," I said, "if you have old scrap, I'll give you a good price on it to feed our smelter. To be honest, I like to try new things, maybe take parts of two or three ships and see if I can make something better. Sometimes it works, sometimes it doesn't."

"Things have been slow, and I could use the credits for some scrap. Let's look around and see what kind of deal we can make."

We took his yard boat, and he took us on a tour of his boneyard. "What in the world is that?" I asked, pointing.

"That is a ship recovery tug. It was the forerunner of those new recovery ships. It has six 100 KLT tugs controlled by a 1,000 KLT control ship. It worked OK but took a good team to work it right."

"Is it operational?"

"Yeah, but it's a bit glitchy sometimes."

"Is it for sale?"

"Son, everything in this yard is for sale except my wife, and that's only because I got so much invested in her. I'd lose my shirt on that deal," He said, laughing.

"Make a note to take a closer look at that one," I joked. "Show us your tugs." He had every size and shape of tug ever made.

"Most of these don't have engines or tanks on them, and they've been stripped for parts."

"I'm looking for good solid frames in the 100 KLT range." I said.

"I've got something you may be interested in. These over here are 150 KLTs, they called them hedgehogs, or just Hogs. They never caught on. They were too small to convert to live on, and too big to get in and out of the small port berths. The company dropped the model then pulled all the engines and tanks for parts. The frames all have low hours on them, and they were over-engineered to handle the bigger engines."

"Yes, I'd be interested in them, how many do you have?"

"12 or 15, I think."

"What about ore haulers?"

He flew us over toward another area. "What size you looking for?"

"The bigger the better." I said, again.

He chuckled, "are those big enough for you?"

I whistled, "I'd say so."

"They call those Super Haulers, they didn't last long because the massive amount of fuel they used."

"What KLT are they rated?"

"Don't exactly know, but they'll haul as much as six big

161

haulers, but they burn as much fuel as 10 haulers, which is why they are still sitting here. I haven't had the heart to scrap them."

"They look complete."

"They are, except for the engines — they removed those before I bought them."

I stared at him, thinking. "What are you thinking young man?"

"I'm thinking I'd love to get them all in service again. How much do you want for them?"

"Are you really gonna fly them?"

"I'm gonna try."

"How many you want?"

"How many you got?"

"12."

"Depending on the price, I'll take them all."

Mr. Hughes stared at me for a long moment, then looked back out at the super haulers. "I'd love to see them flying again." He pursed his lips, "scrap, plus 10 percent, I'll throw in the 150 KLTs, and the ship recovery tug.

"You'll need to refit that first, so you can move the super haulers over to your yard. Also, I'll throw in whatever's inside them, which is mostly scrap.

"Oh, except that one ... that one has another ship inside that didn't catch on. They called them Ore Scouts. They were small recon drones that were to be used to scout the rock field for high concentrations of M-ore.

"But they crashed more than anything else. There are around 50 of them with all the flight remote gear is on that ship."

"I'll take them all. How do you want to get paid, creds or metals?"

"Metals ... gold preferably."

"Let's settle on a weight and I'll have it delivered wherever you would like."

"Delivered here, I have a safe place to keep it." I nodded.

We finally settled on a weight. "*Vee,* have the bank hire

an armored truck and have them deliver the gold here to Mr. Hughes."

"Done."

A few hours later they delivered the gold, and we signed all the paperwork for our new assets. I hired a tug company to move the 150 KLT's and the SRT over to the Hermes shipyard.

"Please go through all the ships," I told Braden, "and make an inventory of everything included and its condition." What was supposed to be a quick day, or two trips, had turned into a month-long endeavor. It was time for me to make a run back to *Duty*.

"I'll be back in a week or so, don't burn the place down."

"Don't worry, sir, we have insurance," Braden said, laughing.

CHAPTER 15

I arrived back at *Duty* in time for dinner. Everyone wanted to hear the news of my "couple of hours" trip. "OK, so it took me a little longer than a couple of hours, but it was profitable."

"How profitable?" Jazz asked.

"We now own a few more businesses." I said.

I gave them a list of all the businesses we had acquired. "We own two banks?" Aunt J asked.

"Yep," I said.

"You bought two banks?" Jade asked.

"No, I bought one bank and traded some bars for the other one."

"You bought some bars and traded them for a bank?" Mal asked.

"Kinda, yeah."

"Kinda?" Jazz asked.

"Start from the beginning." Aunt Jay said.

"What had happened, was …"

"Don't you dare!" Aunt J said, everyone laughed.

I relayed the whole story, starting with the trouble at the plant, then moving to the encounters with Wayne Hall and Wilbur Bryant.

"And he took your generous two percent profit offer?" Mal said, laughing.

"He really didn't like the rug alternative."

"What did you do in your spare time?" Jazz asked, not expecting an answer.

"Bought a few Super Hauler ships, and a few extra parts ships. I needed to have some work for the shipyard."

"What shipyard?" Jazz asked. "Never mind, I'll look at the list."

"All that gold is coming in handy since Hughes wanted to be paid in gold."

"Who's Hughes?" Jade asked.

"He owns the scrap and boneyard where I bought the ships."

"I'm not even going to ask," Mal said.

"I will," Aunt J said, "How many ships did you buy?"

I took a deep breath looking around the table at them smiling, "Well, what had happened was ..."

"Stop!" Aunt Jay said, "you've been hanging around Jocko too much, just say a number." Everyone was laughing.

"Somewhere between 75 and 100," I admitted, and everyone cracked up. It was good to be home.

***

The next morning they took me on a tour of our former asteroid, *Hermes*. Most of the interior spaces were mined out. Since we had moved all our ships inside, Mal had started the bots and some tugs glazing the outside of *Hermes*. The bots were grav-pressuring the outside as well.

Black Ice and *Vanguard* were both out of refit. They had downloaded the gold from *Cargo Three* into *Cargo Four*. *Cargo Three* was now in refit. We sent *Cargo Four* to Titan to unload our gold into the secure warehouse under guard. *Cargo One* and *Cargo Two* continued to make rock runs.

A lot of progress had been made in the Hab areas, but we still had a long way to go. Environmental was still working on the O^2. It was a huge space to fill, and we were going to have a lot of plants.

"Any word on the shops and business owners coming into the Promenade?" I asked.

"Some interest but no takers yet." Aunt J said.

"I'll ask Bill if he knows anyone who might be interested." I

said.

We started letting people take time off to go to Titan for a few days. The P550 provided transportation and brought back new hires on the return trips. All in all, I was pleased with the progress. We were still a few months from completion but coming along nicely.

As a surprise, I messaged our casino hotel and booked the penthouse for the four of us. We loaded *Loki* with enough OFEs and MFRs to refit the processing plant. Once we had that done, we could move our Super Haulers over to the Hermes shipyards.

We did a flyby of Conclave to get a real-time update from *Major*. "Most corporate activities have stopped making headway, since they can't bribe or pressure anyone without it being in the news. Most of the crooked politicians have been thrown out of office, and some are under indictment.

"OEMs business has dropped off considerably, but they are still making a profit. Van Dam's shipyards and HMS Habs are all secured. ESFL ships are still shadowing the Corporation's ships.

"The admiral and CEO Baker are apparently still not talking. None of the admiral's ships have been ordered to the new base. ACE integration into networks and comps continues."

"Re-task *Cargo One* and *Cargo Two* to start making runs to OEM," I said. "Expand Unreported News to Titan, through *Herm*. Good work, *Major*, keep it up." I said.

We landed at our Titan hanger, and Buck supervised the unloading of the parts and equipment. Meanwhile, we four took a G-limo to the Casino Hotel penthouse. The girls loved it. I had the casino boutique send some clothes up for us. There was a chime at the door, and I opened it.

"From the boutique, sir."

"Please come in."

"Ladies, would you care to choose your evening attire?" I asked. That sent them into giggles. The ladies from the boutique helped them try on the outfits.

"Ladies please make a decision ... we have tickets to the show, and we don't want to be late,"

"Out!" They both shouted and laughed.

We enjoyed the show over drinks, then headed to our dinner reservations. Our new restaurant was very nice and very busy. We were shown to the owner's balcony, where we were secluded but still part of the ambience of the evening. The girls looked lovely, even in their undercover faces.

We took a few days off and enjoyed our stay. The girls did the spa thing, and then we went shopping. Mal and I got the privilege of carrying their packages.

"Good thing we're rich." Mal whispered.

"Did you say something, dear?" Jade asked.

"I was just saying how nice this was." Mal said.

"It is, isn't it?" she said, laughing with Jazz.

I let them get a little further away from us, "Have you bought Jade a ring yet?" He shook his head.

"I guess I should do that, huh?"

"Only if you want to live in peace for the rest of your, which I'm sure would be short, life," I said chuckling. Mal found the mall directory and led us around to a jewelry store. "It IS nice to be rich," I thought.

Jade's eyes teared up as we entered the jewelry store.

"May we help you, sir?" "We'd like to see some wedding ring sets, please." Jade couldn't speak, she just nodded.

"Of course, sir, Madam, just over here."

As they were looking at the rings, Jazz whispered in my ear, "Well done, my love." I just smiled. Jade turned and waved Jazz over. The rings they finally decided on were beautiful and Jade clung to Mal the rest of the afternoon.

We met with Bill the next day about the businesses, shops, and restaurants coming to *Hermes*. "What kind of businesses do you want?"

"Everything you would find in a space station." I said.

"Incentives?" He asked.

"First year rent-free," I said.

He nodded, "I'll open a couple of bars and a couple of small restaurants myself."

"That's great," I said.

"I'll pass the word around. Would your bank be willing to do some business loans, if I find some people who want to make the move?"

"We'll cover transporting everything," I said, "But yes, we could make some business loans."

"That will get them moving." He said.

When we got to the Hermes headquarters, Jazz and Jade went to see the new office expansion. We found Buck and Braden elbow deep in the ship recovery tug.

"I'm guessing we're pulling the engines and tanks on it?" Buck asked.

"Leave the tanks on the 1,000 KLT, but pull the engines. Pull both the tanks and the engines from the 100s." I said.

"We're going to make the 100s into bots for the big guy, which will control everything."

"Got it," he said.

Mal and I started digging through the 100s. "Yeah, we can strip all of this out and make them bots. That will give us plenty of room. With the engines and tanks pulled, we'll have more than enough room for the MFRs."

We looked at the 1,000 and saw that after pulling her bigger engines we have more than enough room for our upgrades.

The shipyard teams went to work. They pulled all the parts we would need, including all the emitters. We sold them as used parts. We replaced all parts with M-parts, M-tronics, and M-comps. Mal started writing the program to interlock the six lifting bots through the mother tug.

With all the room we had after removing everything, the six bots became 150 KLT tugs and mother became a 2,000 KLT tug. With the faster M-components Mal had no trouble interlocking and synchronizing the six bots to Mother, which became their new names, "*Mother* and the *Girls*".

With three shifts working on *Mother* and the *Girls*, we were done with their refit in a week. We took her out for her shakedown cruise, of course Jazz and Jade flew. Mal made some tweaks in the program, having the *Girls* separate from *Mother* and fly with us in formation, hover, and a few other maneuvers. Each time Mal would make some corrections, the *Girls* would get better. Once the *Girls* were in sync, Jazz turned the helm over to *Mother*, and she repeated the maneuvers.

Mal was finally satisfied with his programming, and I was satisfied with the performance of the components.

"*Vee*, message Mr. Hughes at the boneyard, let him know we are ready to come get our first Super Hauler."

"Sent and acknowledged," *Vee* replied.

When we arrived at the boneyard Mr. Hughes was on station in his yard ship to watch the show.

"*Mother*, scan the highlighted ship in preparation for recovery and movement," I said.

"Scanning, running recovery calculations, ready to deploy the *Girls*." Mal gave me the thumbs up.

"Deploy the *Girls*." The *Girls* separated from *Mother* and moved to their assigned positions. Once they were set and locked on, *Mother* moved to the stern of the Super Hauler and locked into position.

"All boards are green, all ships locked into correctly assigned positions, *Mother* locked and ready to execute recovery operations."

Mal looked over all his boards and gave me the thumbs up. "Execute recovery operations."

"Executing, all systems operating in the green, structural integrity of the recovered ship in the green." *Mother* and the *Girls* took us clear of the boneyard.

"*Mother*, take us to the Hermes laydown yard."

"In route to Hermes laydown yard."

"*Bones Ship* to *Mother*, that is an amazing sight, I haven't seen the like in many years."

"Thank you, *Bones Ship*, we'll invite you to the inaugural flight of "*Hermes Super Hauler One*" when she's ready."

"Looking forward to it! *Bones Ship* out."

Mother and the *Girls* set *HSH1* down as smooth as silk in our ship laydown yard. *Mother* and the *Girls* detached from the Super Hauler, and the *Girls* docked with *Mother*. We set *Mother* down beside *HSH1*, which we named *Hush One*.

Titan News ships were on site videoing our landing and made numerous requests for interviews and statements. I turned all that over to Joshua and Aaron.

Hush One was hooked up to shore power, and we went to see what was stored inside her hold, and what condition she was in.

"Thank the Lord, they didn't just cut out her engines, they took the time to remove them," Buck said. "That looks like the only thing they removed, everything else is still intact."

We took the lift to the bridge. Everything was in order, just a little out of date. The whole ship was like that, with even the galley still fully equipped.

"So far, we have a diamond in the rough." I said. The lights were on in the hold, and most of what we saw was scrap.

"There are some 50 KLT frames over there, we can put those back to work." Mal said, pointing.

"Are those mining drones?" I asked, pointing.

"Yeah, both mining and haulers, we'll definitely use those." Mal answered. "Over there are some cargo handling drones and Wallys," Mal said.

We heard laughing behind us. We turned and there stood the girls. "What?" I asked.

"Don't you two ever again say anything about us clothes shopping," Jazz said!

"Point taken," I said, "Let's get her opened up and see what we've actually got."

We opened her loading doors and found six 5 KLT cargo handlers sitting at the door. I had no idea how much a Super Hauler would hold.

"Those look in good condition," Buck said, "just need fuel and a jumpstart. Let me get the maintenance Grav-vehicle over here and see what we can do." Once they were refueled and powered, five of the six started right away and ran smoothly. We got the work crews started unloading *Hush One*.

We had them lay everything out, so we could inspect it all. Obvious scrap went over to the smelter to be recycled. The maintenance guys got the sixth 5 KLT cargo hauler running and put it to work with the others.

While the haulers were unloading her, the shipyard crew started removing parts and feeding the M-printer. We changed the crew quarters and Hab into a family crew Hab.

We used the same OFE configuration as we had done on *Duty*, including the emitters for the cone drive. We did have to remove one floor of the bridge and include that into the family quarters to keep everything inside the grav-cone. We added a floor in the old engine room to make up for the lost space.

It took almost a week to unload and separate all that had been loaded into *Hush One*. Mal and I rode around marking stuff that we couldn't use to go to the smelter. Our first time through we just said yes or no as scrap.

The second time through, we started looking a little closer. All the mining and hauling drones were taken over to the factory for refurb. All the tugs, frames, and tug parts were sent over to another area. All the cargo handlers and their parts were taken to the factory as well. All the leftover parts were tested, the good ones were sold as used parts, the bad ones went to be recycled.

"What are you thinking of doing with the drones? Mal asked.

"Putting an ACE program in them and putting them to work," I said.

"And the cargo handlers?" Mal asked.

"The same thing. I think once people see the cargo handlers working, we could make and sell them." I said.

"Or buy them already built and add an ACE comp to them." Mal said.

"Or buy the company that makes them and add the ACE comps to them, and while we're at it do the same thing to the mining drone company." I said.

"I like that idea." Mal said.

Cargo Four arrived with our gold and we had it loaded into our security warehouse. Once a week we'd make a deposit to our banks. *Cargo Four* filled up with supplies for Hermes and departed.

"*Vee,* Comm Joshua."

"Mr. Hermes, how can I help you?"

"We want to buy the company that makes the mining drones and the one that makes the cargo handlers. We also want to buy all the patents for them." I said.

"OK let me make some calls, budget?"

"As cheap as we can get them, I'm sure it's not going to be free."

"Can you tell me why, as it might help in the negotiations."

"Sure, we can put comp programs in them and make them follow a set of rules or do the mundane repetitive jobs with no operator. We could upgrade the old ones, but we want the company that makes them." I said.

"I can work with that, how sure is this programming?"

"100 percent, we use it all the time on the ones we already own."

"Then we have an edge, they either sell to us or we put them out of business when we buy someone else's company."

"That's about the size of it, yes." I said.

"I'll get back to you as soon as I have something."

CHAPTER 16

"Soon" turned out to be two days later. "You have an incoming comm from Ruben Stein, the president of Stein investments," *Vee* said.

"Put him through. Mr. Stein, how are you?"

"I'm doing well, Mr. Hermes, thank you for asking."

"Call me James, please."

"Very well James, and you must call me Ruben."

"I hope you will allow a Mr. in front of Ruben; my mother would smack the back of my head if I didn't respect my elders," I said, laughing.

He chuckled, "Thank God for mothers, young man."

"Amen, sir, amen. What can I do for you, Mr. Ruben?"

"We have found the companies you asked about. Both are owned by the same parent company. The owner also has another small automation security company, and they are all located here on Titan. None of the companies have been making more than break-even profit, so we are in a prime position to buy them at a good price."

"Sounds good so far, what's the catch?"

"How hard you want us to press the deal? How deep do you want to cut our offers?"

"I don't want to draw blood or crush him. I only do that to enemies who draw blood from me. But the patents have to be part of the deal. If they aren't, I'm not interested. But I'm willing to pay a reasonable price for them."

"I understand, then we'll take the negotiations to the next level, and we'll be in touch."

"Thank you, sir."

We held off doing any upgrades to the mining drones or

cargo handlers until we knew the outcome of the acquisitions. Mal did some checking on the automation security company.

"Not bad in its day, but they have fallen way behind the industry. They wouldn't last 10 seconds against one of ours."

"If they sell, are we changing the name?" I asked.

"I think we should, since they need a new face with the new product." Mal said.

We had sorted through all the cargo that had come out of *Hush One,* and her upgrades were on pace. We were ready to bring *Hush Two* over from the boneyard so Mal took Buck and Braden to get her.

It took him three hours to make the trip from the boneyard, but there was no need to hurry. We didn't want any mishaps. They sat *Hush Two* down beside *Hush One*. *Hush Two* was plugged into shore power and we did our walk-through.

The bridge, crew quarters, and engine room were in the same good condition as *Hush One* had been. We opened her loading doors and had the crews started unloading her, laying everything out for inspection.

By the end of the shift 50 percent of everything they pulled out went straight to recycling. I got tired of looking at scrap and told them to comm me when it was unloaded. We had a crew start disassembling parts and feeding the M-printer. We decided to follow the same family crew hab plan for all the *Hush* ships.

"*Vee*, message Bill, and ask if he knows of a cargo ship captain that is looking for a family ship berth."

"Sent."

Mal and I looked over the laid out cargo from *Hush Two*. It was all scrap. "Let's try something." Mal said, heading toward *Mother*. I followed him. He powered up *Mother* and lifted off. "*Mother,* have the *Girls* pick up all highlighted scrap and deposit it into the Hermes SR."

"Understood."

The *Girls* detached and started picking up and moving all the scraps to the SR. They were through in about 30 minutes. "Operations complete."

"Have the *Girls* re-dock."

"*Girls* re-docked."

"Nice job," I said.

"I get a good idea now and then."

"*Vee*, message Mr. Hughes that we are coming for the Super Hauler with the seeker drones in it, please mark it for us."

"Sent."

"*Mother,* take us to the boneyard."

"Enroute to the boneyard."

When we arrived at the boneyard, the *Bone Ship* was hovering over a Super Hauler. "*Bone Ship* to *Mother*, this is the one you want."

"Thank you, *Bone Ship*."

"*Bone Ship,* out."

"*Mother*, recover highlighted ship and return to Hermes shipyard."

We watched as *Mother* and the *Girls* went through the whole operation flawlessly. *Mother* returned us to our shipyard, and we sat *Hush Three* down beside *Hush Two*.

We landed *Mother* and went over to *Hush Three*. Crews were already plugging *Hush Three* into shore power. We did our usual walk-through, and found everything in the same condition as our other Super Haulers.

We went down into the hold. "I don't know how many seeker drones there are in here, but I'd be willing to bet it's more than 50," I said.

We climbed down to look at one. It was not a bad setup. We could remove the tankage and install a small MF/R to power the OFEs and put in Tri-dar. I checked the data plate for the name of the manufacturer, it was the same company that made the mining drones.

Vee, message Mr. Ruben to have the company we're trying to buy include the patents and the tooling for the seeker drones."

"Sent."

"We'll see what that gets us," I said.

"Message from Mr. Ruben, already in the pot, along with a

few other things."

"Thank you."

"Sent."

The crew started working inside *Hush Three's* family crew Hab, but left the cargo hold alone for now.

"Message from Bill, have a prospect for cargo captain, but he has a big family."

"No problem, we have a big ship."

"Sent."

"Message from Captain Smythe, recommend hiring more crew to fill out our fleet."

"Only hire those you personally know and trust your life to. Tell Commander Jones the same thing. Other than that, I'm on board. Let's fill our ranks."

"Sent."

"Let's get a coffee," I said.

"It took you long enough," Mal said, smiling, "You want to take the girls out tonight?"

"Sure, we all need a break."

***

We enjoyed a show in the casino and a wonderful meal at our restaurant and spent the night in the penthouse. We had room service bring in breakfast, and we enjoyed our coffee and family time.

"You have an incoming comm from Mr. Ruben."

"Put him on speakers."

"Yes, sir."

"Mr. Ruben, good morning I have you on speaker with my partners over breakfast."

"I'm sorry to disturb you, James, I can comm back later."

"Not at all … we were just enjoying our coffee, what can we do for you?"

"The deal for the companies you wanted is almost complete, but the owner wants to meet with you."

We looked at each other. "Why does he want to meet with me, and what are we offering him for his companies?"

"We are buying him out at 400 creds to the K-cred, for 80 percent of the companies. That's all four companies, and all the patents held by those companies. He wants his employees to keep their jobs, including the management."

"How good is his management team?"

"Solid, for the most part."

"So, he wants to retain 20 percent, and he wants assurances."

"In a nutshell, yes."

"Downside?"

"His plants need retooling."

"Has he played straight with you?"

"Yes, I believe he has."

"Is he really concerned about his employees?"

"Yes, I believe he is."

"When does he want to meet?"

"At your convenience."

"Let me see if there is a conference room available at 1500." *Vee* blinked a green light on my HUD. "There is, will 1500 here at the Hermes Casino be convenient for you, Mr. Ruben?"

"That will be fine, I didn't know you changed the name of the casino."

"I just decided to, they're now the Hermes Casino, Hotel and Restaurant."

"I guess I better tell Joshua," he chuckled, he's here with us, so I let them know."

"Thank you, sir, we'll see you at 1500."

"At 1500, then."

"*Vee*, have the security squad do a sweep of the conference room, and guard it. We don't want any surprises."

"Yes sir, sent and acknowledged."

"Have the hotel cater coffee, pastries, and fruit for the meeting."

***

We met Mr. Ruben and Joshua at the conference room at 1445 and Randal Scott and his team arrived at 1500 sharp. Joshua introduced everyone. *Vee* gave me a green light on security. Everyone helped themselves to the coffee, pastries, and fruit.

"Mr. Stein says you have some pretty sophisticated programs and tech." Mr. Scott said.

"We do," I answered.

"Would it offend you to give us a demonstration?" Mr. Ruben raised an eyebrow, looked at me, shrugging his shoulders.

"What do you have in mind?" I asked. One of Scott's team suddenly stood up and pulled out a tablet.

Before the tablet had cleared his pocket Sergeant Adams had his hand on it and his pistol at the back of the man's head. The man froze.

"It's just a tablet," the man stuttered. Adams took it, checked it, and handed it back to the man.

"You must forgive my team, we've had some close calls, and they take their jobs very seriously."

"Of course," Scott said.

"The tablet?" I asked.

"Yes, we'd like your program to crack it."

My HUD flash a green light. "We cracked it when you came in." I said.

"That's not possible." He looked at it and then back at me.

"My apologies, sir, apparently it is possible."

"I apologize, Ruben. I guess I'm getting cynical in my old age. We've had so many companies trying to steal our tech over the years, it's hard to believe an honest offer when it shows up. And to you good folks as well, my apologies."

"Of course, sir, one can never be too careful, as you can see with our security."

"Indeed," Scott said.

"I asked for this meeting as a test, and if passed, to ask for some guarantees for my people," he said. "And as you have passed our test, embarrassingly quickly, I'd like to ask if you would guarantee that my people will keep their jobs.

"I'm sure you can imagine the uneasiness these talks have caused. Rumors have run rampant, and I'd just like them to know that they'll have a job if I sell."

"And if I can't guarantee to you they'll have a job?" I ask.

"Then we don't have a deal. No guarantee, no deal." I nodded, looking at him. He meant it ... he would pass on the deal unless his people were taken care of.

"Mr. Scott, I admire a man who looks to the well-being of his people. We'll guarantee their jobs and a 3 percent pay raise across the board. We don't have the time or the inclination to hire and train a totally new workforce." Scott's team look shocked, but Ruben was smiling, nodding his head.

"That's very generous, Mr. Hermes," Scott said.

"Just good business Mr. Scott, we want them to know that they are now our people. We care about our people too."

Mr. Scott stood, looking back at Sergeant Adams, then slowly extending his hand toward me. "I believe we have a deal, Mr. Hermes."

We shook, "Thank you, sir." I reached across to Mr. Ruben, "And thank you, sir."

"My pleasure, son," he said, shaking my hand.

We signed the paperwork buying out Mr. Scott and creating Hermes Automated Security, Hermes Automated Mining (including the seekers), and Hermes Automated Cargo Handling. I had the creds transferred to his account, and that was that.

They took us on a tour of their facilities. Each was a small plant working with outdated machines. They were doing maintenance and repairs on old mining equipment to resell. The seeker plant had been shut down for years. The basic machines were good, but they were way behind their competitors. But luckily, there weren't too many of them. The buildings they were in were leased, not owned. After inspecting everything we decided it would cost just as much to refurb the old equipment as it would to buy good used, new generation equipment.

We told him to continue to rebuild the old mining equipment for resale, so until further notice it was business as usual.

We called the prefab construction company for quotes on two new factories to be built beside our already existing factory. I gave them my requirements, and they sent us plans and a quote. They could have three new factory buildings up in a few weeks. We sent them a deposit and told them to get started. We ordered the new equipment to go into our new buildings. The equipment would start to be delivered in two weeks.

We began unloading *Hush Three*, laying out everything. This whole load was drones and drone parts. There were also seekers, miners, loaders, haulers, and cargo handlers of different types, as well as parts for them all. We had some of our new employees from the drone plant come over and help to separate everything into the correct areas.

***

The day finally came when *Hush One* was ready for its shakedown cruise. We invited Wild Bill, Mr. Hughes, Mr. Ruben, Joshua, and Aaron to accompany us.

"Ship, bring all systems online to safety standby." The bridge screens came to life, showing the status in multiple areas.

"All systems online in safety standby, all boards are green."

I waited for Mal to look over all his programming and give me the thumbs up before proceeding.

"Hush One, close all doors in preparation for departure."

"Door closure in progress… All doors closed for departure."

"Bring all systems online for departure."

"All systems online, all boards are green."

"Raise the ship 1 meter from the surface and hold for complete systems check."

"Ship holding at 1 meter, all systems normal, all boards are green." I looked at Mal, he already had his thumb up.

"Lift the ship to 100 meters and hold."

"Ship at 100 meters and holding all systems normal, all boards are green." Mal nodded.

"Ladies, if you would do the honors."

"Yes, sir." They said, grinning from ear to ear.

"Titan control this is Hermes Super Hauler *Hush One* requesting clearance for local space test flight."

"*Hush One*, this Titan control, clearance approved."

"Ladies, take us out."

"Aye, aye, sir." Our pilots put her through a series of test maneuvers, and everything worked perfectly.

"All right, Jazz, everything looks good … put her through your test."

"Titan control, this is *Hush One* requesting clearance for open space."

"*Hush One*, you have clearance to open space, Titan control out."

"Increasing speed, standby for maneuvers." For the next half hour Jazz and Jade did their pilot thing while *Hush One* operated and responded perfectly.

"How's she handling?" Mr. Hughes asked.

"Not like a hauler." Jazz said, eying me. I nodded slightly.

"Would you like to take the helm, Mr. Hughes?" Jazz asked.

"Really?"

"You should, you looked at them sitting on the ground long enough."

"I'd always hoped to someday, even if it was only to move them around the yard." Jazz got up, and Hughes took her place, initiating a few maneuvers, "My Lord, she handles sweet!" He kept the helm for about 15 minutes.

"Young lady, you better take over, I might quit the boneyard, and ask for a job flying this old girl."

Jazz took the helm from him. "Take us to one Normal Engine Speed," I said.

"One NES, aye." I looked at Mal, he still had his thumb up.

"1.5 NES please."

"1.5 NES, aye."

"Ship, report system status."

"All systems normal, all boards are green."

"Two NES, please."

"Two NES, aye."

"Ship, run complete systems check."

"Two NES and holding all systems normal, all boards are green."

"If you ladies would take us back to base, I think we have enough for a good systems test."

"Returning to base," Jazz said.

The test flight had lasted about two hours until Jazz set us down as light as a feather back at the shipyard.

We hired the captain that Wild Bill recommended. He did have a big family — eight children. We set the maximum speed of *Hush One* at two NES and the captain and his family crew assured us that the crew hab area passed all its tests. Once they were satisfied, we sent them toward *Hermes*, with instructions to contact the base enroute.

With *Hush One* out of the way, we brought over *Hush Four*. We had the movements of the ships down to a science now, figuring we could launch another *Hush* every 2 to 3 weeks, barring the unexpected. One crew would start refits while the other crews unloaded and organizing the cargo that came out of the Super Haulers.

We now knew what we were looking for, so the process went faster. As we were looking over the laid-out parts, something caught my eye and we stopped.

"What is that?" I asked. "It kinda looks like a 3-D printer, but that's an odd shape."

One of the men working near us said, "That's something, ain't it? I haven't seen one of those in years."

"A 3-D printer, right?"

"Yep, one of the original ones. They were better than these new ones."

"Say that again."

"It has a different system of laying the layers. It was slower, but the parts were better made and stronger. When the new printers came out on the market, there was a big legal battle. The original inventor could not outlast the big corporation's lawyers and court costs. The new one is faster, but not as good."

"It must've been big news for you to remember it," I said.

"Kinda, the inventor was from here and my folks knew him. I think he still lives there."

"Take that over to the factory, please, and thanks." I said.

CHAPTER 17

We followed it to take a closer look at the printer, opened it up and compared the old to the new. Mal looked at the programming to see why it was so much better.

"Impressive programming for the time," he said. "The designer used multiple angle printing heads ... that's why they were more precise, and stronger parts. We can have this thing running as fast as the new one," Mal said.

"Let's see if we can buy the company," I said. We commed Ruben and told him what we wanted.

"I know him," he said, "An unusual individual. I'll see what I can come up with."

Meanwhile, Bill found us another captain and family crew for *Hush Two*. We hired them, and they launched later that week, on their way on to the mining colonies and then back to our smelter.

Our crews finished the three new factory buildings, and we had the new machinery installed. We started with the mining bots, as they were the easiest to convert, and we had the most experience on them. We gave the factory the plans for the new models and brought in any new parts for installation.

We gave the sales team a demonstration and videos, then, as soon as we had working models, we sent them out to the mines to demo them. The orders for the new models began to come in. We did the same thing with the cargo haulers, with equal success.

The unions weren't thrilled with this, but the companies loved the new equipment. Not one union man came around to our plants, so I guess Hall took my warning seriously.

The seekers were more challenging. We use the same OFEs

as we had all our Grav-cars, but we were putting mini-MFRs in them as the power source. They would run for 12 months before they had to be brought back to us for refueling.

On the upside, we had somewhere around 100 seekers we could retrofit right away. We were using our Tri-dar program, but we set it up in a way that no one could tell that we were using all three at one time. We got units ready for the sales force to take out on demo rides, and that sold them. Off they went, and the orders came in.

Hush Three left with its new captain and family, and that allowed us to send *Mother* to the boneyard to bring back *Hushs Five* and *Six*. An hour later we received a message from our shipyard requesting our presence.

"On the way."

When I got to the shipyard, the loading doors of *Hush Five* were open. The only thing inside her hold was another ship. The ship took up the complete hold of a Super Hauler. It looked like a giant sausage with the nose cone. I took a moment to realize what it was.

It was a Tri-tanker. Tri-tankers look like three giant beer cans with a nose cone on one end and engines on the other.

"Leave this where it is and get started on *Hush Six*. I need to go to the boneyard." I flew over there, and Hughes met me at the pad.

"You lost or bored?"

"Curious mostly," I replied.

"What about?"

"Didn't I see a big Tri-tanker or two somewhere on the yard?"

"You did for a fact, come along and I'll show them to you." We got in his flyer and he took off. "There they are, I bought them from the same company I bought the Super Haulers from."

"And I'm guessing they got rid of them for the same reasons?"

"Exactly right. Good solid design, but they were fuel hogs. I thought I bought three, but these are the only ones I have."

"Oh, you bought three," I said smiling, "The other one is in one of the Super Haulers we picked up."

He looked at me for a moment and then laughed. "The Old Lady will choke me."

"Well, sell me the three of them and we'll keep this between us," I said.

"Nope, I already sold you one, I just didn't know it," he said, smiling. "I'll sell you the other two at the same price ... scrap plus 10 percent."

"Mr. Hughes, I feel like I'm taking advantage of you."

"Son, I learned a long time ago, in this business sometimes you find Easter eggs, sometimes you find goose eggs. You found the Easter egg this time. No harm, no foul."

"All right Sir, scrap plus 10 percent, and I'll count myself lucky."

***

We applied power to *Hush Five*, and she eased the Tri-tanker out of her hold as pretty as you please. We named her *Tess One,* and could see she would be an easy refit. Her engines were already pulled, and her hull integrity was at 97 percent. Everything was in good shape, just like the Super Haulers. All we needed to do was to mount the OFEs and MFRs and put her to work. Of course, saying and doing are two different things. We took a little over two weeks to refit her, running three shifts a day.

We launched *Hush Four* and *Tess One* a week after they came out of refit. *Hush Four* headed out to the mines. *Tess One* headed to Earth to pick up a load of air and water. She would come back by way of Jupiter, pick up a load of fuel, then continue on to rendezvous with *Hermes*.

Tess One's refit had been so easy that we brought over *Tess Two* and *Tess Three* for refits. "You have an incoming comm from Mr. Ruben."

"Put him through, Mr. Ruben, how can I help you?"

"I found the man that invented the 3-D printer."

"I hear a 'but' in there." He chuckled, "Yes you do, he'll only deal face-to-face with you."

"I hope he's local," I said, laughing.

"He is. He has a small fix-it shop, I'll send you the address."

"Thank you, sir, I'll let you know what happens."

The security team, Mal, and I went to the address that Mr. Ruben provided. A sign said "Al Weaver's fix-it shop." We went inside.

The door chimed, and someone yelled, "in the back." We followed the sound of the voice to the back of the shop area.

"Good morning." I said.

"Morning, how can I help you?"

"I'm James Hermes, Mr. Ruben said you would be expecting us."

"Ah, the man who wants to fight windmills."

"Not necessarily, I'll leave them alone if they leave me alone."

"Well, these won't, they've been after me for 30 years. Mr. Ruben says you want to buy patents, which ones?"

"The ones dealing with your 3-D printers."

"So, all of them, how do you know they work?"

"We don't know they all work, but we've looked at one of your old printers. The designs and the tech are solid."

"If I sell them to you, they will come after you, they'll lawyer you to death."

"They've tried that before, we have good lawyers and plenty of creds to play their games." He looked at us for a moment and went back to working on a power inverter. I reached over, picked up a wrench and held the backside nut while he tightened it.

"You looked at my tech, huh?"

"Yes sir, very impressive, the way you used the angled rail articulating head to lay down the layers." He nodded, "Did you look at the programming?"

"I did," Mal said, "You were ahead of your time. I doubt

most people understood what you are doing."

"And what do you think I was doing?"

"From the way you wrote your base programming, I'd say the small printer was an afterthought. You had something bigger in mind."

He stopped and looked at Mal, "You saw that?"

"I did, it appears you were trying to build a printer that would layer an entire finished product rather than a piece of the time." Mal said.

"After 30 years, someone else sees it," he said shaking his head.

"Like I said, you were ahead of your time."

"If I could have just overcome the power usage problem."

"I don't think it was a power problem Sir, I think it was a sequencing problem. Your program was forcing the machine to do a few operations out of sequence. The other 3-D printer companies dropped that portion of the code and operation. It worked for them, but they make inferior parts." Mal said.

Al walked over to a comp terminal, "Show me where you saw that." Mal opened the program scrolling down.

"Here, here, and here. This operation should come first and those two should be reversed. That would've probably dropped your power usage by half. Al study the screen and got a "far-away" look in his eyes. We waited.

"Oh, good Lord." He said sitting down his stool. He looked deflated. "Thirty years and the answer was staring me in the face." He looked around the shop, "If I hadn't had this place I would've gone crazy.

"Come look at something." He took us over to the back corner of the shop and opened a door. The walls were covered with drawings of different designs of printers, one on which was big enough to print a whole G-car.

"That was where I was headed, and bigger, I couldn't solve what I thought was the problem of power usage."

Mal and I traced his drawings around the room. "This is impressive work." I said.

"What are you offering for my patents and work?" he asked.

"What do you want?" I countered.

"I'm tired, frustrated with the lawyers ... and now I find the answer was in front of me all this time," he said shaking his head. "Give me 100 K-creds and everything is yours."

I looked at Mal, and he turned to Al. "How about we give you 500 K-creds and 20 percent of the company we will start based on your work."

"But," I said raising my hand, "It's a package deal, we want you to come to work with us, and see your creation through."

He stared at us, "you're serious."

"Very."

"Their lawyers will come after us," he warned.

"Just a minor inconvenience," I said.

He held his hand out, "When do we start?"

"We just did. Let's go see Joshua and do the paperwork and let him know we are about to kick over an anthill," I said, laughing.

The Hermes 3-D Materializing Company was born that afternoon, when Joshua and Aaron filed legal papers against the Corporation.

Aaron said Al's old law firm were either idiots, crooks, or both.

We took Al to our factory and told him what we were thinking about doing. As soon as we arrived, 30 years of pent-up frustration burst, and he went at it with a vengeance.

"What's our budget?"

"Whatever you need," I said. Mal set him up an office with the M-Comp with all the programming and CADs he needed. We told him to design his machine, and we would introduce him to some of our inventions and updates.

✳✳✳

Meanwhile, *Hush Four* came out of refit and headed for the

mining colonies to bring back more ore for our smelter. *Tess Two* came out right behind her and headed for Earth and Jupiter to top off her tanks. She would then return to service the belt. The crews then brought *Hush Seven* over to our yard. They unloaded her and started her refit.

The Unreported News was having the same effect on Titan as it had on Conclave. Crooked politicians and corrupt officials were being put in the spotlight. Crooked union bosses and their toughs were being unmasked.

"*Herm*, status of integration into Titans systems?"

"At present, we are at 72 percent, and are building slowly but steadily so we trip no alarms."

"Run a security background check on the law firm that representatived Albert Weaver and send the results to Joshua and Aaron."

"Understood."

I stood looking through the armor glass out across to the Hermes headquarters yard and facilities. Jazz slipped her arms through mine.

"What are you thinking, love?"

"I'm thinking we'll have visitors soon,"

"it's bound to happen sooner or later."

"I know, but it's the 'sooner' that concerns me. I've been holding off on installing shields, since I didn't want to draw attention to their existence."

"But now we are drawing attention with our Super Haulers," she finished for me. I nodded. "You have a plan, don't you?"

"The beginnings of one. We will install shield emitters that look and act like enviro-screens, but will become shields when needed."

"That shouldn't cause a stir, lots of places do that," she said.

"That's my thought, too. We can even do it around the casino, hotel, and restaurant as an added attraction. No one will think twice about it," I said.

"*Vee*, pull up all Hermes properties on Titan. Show me

a standard OFE shield emitter layout and power requirements to cover them. Set the shields to be one-half meter inside our property lines.

"I also want a railgun layout with interlocking fields of fire for the factory, smelter and shipyard areas. Make the rail guns big enough to destroy big rocks or big ships, whichever the case may be."

The plans came up on my HUD, then shifted to VR so both Jazz and I could look around the grounds and see where all the rail gun emplacements will be.

"Make all those emplacements concealed, so no one knows we have them until we want them to." The VR picture changed. "Send those plans to Buck and have him and his team to get started."

"Done and acknowledged."

***

Hush Five came out of refit and headed for the mines. *Tess Three* came out of the yard and headed for Earth. *Hush Eight* and *Hush Nine* were brought over from the boneyard, and went into refit. Mal had shown the guys at Hermes Automated Security a few tricks and they were gaining market share back.

I had transferred all of the gold into our banks. We began to get a rather healthy pile of metals, even with selling some of it here on Titan. *Cargo Three* and *Cargo Four* were both out of refit and back to *Travis*. We brought them to Titan to make a cargo run of metals to Earth.

We sold all the refurbished mining bots, haulers, and seekers at a nice profit. We totally redesigned the mining bots and haulers to work better together. The new redesigned seekers were far better than the refurbished ones since they were purpose built around our OFEs and MFRs. We built 100 of each of the three types of machines to take back to *Hermes*.

"You have a message from Al, he's ready for you to look at his designs and plans."

"Acknowledged ... we'll meet with him at 1500."

"Sent and acknowledged."

Mal and I met with Al in his office, where we found the wall covered in drawings and notes. "You used the CAD program, right?" I asked.

"Oh yeah, those are just notes for me," he said. "Bring up CAD designs for the Materializing Factory." The plans flashed up on a blank wall.

"Nice." I said. He had designed the whole factory around a full-size printer. Mal and I looked over the plans, asking questions. After two hours of study, we made a few changes based on our proprietary tech. We called a halt to work at midnight. We all needed sleep.

We began again the next morning and finished our modifications to Al's plans and designs by lunch. We gave him the go-ahead to tool out his design. "Can our power grid support this?" Al asked.

"Easily," I said.

He shrugged, "OK, I'll get started."

"You have a message from Captain Smythe, all security ships fully manned, including the Marine contingents."

"Acknowledge."

"Sent."

Hush Six came out of refit, and left for the mines, and would take its loads to OEM. We pulled *Cargo One* and *Cargo Two* to support the *Hermes* on supply runs. P550 had been making the Titan run every two weeks, bringing new hires in and taking work crews out on breaks. Everything was running smoothly, which made me nervous.

Hush Eight, *Hush Nine*, and *Hush Ten* were brought over from the boneyard and started their refit process. Half of the cargo we were getting out of the Super Haulers went straight into the smelter. The rest was being separated, cataloged, and the parts repaired to be sold.

Jazz and Jade have been busy furnishing the office complex addition of our headquarters and flying wrangling missions with the hybrids.

"We'd like to make an addition to the office complex," Jazz said.

"And it will not be cheap," Jade seconded.

I nodded, "What do you have in mind?"

"A Med-bay." Jazz said.

"We have a Med-bay, a good one, you want to move it?"

"No, we want a new and expanded one. One that can provide health care for our people and also for the less fortunate in the area. I'm sure you've noticed this isn't the nicest part of Titan."

I nodded, "How big are you thinking?"

"As big as A14 has, maybe bigger," Jade said.

"What's happened?" I asked.

They looked at each other. "The women who have been working with us in the office complex were talking about the health care in the area. They said, thank God their husbands were working here and had health insurance. It is especially bad for independent rock hounds and their families. There are also a lot of widows ... you know how dangerous the belt is."

I nodded, "I like it. This is a way to give back to the community."

"This is a good thing, Nic," Jazz said, kissing me.

"*Vee*, comm Bill."

"Nic, how's everything going?"

"Busy ... a quick question for you."

"Sure, what do you need?"

"There seems to be a lack of medical services in my area. Was there ever a med center or urgent care facility around here?"

"There used to be one, right by your warehouses."

"Where?"

"Square building, 3 or 4 stories"

"That was a med center?"

"Yep, closed two years ago, lack of funding."

"You don't happen to own it, do you?"

He chuckled, "no, but I know who does."

"I want to look at it and maybe buy it."
"I'll have him you comm you right back."
"Thanks."

CHAPTER 18

"Mr. Hermes? This is Dan Thompson. Bill said you may be interested in the old med center building."

"Possibly, I'd like to look at it."

"I can be over in about 20 minutes to show you around. Bring lights ... all the power is off."

"See you then."

Dan arrived in coveralls, "Please excuse my clothes, I was on another job site when Bill called."

"No problem, coveralls save on good clothes."

"Amen. I'll show you around." I followed him in, and he started our tour. "It was originally a 400-bed hospital, but they lost rooms during upgrades, and Auto-docs made long-term stays less of a requirement. What are you going to put here? You going to tear it down or renovate?" He asked.

"I want to reopen the med-center." I said.

He stopped, turned and looked at me. "Seriously?"

"Yeah, there's none in the area, and my people all live around here."

"Funding?"

"Tax write off. My corporation will completely fund and staff it."

"You're serious?"

"I am."

He nodded his head, "Let me stop my sales routine. I'm a property owner in this area, and since Hermes has come in, my property values have gone up and so have my occupancy rates. You and your corporation are good for business. If you will reopen this center, my property values and occupancy rates will both go up."

"Likely." I answered.

"You going nonprofit?"

"Probably."

"You get your nonprofit paperwork approved, and I'll *give* you the building, if you give me the value of the building as a tax writeoff."

I reached out my hand, "You have a deal."

I commed Joshua and told him what I wanted and what I was doing.

"No problem," he said, "Good for taxes. I'll get everything started."

Funny how creds spent in the right places makes things happen. Within the week the building was ours, so we hired cleaning and maintenance crews and got them working on the building.

Joshua, Aaron, and Mr. Ruben put the word out for anyone who wished to donate medical equipment and creds for a tax writeoff. The creds and equipment rolled in, and none of the equipment was used or second rate. This was all top-of-the-line equipment. We hired enough medical personnel to staff three shifts. The maintenance crews worked 24/7 until they finished it.

It took five weeks from start to finish, and the Hermes Med-Center was opened, fully staffed, and fully equipped. The newsies wanted interviews. I let Joshua handle all of that.

Hush Seven and *Hush Eight* were now out of refit. We sent *Hush Seven* to the mines and OEM. We loaded *Hush Eight* with the 15 hedgehogs that needed a refit and 300 pieces of new mining and seeker equipment for *Hermes*. *Hush Eleven* and *Hush Twelve* were brought over from the boneyard to prepare for refit. We had been away from *Duty* and the *Hermes* for almost 6 months. We felt like it was time to go home for a while ... it would be good to see everyone again.

"Commodore, you have an incoming comm from Mr. Hughes." The "Commodore" got my attention. "He is asking for 'Hermes' and said it was 'Hughes' this is not normal for him and his voice stress levels are elevated," *Vee* said.

"Understood, put me through. What do you want, Hughes?" I asked. The corner of his mouth lifted slightly.

"I'm calling in that favor you owe me."

"You believe in collecting quick, don't you?"

"You owe me the favor, I can call it whenever I want it."

"Yeah, yeah, what do you want?"

"I want to use the SRT. I need to rearrange my yard since you moved those ships."

"Seriously, you could've said something while we were over there."

"I don't need your pilot I can fly it better than he can. Have it here by 0800 in the morning."

"I'll have it there by 0900, but this is all, old man, the favor is done." I cut the connection. "Yeah, he has trouble all right, and I bet we are the cause of it. Message Mal and Sergeant Adams to meet me on *Loki*."

***

I played the comm recording for them. "I suspect someone is using his wife as leverage to force him to get the SRT from us."

"Why the SRT?" Adams asked.

"It's a good example of all our tech, and this wouldn't raise too much suspicion." Mal said.

"No problem, it's a basic hostage rescue," Sergeant Adams said.

"Yeah but let's not chance anything, if the hostage takers are high paid, they may have high-tech gear. Approach it like you would if you were facing someone better than yourselves." I said.

"In that case, I don't have all the tech I need," Sergeant Adams said.

"Let's call in the Commander for support. They can be here in an hour." He nodded, "That way we'll be sure."

"*Vee*, message Captain Smythe and Commander Jones. Include all info including our best guess and discussions here.

I want the hostages rescued, so bring whatever assets they feel they need to cover all contingencies. Dark, ASAP, all speed restrictions lifted for this mission."

"Sent."

"*Vee*, pull all surveillance feeds from around the boneyard, gather all Intel on the who, what, when, where, and how of this situation."

"Yes, Commodore."

Shortly thereafter: "Commodore, *Black Blade* and *Black Ice*, are on station. *Black Blade* has assumed high cover. Commander Jones is enroute in the *Ice*'s pinnace, ETA three minutes."

"Understood."

Commander Jones came aboard *Loki* and saluted, "Commodore."

I returned the salute, "Commander."

"Any additional Intel sir?" He asked.

"*Loki,* show us what you've got."

"There are two separate groups in this operation. These five are local muscle and beaters, hired by this man, the probable leader of the second group. His picture flashed on the wall. The second group numbers 30 and are well-equipped judging by their comms and security equipment.

The larger group arrived in the ship shown on the wall. Once they left the ship, it left the port and is sitting at these coordinates."

"Have *Blade* moved to cover that ship … I don't want it to get away."

"Done."

"The group of five went to the boneyard and took Mrs. Hughes hostage, using her to force Mr. Hughes to comm the Commodore. Once that was done, the group of 30 took up positions around the boneyard — covering the house, landing pad, and entrances. Tactical analysis is that the main assault team is using the five toughs to draw you in, Commodore, and the assault team is the trap to close around you. Their objectives are to get both you and the tech, but at least one or the other."

"I concur," Commander Jones said.

"It looks that way," I agreed.

"Any ID on the group of 30?" Mal asked.

"Most likely corporate mercenaries," *Loki* answered.

"Mission parameters, sir?" Jones asked.

"Our top priority is to rescue the Hughes, I'd like some mercenaries to talk to afterward. Their ship gets hammerheaded for intel. Other than that, they started it, let's finish it."

"Roger that. I'll have a mission brief for you in one hour."

***

"Commodore, the safest scenario, and the one that has the highest probability of accomplishing all our objectives is this one," Commander Jones said a short while later.

"So, I fly the SRT over there, walking to their offices, spring the trap. When the 30 come in, you take them down?"

"In a nutshell, yes, sir."

"Your shield will protect you and the hostages. According to our test, your shields will easily expand to an 8-foot circle."

"I never thought of that," I said. "OK, I'm sold, I told him I'll be there at 0900. Let's be ready to use the hammers, or the Mechs if you need to. Jim, issue everyone on the op our shield belts. We want none of our guys getting hurt."

"Yes, sir."

Once we were all in place, I took my normal approach to the boneyard, and landed outside their office, blocking half the yard from seeing the entrance. "*Mother*, lock out flight systems, keep shields up, maintain comms."

"Understood."

I got out of *Mother* and walked into the office, Mr. and Mrs. Hughes were sitting there, and another man was sitting in their waiting area reading.

"You got any coffee, old man?"

"Help yourself." He pointed to the pot. I pulled me a cuppa, went back and sat down in the chair next to them. *Vee* gave me a green light, letting me know I had them covered with my shields.

"Mrs. Hughes, I'm terribly sorry about this, some people are just plain rude. I'll pay for the breakage."

"That's all right, dear, thank you for coming." She said.

I took a swallow of coffee, looking at the reader. "Are we supposed to wait for your friends, or are you going to do something stupid?"

He looked up at me, "they said you were cool under pressure. No, we'll wait. We got him, come on in."

I chuckled, "yes we do." I said, sipping my coffee. *Vee* had me keyed in, monitoring the operation outside.

"Op-force are on the move, half on overwatch." *Vee* said.

"OK, they're on the way, just relax and this will all be over soon," the reader said.

"I was about to say the same thing to you," I told him. The other four men came into the room with us, holding guns. "Gentlemen, no need for those. It would be better if you put them away. That way, no one will accidentally get shot," I said.

"I don't think he's cool under pressure, I think he's crazy." They laughed, and so did I.

"Point taken," I said. I looked over at the Hughes, "Whatever happens, do not move from that spot." They both nodded.

The firefight erupted outside. The five moved to the windows to see what was happening. While their attention was at the windows, Sergeant Adams and three of his men walked quietly into the room, taking up firing positions.

"You guys really aren't very good at this." I said. They spun around and raised their guns, and Adams and his men dropped them with stun shots.

He disarmed them, his men took up positions covering all entrances. The firefight continued outside.

"Fast attack Marine landing craft on approach, hammers are intercepting," *Vee* said.

"Let it land in the boneyard, then hammer-head it," I said.

"Understood. They have missile lock on *Mother* ... firing." Two missiles came streaking in and exploded on *Mother*'s shields. "No damage to *Mother*."

The fast attack ship landed and was immediately hit with an HH missile. "No further movement from the attack craft," *Vee* said. "Their support ship has started this way, *Blade* has engaged with HH missiles. Support ship neutralized," *Vee* said. "Their ground forces are laying down their weapons."

"Sergeant, if you would take out the trash please?"

"Yes, sir." He and his men removed the five toughs from the Hughes's office.

"Mr. Hughes, it appears you have another ship in your yard. I'd be interested in buying it."

"Which one were you thinking?" he said, smiling. His wife slapped him on the arm.

"That one," I said pointing, "And I'd like all the associated equipment that came with it."

"I don't know, I was thinking I might like me one of those fancy fast ships," he said, pulling on his chin in thought.

"Hughes!" His wife slapped his arm again.

"I'm glad I'm the one in charge around here," he said. We all laughed. Adams had rejoined us. "OK, scrap plus 10 percent, like always," Mr. Hughes said.

"Done, thank you for the coffee Mrs. Hughes, and since I'm here, I'd like to invite you to my wedding."

"About time!" Sergeant Adams mumbled.

"Please excuse my Sergeant, he apparently hasn't learned that to make Lieutenant he has to keep those stray thoughts from his mouth," I said, smiling.

"Begging your pardon, sir. That wasn't a stray thought, but an observation, sir."

"He recovers well," Mr. Hughes said. We all laughed.

"We'd be honored to come, dear, just let us know when," Mrs. Hughes said.

"We'll send you an invitation."

"Commander, gather all our new gear and our attack ship. I'll meet you on the *Ice*, so have *Blade* recover the other ship."

"Roger."

***

I flew *Mother* back to Hermes headquarters and had Mal join me on *Loki*.

"All went as planned, I'm guessing?"

"One small surprise. They had a fast attack Marine landing craft that we didn't identify until she started her attack run. A hammer took care of her, so we captured her too," I said.

"Are the Hughes OK?"

"Yeah fine, the Marine craft landed in his bone yard, he was happy to sell it to us. That smoothed any ruffled feathers. He wasn't upset with us. We're going up to *Ice* to talk to the prisoners. Maybe we can find out who sent them and why."

Loki docked with *Ice,* and Commander Jones met us and took us to the brig. I was still in the guise of James Hermes. "What have we found out?"

"Nothing yet, we were waiting for you before starting."

"How many did you take alive?" "All 30 ... we stunned them. The only casualties they suffered weres their ship's crews," He said.

I nodded, "No use killing anyone if we don't have to."

"Commodore," said *Vee*, "we have a positive ID on the Merc personnel. They are all ESFL special ops Marines. I stopped, and so did the commander. I held up my hand while he waited. "Verify."

"Verified."

I looked at Jones, "The Mercs we took are Legion Spec Ops," I said.

"You sure know how to keep things interesting, sir."

"It's all part of your bonus package. No need to thank me."

Vee, have *Blade* stand down on searching the captured ships comps."

"Sent and acknowledged."

"Let's go crack their comps before we interrogate them," I said.

"Yes sir, we'll await your return."

Loki docked with *Blade*, and we checked in with the captain. "No one's been on her sir, I recommend taking a squad of Marines in with you."

"Sound advice Captain, assemble the team, then we'll go in."

The hammerheads had done their job, and no one survived. We went straight to the bridge and Mal went to work on their comps.

"Ooow sneaky!," Mal said, "Self-destruct trip program disabled." He worked for while, putting his cracking codes in place. "We're in, all automated self-destructs, and booby-traps disabled. No way to tell about the mechanical ones, but I doubt they set any since we took them before they knew we were on to them."

"OK sergeant, recover the bodies, take them to the cargo bay."

"Yes, sir."

"Anything interesting yet?" I asked.

"There are two comp systems here. One looks like a normal ship for their cover, the second is their spec ops unit. They are definitely Legion Spec Ops on special assignment from Admiral Cole." Mal said.

"Does it give mission specifics?"

"Yeah, seems the Hermes Grav-drive tech, the SRT, and James Hermes are targets. If only one is possible, take the SRT, and James Hermes is expendable."

"So, they don't know or aren't saying anything about us, the Haydock us, I mean."

"So far everything points to them being after the Grav-drive tech."

"Thank God for small favors."

"Why didn't we know about this before they got here?" I

asked.

"The ship is not part of their normal comm network. Theirs comms run through a different system and network."

"Where do they operate out of?"

"According to this, their home port is ESFL home base."

"So now we know what we are looking for. Gunny's ACE, that seeded their system, should be able to integrate with it, correct?"

"Should, if it comms with the Base Comp."

"*Vee,* send a message to Gunny's ACE, find and integrate with the Spec Ops comp systems."

"Sent."

"So, we don't have to send this ship back to them to subvert their system?"

"Nope." Mal said.

"As far as they know someone unknown destroyed the ship."

"As far as they know, yes."

"OK, we'll turn the Commander loose on her and see what goodies he comes up with."

CHAPTER 19

We went aboard *Ice* to interrogate the fake mercs, first briefing Commander Jones on what we had found.

"So, how do you want to play this?" he asked.

"Let's let them think their merc story is holding, and see where that takes us, who's to blame, who hired them, and what they wanted. Let's see what that shakes loose. I wonder, when all is said and done, will the ESFL disavow them?" I said.

"That's the way it's supposed to work. This admiral will no doubt cut them loose. The Commander said.

Mal and I watched on video as Jones started the interrogation. "Name?" he asked.

"Captain Hans Foller, of the Foller Mercenary Company. And I claim prisoner status for me and my company under article 12 of the Mercenary Code Charter."

"So you and your men will become noncombatants against Hermes Corporation, and you want to buy your freedom and your equipment from us."

"Yes, that's why we have insurance."

"True, it comes in handy."

"How many of my man survived?"

"30 of your ground forces, but your ship's crews were not so fortunate."

"The ship was destroyed?"

"We gave them a chance, but they declined. Who contracted you, Captain Foller?"

"The Consortium."

Jones left the interrogation room to confer: "The Consortium, another order from the admiral — if caught, blame CEO Baker."

"Good cover. How would we ever know? Well, except that we know," I said. "Let's shake things up, shall we?" I said, putting on my Mr. Wright guise.

I went in to see the captain, who I knew was actually ESFL Spec Ops Major Goodard. "CEO Baker hired you to steal a Hermes ship and kidnap Mr. Hermes?"

"I don't know specific names, this was an open contract from the Consortium."

"And the hostages were collateral damage?" He didn't answer. "So, you have no useful information for Mr. Hermes then ... there is one other issue though."

"What's that?"

"Members of the ESFL, specifically Spec Ops, can't claim mercenary status, Major Goodard." The major was good ... he never even blinked.

"My name is Captain Foller, of the Foller Mercenary Company, and I claim ..."

"Let me stop you before you run through your whole spiel. Do you really think that ESFL intel are the only ones who have people who infiltrate other organizations? We know exactly who you and your men are." I pointed to the wall, and a list of his men with their names and ranks started showing.

"You get points for throwing CEO Baker under the bus, though. I'm guessing that order came personally from Admiral Cole. They really don't like each other."

"My name ..."

"Is not important," I interrupted. "Let me ask you, how long will it take the admiral to disavow all of you? As far as anyone will ever know, you and your men were pirates on stolen ships. All of your honorable service is down the tubes, because you know, and if you don't you should, that the admiral will let none of this stick to him."

"My name is Captain Foller ..." I held up my hand to stop him, once again.

"Major, I admire your loyalty, but Admiral Cole doesn't deserve it." Looking at the overhead, I said, "Play that last recording where the admiral talks about that battalion of Marines." The video started and the major watched.

The admiral was saying, "Those people are meaningless, I'd have sacrificed them all and executed the two battalions of Marines for atrocities if it would've gotten me all the tech and all of my appropriations." The video ended.

"So you see, as the admiral likes to use chess analogies, you and your men are pawns to be sacrificed. Just pieces on the board in his grand game that no one cares about except him. I suppose it wouldn't be so bad if he weren't skimming 20 percent of all appropriations for his personal retirement accounts.

"Don't worry about the money he stole. Supposedly, CEO Baker found out about the gold and sneaked it away from him. He will love that. CEO Baker also destroyed the secret base where he was hiding it. Unfortunately, his loyal Gunny was killed in the process.

"So, here is what we will do: we will send all the intel we have on you and your men to the ESFL. They will disavow you, then we'll let you and your men go. The newsies will pick the story of pirates up, so you must be careful. I'm sure the Foller Mercenary Company is up to the task." I stood and left the room.

"Are you really going to do all that?" Commander Jones asked.

"Maybe not all of it. *Vee,* how good a cover is the Foller Mercenary Company?"

"Pretty good, you'd have to dig deep to catch any flaws. There are no obvious ties to the Legion. All payments come from third parties on open contracts."

"Interesting, run everything down. Build a file on them and their operations. Let's see what the admiral has been up to."

"There may be a better way to use the good major," Mal said.

"I'm listening."

"Tell him that Mr. Hermes understands he's just a pawn and has no control over his orders. If we turn them out and get he and his men disavowed, that would not bother or hurt the admiral one bit. So, let's just send them back to the admiral with a message ... leave the Hermes Corporation alone or we'll release the video."

"That, and all the other doubts you've planted, will keep them busy for a while. Which gives us more time to continue preparations."

"I like it ... Commander?"

"I like it too. They will rotate most of these guys back to regular Marine berths, but they'll still have a career if they want it."

***

We let them stew for a day, then had the major brought back to the interrogation room. The guard sat him down and handcuffed him to the table. He said nothing, just stared at me.

"Mr. Hermes has reconsidered. He has decided that to turn you and your men over to be disavowed would hurt no one but you and your men. It surely wouldn't hurt the admiral. Ruining you and your men's lives serves no purpose for Mr. Hermes.

We will release you and your men and send you back to the admiral, to deliver a message to him: leave the Hermes Corporation alone, and leave Hermes ships alone. If he does not, we will release information that will probably put him behind bars or facing execution as a traitor to the Legion.

"Someone will take you and your men to the passenger terminal on Titan. Tickets will be there taking you back to Earth Station. I'm sure you can get home from there. I honestly hope we never meet again, major."

The passenger liner left for the next day with the Legion Spec Ops teams on board. "*Vee,* message *Ice* and *Blade* to return home. Have them put the new ship into refit."

"Sent."

"Message Buck and Riley to put more crews on the envirodome shields. I want that installation finished, ASAP."

"Sent."

We left Buck at Hermes headquarters to finish the envirodome. The four of us boarded *Loki* and headed for *Duty*. We'd been gone a long time but had been so busy that the time had flown by.

Hermes looked different. They had smoothed and compressed her outside. The tugs were unloading rock into her smelter/refinery and were going back to get more. We flew inside *Hermes* to dock with *Duty*. *Hush Eight* had arrived and unloaded all the mining equipment and the 15 hedgehogs.

We dropped our things off at our apartment on *Duty* and went to find Aunt J. We found her and Jocko on the Promenade on Hab level One. The transformation was breathtaking. People were walking around everywhere. Small shops and kiosks were open and doing business. When she saw us, she grabbed us all in a group hug. Even Jocko joined in.

"It looks like we've missed some things," I said.

"She's 95 percent complete but the 5 percent remaining is in the Hab areas. She's fully operational. Families have moved in to the Habs. We are filling them one level at a time... and we made Jocko mayor of the *Hermes* Habs," Aunt J said.

"If nominated, I will not run. If elected I will not serve," Jocko said, we all laughed.

"I see we got businesses to come on board with us." I said.

"It was your bank loans that started it. Then Bill sent people out to open a bar," Jocko said.

"They got beer?" Mal asked.

"Humanity goes nowhere without beer," Jocko said.

"In that case let's go get a cold one and catch each other up," I said. When we arrived at the bar, I stopped to read the name over the door.

"I wonder how many thousands of times that name has been used." I mused.

"I like it," Jazz said.

"It does make you smile," I said. The sign read "The Dew Drop Inn".

We spent the next several hours drinking beer, telling tales, catching up on the work that had been done. We also talked over work still waiting, as well as the latest moves — that we knew of — that our enemies were making.

"So, the huge item is the Founder's Day celebration," Aunt J said. "It has been almost a year since you brought us safely out here and started creating *Hermes*. We decided to mark that day was a celebration, and we're calling it Founder's Day."

I nodded, "the people need a reason to celebrate, and they deserve it." Aunt Jay looked at Jazz and Jade, they both nodded.

"It will also be your wedding day, a double wedding." Aunt J announced.

"Aw man, we'd love to be there, but Mal and I have that thing we have to go to," I said looking at Mal.

"Yeah, that thing," Mal said. I think it was their augmentation that got me. Both girls sprang across the table and landed on top of the both of us.

"Bouncer! Bouncer!" I kept yelling.

"You are on your own," came a shout back from the bouncer.

"Wrangled, roped, and branded," Jocko yelled.

The whole bar was in an uproar. Since Mal and I couldn't get away, we turned the uproar into a pre-wedding party.

The next day, despite my hangover, we had a manager's meeting. They gave us updates from every department, and of course Aunt J and Jocko had kept everything running smoothly. We now had a mining department that coordinated the mining tug operations.

"We brought 100 seekers, 100 mining bots, and 100 hauler bots back with us. Send the seekers out and map everything within one hour's flight time. Let's find and mine the highest concentrated Mithrilium rocks in the area. Once found and mapped, put the mining bots and the hauler bots to work.

"Once the 15 hedgehogs are out of refit, get them started bringing the ore back to Hermes. They will be ACE autonomous, so they can run 24/7. Let me assure you that the ACE miners will replace no one. So, no one is losing their jobs. They are in addition to your normal operations." There was a look of relief on their faces after that assurance.

After the managers' meeting we went up to the ship's operations level, and then to the flight deck and bridge. They gave us a tour of all ship operations consoles and area.

"Everyone has done an outstanding job. Better than I had ever dreamed possible," I announced to everyone.

We finally made it to the bridge, vid screens covered the forward bulkheads giving the appearance of looking out of the front of the ship. Each station had its own dedicated console and vid screen. Should an event occur where we would have to operate the ship without *Hermes'* ACE, we would be ready.

I stood there soaking it all in. "*Hermes*, ship and systems status?"

"All operations systems, and ship's systems are online, all boards are green. Ship is at station keeping, and GCD is online in safety standby, all boards are green. Shields online, all boards are green. Weapons systems online in safety standby.

"All scanning systems are online, all boards are green. Scans are all clear of any unauthorized ship out to one day's travel. All ACE programs are online and have 100 percent integration," *Hermes* reported.

"Very well, continue normal operations."

"Continue normal operations, aye."

We toured our family quarters. They were set up much like those on *Duty*. All the furniture was moved in, galleys were fully stocked, and everything was 100 percent operational.

"When are we moving in?" I asked.

"Anything wrong with right now?" Mal asked. Both girls nodded their heads.

"Well then, let's get to it." I said.

Mal and I stayed out of the way of planning both the Founder's Day and the wedding day celebrations ... discretion being the better part of valor. The seekers that we had sent out mapping were already paying off. The production rate of our ore mining was way up.

Cargo One and *Cargo Two* were continuing to bring supplies in, filling Hermes's massive storage bunkers. We didn't want to be held hostage over food. We could get water from asteroids if we had to.

"*Vee*, open a new ship design file under the name "Sledgehammer". The design will be like the existing Hammers. "Design the ship large enough to carry six HH missiles, four ECM missiles, two small rail guns, one large railgun, ECM broadcast capable, and long-range scanner and Tri-dar capable. No crew, ACE autonomous controlled, redundant MFRs, shields and GCD."

Vee put the plans up on my HUD wall. It looked almost like a normal Hammer ship. "Show Hammer and Sledgehammer ships in a side-by-side comparison." The Sledgehammers were twice the size of the Hammers. "Good, send plans to Mal and ask for improvements and/or changes."

"Done."

"Message from Mal, Cool, no changes, there is room enough for my tweaks."

We sent the plans to the ship designers. They had no changes. I ordered 36 Sledgehammers and 100 more Hammers made. That would keep everyone busy for many months.

***

"Message from Buck, *Hush Nine* and *Hush Ten* are out of refit and in-service. Enviro-dome complete and operational."

"Acknowledged."

Two weeks before the wedding we sent invitations to all our friends on Titan and had the P550 liner ready to provide transportation. Just about everyone accepted their invitation.

The celebration day plan was that it was a stand down day. The only ones working would be security. Everything else would be at minimal manning. They had set a large grandstand up on Promenade One for the wedding, and the band to play afterwards. We wanted no long speeches, just a well-deserved celebration of the day.

Everyone's family made it, Mal's, Jade's, and Jazz's. Jazz and Jade's father's gave away the brides. The brides were beautiful. It amazed me at how lovely they were.

Our vows were traditional before the minister and 5,000 family, friends, and employees. I was so nervous the only thing I remember about the vows was to say, "I do", and I did, without messing it up.

The celebration lasted all day and into the night, it was a great day, and everyone had a great time. We newlyweds took a few days off to ourselves before getting back to work.

***

It had been a little over a month since we had sent the Legion Spec Ops people back to earth. Our intel said they had arrived at Earth Station and then went to the ESFL base.

"Commodore, Intel reports they have dispatched an ESFL ship to the NL base, ETA 37 days. All Spec Ops people we sent back have been reassigned to other units, except the major, who is being listed as MIA."

"So much for loyalty!"

"*Hush Eleven* and *Twelve* are out of refit and were dispatched to fill their holds with supplies for *Hermes*."

"I think it's time to see if this big baby can move," I said at breakfast the next morning. Jocko had started joining us for family meals, I think he had finally worn Aunt J down.

"How much of a move are you talking about?" Mal asked.

I shrugged my shoulders, "Enough that we are sure she'll perform as expected," I answered.

"And the ships we have working outside?" Aunt J asked.

"We'll recall all ships to *Hermes*," I said, "That, in itself, will be a test."

"Make it so, number one," Mal said, everyone laughed. "He's been watching Star Trek-NG again," Jade said.

"*Hermes*, recall all ships, in preparation for departure at

1300."

"Recall issued," *Hermes* said. All ships were recovered by 1400. As this was our first move, we checked and rechecked everything.

"*Hermes,* cross check all systems in preparation for departure," I said.

"Cross check complete, all ships secured, all boards are green, all systems online and ready for departure," *Hermes* replied. I looked around the bridge operations, we had all green lights and all thumbs were up.

"*Hermes,* take us to open space, ahead slow."

"Enroute to open space, ahead slow, aye." We could only tell we were moving by watching the big screens. Internal-grav was rock-solid. Everyone was watching their boards and listening to reports from around the ship.

"*Hermes,* when we have reached open space, and it is safe to do so, increase speed to one quarter normal engine speed."

"Roger, One quarter NES."

"*Hermes,* report all ship statuses."

"All ship boards are green, external Grav-fields are green, all systems normal, all boards are green." We were all watching the screens. Mal was watching his readouts.

"Mal?" I asked. He never looked up but gave me a thumbs up.

"We have cleared asteroid field, and are in open space, at one quarter NES."

"Plot a course away from Earth, 50 percent NES."

"Course plotted away from Earth 50 percent NES, engaging." I waited five minutes, watching screens from the Captain's chair.

"*Hermes,* status of the ship?"

"All systems normal, all boards green."

"How's our power usage Mal?"

Mal looked up smiling, "10 percent."

I shook my head, "Amazing."

"*Hermes,* slowly take us up to 100 percent NES, report any

problems."

"Increasing speed to 100 percent slowly, report problems, aye. 60 percent NES all boards green... 70 percent NES all boards green... 80 percent NES all boards green... 90 percent NES all boards green... 100 percent NES all boards green, no problems to report." *Hermes* announced.

I looked around the bridge, "Any reports of problems from the crew?" Everyone was shaking their heads. There were no problems reported.

"*Hermes*, increase speed to 200 percent NES."

"200 percent NES all boards green..."

"Increase speed to point one C."

"Point one C all boards green..."

I looked at Mal, "Power usage?"

"12 percent," He said smiling.

"*Hermes*, increase speed to .3 C."

".3 C, all boards are green, power usage at 13 percent..."

I looked at Mal, he shrugged his shoulders and smiled, "Learning program." I nodded, smiling.

"*Hermes*, increase speed to .5 C."

".5 C, all boards are green, power usage at 15 percent."

"Ladies and gentlemen, we have just set another record." I announced. We continued following the plotted course for another 30 minutes, "*Hermes*, ship status?"

"All systems normal, all boards green, power usage holding it 15 percent."

"*Hermes*, return us to our starting point, safe entry speeds."

"Returning to starting point, safe entry speed, aye."

"Let's take a walk," Jazz said.

"*Hermes*, you have the helm."

"*Hermes* has the helm, aye."

CHAPTER 20

The four of us walked the Promenade talking to people and found they could not believe we were moving. There was no fluctuation in gravity. Some even asked when we would start the test flight.

"Soon," I answered, smiling.

"Anyone for a beer?" Mal asked. We all raised our hands.

As we sat enjoying our brews, "We have arrived at our original starting point, propulsion is at station keeping, all boards are green," *Hermes* announced.

"Redeploy the fleet. Everyone can go back to work, test flight concluded successfully." I answered.

"Roger, redeploying fleet," *Hermes* replied.

***

"Commodore you have a message from *Major* that a combined corporate battle group was in the Conclave area, and have now left, following *Hush Six*, heading back toward the mining colonies. Their orders are to seize *Hush Six*. The fleet includes a space fighter carrier, a battleship, two frigates and four tenders," *Vee* reported.

"Contact *Hush Six* and instruct her not to go dark, but to continue on course."

"Sent."

"Scramble the fleet. Send all info to Captain Smythe. Our fleet will intercept the corporate battle group, dark. Once out of range of prying eyes, hammerhead and recover the new additions to our fleet. *Hush Six* to continue on scheduled contract. We will join you on the *Anvil*."

"Sent." Just enough time for me to change into my uniform, and tell the girls we have to run, and still make fleet deployment.

Some 45 minutes after the fleet left *Hermes,* we found the corporate battle group.

"Captain Smythe deployed our fleet into attack formation. Let's wait for them to make their move before we make ours. Once they do, they are pirates. Double check for additional followers. We told *Hush Six* that we would handle the comms, to just continue on course.

We cruised towards them for another hour, until we received, "Shut down your engines and prepare to be boarded. If you do not do so, we will destroy you."

"And so it begins," I said,

"Unknown ship," we replied, "we are in free space, if you fire on us that's piracy." They fired a railgun shot across her bow. I nodded to Captain Smythe, "Take 'em."

"Hermes battle group target all enemy ships and fire HH missiles." It was over almost before it started. We had hit the carrier with four HH missiles in case the pilots were inside their fighters. Our crews had trained for this so much that in less than two hours we were on the way out of the area with our new ships. *Hush Six* had gone dark and continued on course.

"These people don't seem to learn very fast," Captain Smythe said.

"Or care about how many people or ships they lose," I replied.

"We're going to need to hire more people." Captain Smythe said.

"We sure are, Commodore Smythe, why don't you plan that while we get our new ships into refit," I said.

He stared at me for a moment, "Yes Admiral Hermes, I'll get right on that," he said, smiling.

"Crap," I said, "I guess it comes with the territory."

We arrived back at *Hermes* and docked our new ships.

Our fleet docked inside. It appeared that the corporations were trying to show each other who had the best ships. They had all sent relatively new vessels, and all of them were fully loaded.

The carrier was of a new design — she housed 80 fighters, 20 bombers and bristled with multiple missile launching sites. She had close in missile defense systems, rail guns, and ECM capabilities, and also housed a battalion of Marines.

The first thing we did was let the Intel guys go over the ships, less the comps. As always, Mal handled the comps. Mal had created a special ACE Intel M-Comp that stripped all the Intel from a system, deactivated any fail safes, and any self-destruct programs. Once that was done he installed ACE programs on all our new ships. All the crew's bodies were given last rites and cremated with due ceremony.

The carrier, which we renamed *Shogun,* took priority and went into refit right away. By removing her engines and fuel systems we made room for fast attack Marine drop ships. All the fighters would be ACE controlled, so that cut down on personnel needs for crew her.

We put the new battleship, renamed *Tundra,* into refit next. We had enough people now we could run three full shifts on both the *Travis* and the *Hermes.*

We decided to rebuild *Tundra* with the same design plan that the *Anvil* had, including the Hammer ships. I put the Sledgehammers and the newly designed Hammers on hold until the new ships were out of refit.

"Admiral, you have a message from Al, the 3-D plant is ready for its first test run of a product."

"Acknowledge, we'll be there in a few days."

"Sent."

We set everything on schedule and would be ready to leave for Titan in a few days.

"Admiral, the ESFL ship has reached the NL base site. They sent a message back to the ESFL base." The message started, "Base destroyed by nuke strike. Request further orders."

"That should kick over an anthill," I said.

***

We landed *Loki* at the Hermes headquarters and Buck met us and gave us a quick update on where we were with the ongoing projects.

"The shipyard is almost at a work stoppage, we have worked ourselves out of a job, literally. The enviro-dome is complete, and all security systems integrated into it."

"OK, let us finish with Al, then we'll go shopping at the boneyard for more work for the shipyard," I said. Al was a proud father of his 3-D Factory Level Printer. He showed us around and answered all of our questions. Mal checked the M-Comp's, then installed an ACE program for the factory. While Mal did that, Buck and I went to visit Mr. Hughes.

"Good morning, Mrs. Hughes." I said as we entered the boneyard office.

"Good morning," she said coming over and gave me a hug.

"Coffee is fresh, won't you have a cup?" She asked.

"Yes ma'am. Where is that old man you used to have working for you?" I asked.

"I heard that!" Came from the back office. Everyone laughed. Mr. Hughes came out and shook everyone's hand.

"What can we help you with?" he asked.

"To be honest, I'm looking for something to put in my shipyard to keep my people working. They've worked themselves out of a job," I said, smiling.

"Any idea what you might want?" He asked.

"Not really, I thought we might have a look around and see if anything jumps out at me."

"We can do that, let's take a ride." We loaded into his yard boat and looked as we flew around the boneyard.

"Let's check out your bigger ships: your ore haulers and large ships that have no engines," I said.

"The biggest ships I have left are two container ships." We flew over to them and I saw that they weren't as big as the Super

Haulers but didn't miss by much.

"I'm guessing these were fuel hogs, and it cost more to feed them than they were making."

"Got it in one," Hughes said.

"Do they still use the same size and style containers?"

"Yep, those are universal standard."

"We'll take both of them What are those over there, passenger liners?"

"Yeah, older engines, new ones get better fuel economy, they phased out these. There are some PL3000, P600, and I think one is a 1500, or 2000."

"I may want those, but I need to check on some things. Show us your haulers, please, sir."

He swung the ship around. "Those are just over here, they are all larger standard size haulers and none of them have engines."

"We'll take those four, and two container ships, what's your price?"

"Let me show you one other ship first," he said. We flew back around to his office and landed by a medium sized cargo ship. "This has been my project ship for when me and the Mrs. retire. We want to travel and pick up a few loads here and there to make it pay for itself."

"She looks like a solid ship," I said.

"She is, she's a workhorse."

"You change your mind about using her?"

"Nope, but I want you to upgrade her. I know you're careful about your tech, and who gets it. I'll abide by whatever limits you place on her.

"If you will upgrade her, I'll give you the four large haulers in trade, and sell you the container ships for scrap plus 10 percent."

"I'm sorry sir, I can't do that," I said. He nodded, "I understand."

"I don't think you do. You have helped me, selling to me at good prices, and even when you could have raised your rates, you didn't. When dealing with me put you and your wife in harm's way, you never blamed me for it and stayed friends.

"I'll give you scrap plus 10 percent for all six ships, and the Hermes Corporation would like to refit and refurb your ship as an early retirement gift. If you want to reconsider the ship you want us to refit, that would be fine, too. "We're going to strip her out, anyway. Why don't you sell that one and give us a good frame to work with? That way you could go bigger and have more room, in case your family wants to ride somewhere. Once we're finished she won't cost anything — or very little — to operate."

He thought a moment. "That's a kind offer, and I'm not one to look a gift horse in the mouth."

He took us over to a larger cargo ship of a newer design. "This is the one I originally planned to use as a retirement ship. But we were being cautious about the operating cost. She has no engines, but most everything else is there."

"We'll take care of the rest. *Vee*, have *Mother* come get this ship."

"*Mother* is on the way, Sir."

***

"*Vee*, what is the name of that company that builds those high-end corporate yachts?"

"Executive Yacht Inc."

"Yeah, that's the one, let's go over there and see what they have." We arrived and sat down in a genuinely nice sales lot.

We went inside, and one of the salesmen looked up at us, "Deliveries are around back in the other building," and walked off. Buck laughed, I smiled. We walked over to the receptionist.

"Good afternoon, sir, how can we help you?"

"Who is your youngest and newest salesman?"

"That would be Leo, Leo Myers."

"That's who I'd like to see." She called for him to come to the reception desk. When Leo arrived, he introduced himself and shook our hands. He was wearing a nice, but off the rack suit.

"Just starting in the business, Leo?"

"Yes sir, just finished the sales training."

"I'm sure you'll do fine, just don't do what that guy does." I chin pointed at the guy who thought we were delivery people.

"Yeah, he thinks he's God's gift, but he does make sales."

I explained what I wanted to do was to bring in a cargo ship to have them upgrade the interior. My yard would take care of the rest.

"Your yard?"

"Yes."

Then it clicked for him, "Hermes yards, you're that Mr. Hermes." I nodded. "It is a pleasure to meet you, sir. Let me ask you, are you open to other options?"

"I'm open to most things, what do you have in mind?"

"We have an older ship that's been traded in that's along the same lines as what you're talking about. It might be a little bigger than what you are looking for, but I could get you a great deal on her. A well-to-do businessman who wanted to travel owned her, but wanted the ship to pay for itself. She needs refit because of her engines. Everything else is in excellent condition, and she has well-appointed finishes."

"Let's look at her."

Leo had said it was an older ship, but it was actually newer than what Hughes had given us to work with. She was roughly the same size but could carry more cargo because of her configuration. She had four master suites and crew quarters for 10. The galley was well appointed and had two dining areas, one for the crew and one for passengers and owner.

The bridge and operations were all nicely done. "How much are we talking here, Leo?"

"She needs new engines but I'm betting you will put those new design engines in her like you did your Super Haulers." I nodded. "Let me ask you, have you considered selling an installation package of your engines? Before you answer. For conversation's sake, hypothetically, could you install one of your packages into one of our luxury ship's packages?"

"I have sold some of our tech, but too often find someone is trying to steal the tech rather than using it as intended."

He nodded, "I can see that. What if we sell the unit with a sealed compartment? If they open the compartment, it voids all warranties. I'm sure you have your own safeguards against tampering."

"We do."

"Our customers are rich, and their friends are rich. We'll sell the package for three times the price and they'll pay it because no one else has it. Then everyone else will have to have it.

"Sir, most of the people who buy these do it as a status symbol, they want to show off their newest toy to their rich friends. Then everyone else will have to have 'the Hermes package' because they don't want to be outdone.

"They couldn't care less about the tech. I'm sure there will be those who try to cheat, but as soon as they open that sealed door, that whole section is toast, and we will not replace it. We could both make lots of money on this deal, and when I say both, I mean Hermes and Executive Yacht's. I'll make my commission, but these will sell themselves. Before you decide, at least talk to my boss."

"You make a good case, Leo. I'll give you your shot. Let's go see your boss."

We were in the waiting area getting a cup of coffee when Mr. "deliveries are out back" came over. "That coffee is for customers! You two are not customers, so you need to get out of here and get to work."

Buck busted out laughing.

"I will comm security."

"I think you need to," I said.

"Fine." He pulled out his comm and made a call.

Security, Leo, and Leo's boss arrived at the same time. "No need to worry Mr. Taylor, I've taken care the problem."

"What problem?"

"Pencil neck here," I interjected, "just threw us off your property and commed security to get it done," I said, sipping my coffee.

"Did he now?" Mr. Taylor asked.

"Yes, sir I did," the salesman said, throwing out his chest. "We can't have people like this in the showroom, it's bad for business."

Taylor shook his head, "Allow me to introduce Mr. Hermes of the Hermes Corporation. You know, the one that has his name on banks, casinos, hotels, restaurants, shipyards, things like that. Security, since you are already here, escort 'pencil neck' to his desk. Let him clean it out, then escort him off the property." Security took the astonished man away, so shocked he couldn't even speak.

"My apologies Mr. Hermes, Raymond Taylor, owner of this circus … and monkeys are part of the package," he said smiling.

"Good to meet you sir. Leo was sharing an interesting proposal with me." I said.

"I hope he didn't overstep himself," he said looking at Leo.

"Not at all, he baited the hook and went to get the master fisherman."

After several hours' negotiations, we came to an agreement. I got the executive cargo ship at cost. We would install and seal the engine and power rooms and then split the profitsm with 60 percent going to Hermes Corporation and 40 percent going to Executive Yachts Inc. Leo would be the liaison to Hermes and get a percentage of each sale no matter who made it.

I guess it was his lucky day.

We set Hughes' old cargo ship hull to the side and put his new executive yacht/cargo ship straight into refit.

"What made you decide to put the GCD in ships to be sold?" Mal said.

I shrugged my shoulders, "the tech will come out eventually, we might as well get some rich guys on our side.

Besides, we will limit the speed to twice normal engine speed. And the ACE programs would keep our tech safe, so let's make money before crazy happens." I said.

"Sounds good."

For the first project on Al's 3-D factory printer, we built a newly designed 50 KLT ACE tug to would work in concert with the mining bots and an ore hauler.

We fed the design specs into the factory ACE and started the printer. We took it slow, so we could tweak and calibrate all the printing nozzles and mediums. We spent two days adjusting equipment, programming, and medium loaders. We were finally satisfied with the process but kept it slow, crosschecking everything on the first run.

We took a week to print the first tug, and we estimated it would have taken a tug factory three weeks to make one start to finish if they had all parts on hand. The next tug through the printer took four days, less the M/U core.

The next printing took three days, we finally got it down to printing one every 42 hours. We ordered 24 more to create the Hermes Ore Hauler Combine package, which would be financed through our banks. While we waited for our new H50 KLTs to be printed we started another hauler through refit.

***

We promoted Sergeant Adams to Lieutenant Adams and added the counter Intel M-nite infusion nanites to his systems. We had him select another man and two women to become our security detail. Upon approval we would also give them the treatments. All of our security people now wore the shield belts as part of their uniforms.

We set up a whole new refit line just to service Executive Yachts Inc. They wanted one of their current ships refitted as a demo so we started work on her the same day.

Mal had done his usual magic with the ACE comp's. He had been installing ACEs on the H50s as they came off the line. We installed the ACE M-Comp in the Hughes Executive Cargo Ship and got it ready for its shakedown cruise. We also installed rail guns for protection and added a full internal security protocol package. Her shakedown cruise went perfectly, and we had her fully stocked, and all of her tankage filled.

We flew her over to present her to the Hughes. To say they were speechless may overstate it, but not by much.

"Oh, my!" Was all Mrs. Hughes could say as tears ran down her face.

"What did you name her?" Mr. Hughes asked.

"We didn't, that honor goes to you." I said.

He thought for a moment, looking around. *"Boneyard's Envy."*

"Perfect," His wife said. We took *Envy* out for a cruise. The Hughes's were ecstatic with their new ship.

CHAPTER 21

The big hauler came out of refit, and we put the Hermes Hauler Combine Package together. The package included six H50s, six mining bots, six hauling bots, and one seeker.

We turned it over to the mining equipment company sales force and told them to sell it. We would include our bank financing as part of the deal. We had the order for the first package three days later. We pulled two more haulers from the boneyard and put them into refit.

"*Vee*, comm Mr. Reuben."

"Hello James, how are you doing?"

"Fine sir, and yourself?"

"Fine, fine, how can I help you."

"I would like you to find us a passenger carrying company to buy or to buy into. One with a good reputation but who are being pushed out of business by a big corporation. We will provide ships that will go twice the speed of any other carriers, and they provide the crew and passenger services."

"How big are you thinking of starting?"

"I'm open to all options."

"We'll see what we can find and get back with you."

"Thank you, sir."

"Sir you have a comm from Mr. Hughes."

"Put him through, Mr. Hughes, what can I do for you?"

"Buy the boneyard."

"Excuse me?"

"Ever since you delivered the *Envy* to us, we have been ready to go. The only thing keeping us here is the boneyard. We want to sell out and get traveling. I'll give you good terms."

"I'm listening."

"As you sell, use, or scrap a ship, you pay me scrap prices. What you make on it is your business."

"No down payment?"

"No, I trust you for it."

"When do you want to leave?"

"As soon as you agree to take the place over."

"Take your paperwork to Joshua, I'll tell him to expect you. Have a nice trip." I said, laughing.

"*Vee*, message Joshua, tell him to expect Mr. Hughes — we are buying the boneyard. Ask him to hire a caretaker to manager it, doing business as Hermes Boneyard."

We moved two of the P300 hundred passenger ships over to the shipyard and started their refit. Al's factory easily printed new seats, M-tronics, and M-instrumentation for the P300 ships.

Our smelter/refinery was running at capacity, and ore was waiting to be processed. We were hauling product out as fast as we could load ships … half going to Earth, the rest going to Mars and other stations.

"*Vee*, message Mr. Rueben, ask about another smelter for sale."

"Sent."

"Sir you have a message from Joshua and Aaron Stein. The corporate lawyers would like to meet with you to discuss a settlement on the 3-D printer issue."

"Tell them we can meet them here at our offices at 1500 tomorrow."

"Sent and acknowledged." I gave Lieutenant Adams the schedule and had them set up security for the meeting.

At 1445 the Steins showed up along with a lawyer representing the Corporation. *Vee* had a green light on my HUD for security.

Coffee offered, introductions made, we got down to business. The corporate lawyer, Bailey, kept looking at his watch.

"Mr. Hermes, surely you can see what a waste of your resources this lawsuit is. We have drawn this litigation out for 30 years. Do you think we will stop now? We are prepared to leave you and your inferior printer alone if you drop your suit and sign over our portion of the tech."

I looked at the Steins. They shrugged their shoulders. "I'm sorry, I thought you wanted to meet to discuss a settlement."

"This is a settlement offer, I assure you."

Vee spoke into my ear, "There has been an explosion at the Stein's law offices. No injuries reported, but quite a lot of damage to the building." My expression never changed. Bailey looked at his watch.

"Do you have somewhere else to be, Mr. Bailey?"

"No, I'm right on schedule," he said, smiling.

"Mr. Adams, have someone show the Steins to the galley, please."

"Gentlemen." He opened the door and they nodded and left.

"I presume you got a message," Bailey said.

"I did," I said looking at him.

"I would suggest you heed the warnings and drop the lawsuit. The next time," he tapped his watch smiling, "it won't be just a building."

I stared at him for a moment. "Mr. Bailey do you know where the saying 'don't kill the messenger' comes from?" I leaned forward. He frowned, hands folded on the table in front of him.

"I'm afraid I don't."

"I don't either, but it apparently happened quite a bit, because it became a saying."

"You will not lay a finger on me, I'm …" That's as far as he got when my cyber palm impacted on his folded hands, breaking both of them. He screamed and fell out of his chair.

He sat up on the floor, looking at his broken hands.

"You see, that's the thing with you people, you think you can do anything you want with impunity, no consequences. You have been doing it this way for so long, you are shocked when you meet someone willing to be just as ruthless as you.

"As you may have noticed, I'm more of a 'hands on' type of

guy, pardon the pun. I don't send others to do my dirty work.

"Now that I have your attention, I will ask you some questions, and you will answer them. We can do this the easy way or the hard way. The hard way having been demonstrated."

He broke out in a cold sweat from the pain. "Do you understand?" He nodded. "Who sent your little bomb message?"

"We are a subsidiary of the Consortium."

"Who, specifically?"

"CEO Baker." He said holding his hands to the front of his chest.

"Since CEO Baker has used you as a messenger, I have a message for you to take back to him. Tell him the settlement price is 10 billion creds, or ownership of the 3-D printer company."

"Are you crazy?"

"I thought that would be obvious at this point. Was there anything else you were supposed to tell me?"

He shook his head, "No."

"Good, now if you will go with Lt. Adams, we'll have those hands seen to." They left the meeting room headed for Med-bay. "*Vee*, message Med-bay and tell them not to put him in an Auto-doc, but simply put his hands in casts and send him on his way."

"Sent."

Lieutenant Adams came back in, with the Steins in tow. "We'll pay for the damages."

"Thank God it hurt no one," Joshua said.

"Have you thought about moving your offices out here with us, in our office complex?"

"We have now," Joshua said.

"Why don't you walk over there and pick out some office suites."

"I think we will." Aaron said, Joshua nodded.

"Herm, have the Unreported News leak stories about the Consortium and CEO Baker. If he has a mistress, make sure his wife finds out about it. Include all his hidden bank accounts with that info."

"Yes, Sir."

"On another subject, infiltrate the systems in CEO Baker's G-car. When it's in the parking area with all the other board members cars, overload the systems and blow it up. Ensure it harms no one, only the vehicles. Even better, blow all the board members' G-cars up in the corporate parking area."

"When would you like that happened?"

"As soon as CEO Baker gets the message from Mr. Bailey."

"Yes, sir."

***

We completed the Executive Yacht's demo ship, and they loved it. "It will sell itself." Leo said.

Another Hermes Hauler Combine Package was completed and put out for sale.

Al finished printing all the parts we needed for the P300, and crews were installing them.

"*Vee*, design a security grav-hover bot with full scan capabilities, stun capabilities, and shields. We'll integrated them into our security forces around the Hermes properties."

"Size?"

"1 meter across and 10 centimeters thick as a guide, not a locked in measurement." The plans came up on my HUD. "Looks good, send it to Al and have him print one for testing."

"Sent."

Once Mal finished tweaking the bot, the security teams loved them. They integrated a dozen into *Herm's* security net. Our security detail, headed by Lieutenant Adams, now had three new team members. Two women for Jazz and Jade, and another man for Mal.

"Sir, a message from Gunny ACE. An ESFL ship tried to stop and board one of our Super Haulers under the guise of a safety inspection. We declined, and as they were in free space, they continued on their way. The ESFL ship is following, awaiting further orders."

"Understood, have our ship continue on as contracted, allow no one to board them."

"Sent."

"Sir, they have sent you a summons to appear before the UNSA regarding the new engine technologies we are using in our ships." *Vee* said.

"Decline their summons, they have no legal jurisdiction over me or our companies."

"Sent."

"Sir, you have a message from Gunny ACE. They have recalled the ESFL ship to the Legion base."

"Acknowledged, forward all of those messages and my replies to Jazz, Jade, and Mal."

"Done."

***

"Sir, Mr. Bailey arrived at the Consortium headquarters building to brief the Board. We carried the G-car destruct order out. Destruction of all grav-cars was accomplished with no harm to anyone," *Vee* said. "Mr. Bailey delivered your message, related the events that transpired and was dismissed."

"The following is a video of the meeting after Mr. Bailey was dismissed: "It seems Mr. Hermes is not so easily cowed," CEO Baker said.

"Perhaps we should consider a settlement," a board member said.

"Of 10 billion creds? Out of the question."

"I'm sure that number was because we threatened him, maybe a legitimate settle offer would yield better results. The corporate G-car parking garage destruction was his answer to that."

"Your proposal?"

"2 billion, and he stops all litigation. We leave him alone, he leaves us alone."

"It would be cheaper to kill them."

"I'm not so sure about that, besides he may feel the same way about you. He has shown he will resort to violence when pushed."

"Very well, make your offer ... if he turns it down, then we'll kill him."

"*Vee,* message Joshua that they will offer us two billion creds in the settlement. Take the creds. We'll stop pursuing the lawsuits and leave them alone, and they stop pursuing their lawsuits and leave us alone."

"Sent."

"On another subject sir, Rep. Johnson and Admiral Cole had this conversation:"

"So, your ploy of a safety inspection did not work, what's your next move?" Johnson asked.

"Maybe a personal meeting will open some doors," The admiral replied.

"I want those engines and power sources. With them we could push out into space faster and get rid of some of the freeloading people here on earth. I don't care how you do it, just get the tech."

"I may have to apply direct force to get what we want."

"I don't care, elections are coming up and I need this. Do what you have to do, but get the job done. No messing around like with that Haydock mess."

"All right, I'll pay Mr. Hermes a visit, and see if he's open to negotiations."

"End of the message."

"Gunny ACE reports that the admiral and an ESFL battle group of 12 ships have left Legion Home Port headed for Titan, with an ETA of two weeks," *Vee* said.

"Understood, send Commodore Smythe a warning order to have the fleet ready to meet the incoming ESFL Battle Group. Attach the video as background information."

"Sent."

***

"You have an incoming comm from Mr. Reuben."

"Put him through. 'Mr. Reuben, what can I do for you?' "

"We have found a passenger transportation company that fits your criteria. They are based here on Titan and make runs to Conclave, Mars, and a few other stations. They were doing well, but the bigger corporations are undercutting them. They are now barely breaking even."

"How big is their fleet?"

"They have six P300s, all in good condition, and an excellent customer service rating and maintenance record."

"Are they ready to talk to us?"

"They are."

"Good, we have one of our HP300s out of refit, we'll take it over and let them see it. Then we'll talk. Set up the meeting, and I'll be there."

"Will do."

***

We landed the HP300 on the Peterson Flight Services tarmac the next morning at 1100. The Petersons came out to meet us. "Before you say it, she's not much to look at," I said, smiling, shaking his hand.

"So, you read minds, too," he said, laughing.

"We'll have her painted in whatever livery you want. What you really need to see is inside." I led them in and showed them around, then let their pilots take the controls, but had the HP ACE take us on a test flight.

Once we were in free space, I let the pilots fly her, so they could see what she could do. "Top speed?" the chief pilot asked.

"Twice a normal liner's speed," I answered. He gave me a skeptical look. "Push her and see." I said.

He did. "She handles like a dream," he said. The copilot got stick time and fell in love with her. Peterson and I took seats in first class.

"I see the carrot, where's the stick?" Peterson asked.

"The stick is you can't touch the engines or power supplies. They are proprietary and only my people will have access to them."

"Why?"

"Honestly, because every corporation in the system is after the tech and would literally kill to get it. So no one gets it. One reason we chose your company is you've been pushed around by the corporations as I have and understand what it's like."

"I do indeed. OK, what are we talking about in percentages?"

"Simple 60/40 split of net. 60 percent to you, 40 percent to me. I've no interest or experience in running a passenger carrier. Hermes will be a silent partner. However, with these engines we can expand to cover Earth as well. I have more ships I'm putting through refit. We have a PL2000 we can put into service when we expand service to Earth." I explained.

"Will you put all of that in writing?"

"I will."

"Then we have a deal."

"I think we do. Keep the HP300, send her to the paint shop, and send me the bill." I said.

"I'll have her there first thing tomorrow."

***

"You have an incoming comm from Joshua," *Vee* said.

"Joshua, how are you, how can I help you?"

"I'm fine sir, I called to let you know we have accepted the 2 billion creds settlement from the Consortium and have the money in our accounts."

"Congratulations, well done. Send half to Al Weaver, 20 percent to your law firm, and 30 percent to the Hermes Corporation. Thank you for the hard work."

"Thank you, we appreciate the business."

***

The third and fourth Hermes Hauler Combines came out of refit and were sent over to be sold at the mining equipment company. They'd already sold the first two. We brought over one of the big container ships from the boneyard and started her through refit. I toured the Hermes Shipyards — we were very busy. The second HP300 came out of refit and was delivered to Peterson.

"Admiral, Commodore Smythe and his task force of *Anvil, Ice, Blade, and Vanguard* are in position and dark." *Vee* said.

"Acknowledge."

Dinner was subdued that night. "What are you going to do?" Jazz asked.

"That depends on the admiral. I hope to give him enough rope to hang himself. What I will not do is run, or turn over our tech. I hope I can do so without starting a war with the ESFL." I said.

"We should be ready to broadcast the video feeds of that meeting between the admiral, Rep. Johnson, and CEO Baker. We'll wide beam the broadcast so all of his ships can hear it." Mal said.

"I agree, give Joshua, Aaron, and Mr. Reuben a heads up. They probably have contacts in the government here on Titan. That way they'll be ready to react to things go badly."

"We definitely need to do that," Jazz said.

We were in my office with the admiral comm'ed. "*Vee,* keep the camera tight on me and answer." What can the Hermes Corporation do for the ESFL?" I asked.

"This is Admiral of the ESFL Cole, we want your engine and power tech."

"I'm sorry you made the trip for nothing, Admiral. Our tech is not for sale." Out of the corner of my eye, I saw Mal working on his programming. He sat back and gave me a thumbs up.

"You misunderstand, we're not here to buy it. You will turn it over to us as a matter of Sol system security, so we can better protect Earth and the Solar System."

"Protect us from what? As far as I know, there is no alien menace or impending invasion. No, Admiral, you cannot have our inventions. Did you get the message I sent you via Major Goodard?" I asked.

"You don't issue ultimatums to the ESFL."

"You misunderstood, that message was a personal message to you. I have nothing against the ESFL as a whole, just you."

"Son, I have 12 ships of the line above you, I will land two battalions of Marines on your compound, which is a known terrorist haven. We'll take the tech after we root out the terrorist."

"Is that the same two battalions of Marines you were going to have killed after they killed the hostages from Conclave? You remember the ones you were taking to the new Legion secret base? That was a threat you made to Nic Haydock if he didn't turn over *his* tech to you.

"You said you would have your Marines kill all the hostages, then have all the Marines executed for crimes against humanity or whatever cover story you concocted."

I pointed to Mal, and he played the video conference where the admiral had said that. "You are a traitor, Admiral. You are a pirate leading ships of pirates. If you fire on this civilian corporation complex, one hour from now the only ships the ESFL will have left will be the ones you left at your home port."

"That video is a fake. I declare you a terrorist in the name of the ESFL and demand your immediate surrender," he shouted.

"That's all you got? Is Johnson going to back your play?" I pointed at Mal and he played the video of Johnson telling the admiral to come and take our tech.

"Oh, I guess he will back this play, since you seem to be his lapdog."

"Another fake video."

"I'll make this easy, and less time consuming for you.

Either strike up the band and let's get this dance started, or go home, Admiral. You'll either have to steal it, or come take it, because we aren't giving it to you."

The admiral's screen went blank. I looked at Mal. He shrugged his shoulders. "We'll give it a minute, he might have had to go to the little boy's room." I said. Everyone smiled.

"There is a lot of comm traffic between his ships." Mal said. I nodded, and we waited. "The two Marine deployment ships are breaking formation and heading back to the ESFL base. Others are turning to follow. Three, no, four more are turning toward home.

The admiral screen came back on. "Now that we have separated the pups from the wolves, where were we? Oh yes, this is your last chance to surrender or we open fire."

"And this is your last chance to leave and live another day, if there is one impact on the Hermes Corporation there will be nothing left of your task force but a debris field of destroyed pirate ships." The Admiral looked to his right, "The shipyard, fire."

"They have launched missiles, impact on the shipyard in six seconds," *Vee* said.

The admiral looked at me, "I warned you, Hermes."

"Impact on shields, no damage." Herm said.

I looked at the admiral, "If that's all you got, you'd better go home now, that was embarrassing."

"All ships open fire … destroy that compound." His ships opened fire on us with all they had. Missiles and rail gun rounds impacted on our shield.

I looked at Mal. "No damage."

"I warned you Hermes, this is your fault."

I looked at him, letting my eyes turning black, "And I warned *you*, Admiral. Do you remember Captain Smythe? He's a commodore now. Pawn takes King, Checkmate." It seemed to finally dawn on the admiral, and his expression changed. "Commodore Smythe, you have your orders."

"Wait!" The Admiral shouted.

The Hermes task force came into the clear and unleashed their Hammer drones on the six former ESFL ships. The Hammers made strafing runs through the six ships and pulled away. Their shields were taking hits from the ESFL ships, but they just shrugged them off and kept going.

The Hermes task force held their formation, targeting the pirate ships. *Anvil* fired her main rail guns, turning one ship after another into spreading clouds of debris. There were no survivors. My eyes are no longer black, but maybe a little of my soul was.

"Mal have the Unreported News broadcast the entire event along with all the video of the Admiral, Baker, and Johnson's videos and comm traffic.

Vee, message Commodore Smythe, have his task force go dark and remain in the area. Well done!"

"Sent and acknowledged."

"Sir, the ESFL Ships are asking permission to come back and recover the bodies from the wreckage," *Vee* said.

"Granted." I answered.

CHAPTER 22

They arrested CEO Baker and Representative Johnson on conspiracy, murder, and many other charges and then issued me another summons, which I again declined. Once the ESFL ships had finished their recovery operations, Hermes Corporation and everyone else with a tug cleaned up the debris field.

Many millions had seen the Unreported News about "The Event" as it constantly replayed on every station. Every government on Earth wanted our tech, by whatever means necessary. "One man should not control that kind of tech, it belongs to everyone!" was the new mantra.

I had to recall all of our ships to *Hermes* after they tried to seize one of our haulers. It gradually became clear that it was only the governments of Earth who were crying about how unfair it was that they didn't have our tech.

So we quit going to Earth with our ships.

The UNSA decided that Earth would not buy or sell anything to or from the Hermes Corporation until we shared our tech with them. Of course, when they said "share" they meant give. The Hermes Corporation no longer bought or sold to Earth.

Middlemen made a lot of money, but merchandise still moved. I ordered all our ships to buy all the supplies they could and take them to *Hermes* as fast as they could for as long as they could.

The governments of Earth were in an uproar over our tech and were applying pressure in whatever way they could to make us turn over our carefully crafted technical secrets to them.

Their propaganda machine was painting the picture of us holding back humanity from the stars, charging that we were withholding tech that could save lives and make the Sol system safer for all mankind.

I was being subpoenaed daily by the UNSA, which I continued to ignore. Once the video of Admiral Cole's ships attacking our complex, clearly showing that their missiles could not penetrate our shields, everyone wanted them. Orders came in from every sector of Sol.

"Sir, you have a comm from the UNSA Secretary General."

"Him personally, or his office?"

"Him personally."

"This should be interesting, put him through."

"Mr. Hermes, thank you for taking my call."

"Good morning Mr. Secretary, how are things on Earth?"

"To be honest, things are tense."

"Greedy, power hungry people tend to create that kind of environment."

"You and your corporation are the ones causing this. Don't you see you have an obligation to humanity, to Earth? Earth needs this technology, humanity needs it. With it, we can push out farther into the stars. We can find new worlds, just imagine what humanity could accomplish!"

"Who will control the tech and who decides who goes out into the stars?"

"The UNSA will form a consortium of countries that will oversee development."

"So, I should turn my tech, the basis of my corporation over to the UNSA. What's in it for me?"

"So, you can be bought?"

"I'm a businessman, I could have always been bought. No one made me an offer, just tried to steal what was mine."

"I'm afraid, in this case, you have waited too long to sell us your product. Circumstances have gone too far, too many people know too much about this.

"Here is your offer. You have 60 days to turn over all your tech to us. If you don't, Earth will no longer export anything off planet. No food, No water, No air, nothing to anyone. We will starve you into submission. You will have no safe haven, Titan, Mars, Conclave will all be starving, and they will eventually turn you over to us."

"So, as they say, we can do this the easy way or the hard way."

"Is that your final offer?"

"Final and only." The comm ended.

I looked around the table at the family, including Jocko. "So, we have 60 days before they move against us," Aunt Jay said.

"I doubt it," Jocko answered. "They are probably already making moves against us."

"I agree, he was giving us false hope so we would think we may have that long to prepare," I said. "Suggestions?"

"Short of direct interdiction, Let's sow dissention in their ranks," Mal said.

"How?" Jazz asked.

"Easy. They are power hungry, greedy, distrustful people. Give them a reason to be distrustful of each other," Jocko said.

"*Vee*, what is the most power-hungry government on Earth?"

"The African-Western Bloc … they are radical and well-funded."

"Let's drop Intel crumbs that we are in negotiations to sell our tech to either the African-Western Bloc or to China. Whichever offers the most creds and will support us in space. Plant comm traffic to both governments, so someone can find them if they look."

"Roger."

"*Vee*, assuming no support from Earth, how long can we support ourselves with supplies on hand, and how long can everyone else in the belt support themselves with existing supplies?" Mal asked.

"Hermes Corporation and all its ships can support themselves for 18 months, plus or minus 2 weeks. All other entities can support themselves for 4 months if they work in concert. If not, some will last 6 months, others 45 days."

"So, worst case we have 45 days before crazy stuff happens," Jade said. I got up and moved to the armor glass and looked out at the stars.

"If we give them our tech, it's over. They will take everything we've built. All those deaths will have been in vain," Jazz said.

"*Vee*, what is the closest solar system with habitable planets?"

"Gliese 876 has 4 planets at 15.3 light years away. Spartan 23 has 7 planets, 3 of which are in the Goldilocks Zone, at 23 light years away."

"How close in alignment are those two systems?"

"They lie almost in opposite directions of each other."

"Which has this highest probability of planets that can support humans?"

"Spartan 23 has the higher probability at 67 percent."

"Hmmm… 23 seem to be your lucky number," Mal said.

"Let's hope my luck holds, I said "*Vee*, how long would it take *Duty* to get to Spartan 23 at max speed?"

"Unknown."

"Theorize."

"Not enough information to form a theory."

"What information are you missing?"

"*Duty's* top speed is unknown."

"Theorize, based on current theoretical mathematics." I said.

"There is the possibility that *Duty* could enter FTL travel."

"Show me the equations." The equations flashed up on the wall screens, and I studied them, intently. In fact I don't know how long I stood, turning the numbers over in my head. At some point I realized I was alone. My brain was mush and I needed sleep, so I went to bed.

The smell of coffee lifted me out of a deep sleep. "Good morning, dear."

"I don't want to go to school."

"Don't tell that lie, you loved school. I brought you coffee."

I sat up and took the offered cup. "Did you learn anything last night?"

"Yeah, I need to brush up on my math. Whoever wrote that equation was exceptional."

"Who wrote it?"

"It's called the Hightower theory of FTL travel. So I'm guessing Mr. Hightower."

"Or Miss Hightower."

"Or Miss Hightower, but Mr. Hightower probably helped," I said, smiling. I stopped, something was tickling the back of my brain.

"Hightower, where have I heard that name before? Vee, who wrote the Hightower theory of FTL travel?"

"Emanuel 'Manny' Hightower. Most notable achievements include the design and building of *ESS Duty*."

I sat for a moment. "Oh, my!"

"Oh my, what?"

"He was building *Duty* to prove his FTL theory, and he almost did! The Gantry! That's what The Gantry is for!"

"What? What's it for?"

"The Gantry pushes the lead emitter forward to push through or break through the bow wave, like breaking the sound barrier. Once that is achieved, you enter FTL, or at leasy that's the theory."

"Dear ... put that into pilot, I mean I understand the sound barrier, but everything else."

"OK, the lead emitter breaks the bow wave of gravitational harmonic layers. Hyperspace, subspace and normal space are all layers. This opens them enough to create a bubble that the ship can enter. Once inside, theoretically, you can go faster than light. How much faster is unknown, since no one has done it ... well, as far as we know."

"So, we could reach other solar systems in, what?" She asked.

"Days, weeks, months ... depends on the distance and the speed of our ship."

"Are we going to take *Duty* to test this theory?"

"No, there is no need to risk *Duty* or any lives. We'll build an ACE equipped probe to test it. If we lose the probe, we've lost nothing that can't be replaced."

"I like that idea better. Get a shower and we'll go to breakfast."

While I was in the shower, I set *Vee* to work on our probe ship plans. "Build in an additional 50 percent safety factor. We don't know what kind of stresses will be involved crossing the bow wave."

"Understood."

We joined Mal and Jade in the galley. "I've got an idea, and yes, this will get us killed. Well, if it works."

"You're thinking of trying to go FTL," Mal said.

"No, that's just a theory, I want to build a new pinball machine."

"Oh, I love those things, make one that will pay out creds like a slot machine," Jade said, excitedly.

"They have finally infected you, haven't they?" Jazz said, rolling her eyes. We all laughed.

"Yes FTL, that was what they built *Duty* for." I told them about what we had found out, and what I believed, based on Hightower's theory. "We will build a probe; with an ACE to pilot it. We'll send it out one light year, let it take readings for 15 minutes and return. If all goes well, based on the time it takes to go and return, we'll know if FTL is possible, and what our next steps should be."

"Well, let's get started!" Mal said.

***

We were building the probe in the shape of a cone from which a gantry could be extended. We used the same emitters, MU/R, and GCD that we used on the battleships. We wanted to make sure she could take punishment if needed. It would take a week for the probe to be ready.

Meanwhile, our ships continued to bring in supplies as fast as they could.

We didn't know how much more time we had and did not want to waste any of it. I had lifted speed restrictions on all of our cargo ships once they went dark. If someone followed them, their orders were to outrun their pursuers.

"Admiral, message from Gunny ACE. The UNSA has ordered The Legion to interdict Hermes shipping. The Legion Admiral responded that Hermes has broken no laws and his forces no longer were involved in politics. The UNSA ordered the Legion to at least follow Hermes ships and find our home base.

The Legion Admiral replied they would shadow all corporate ships and enforce the law. Then he dispatched Legion ships from their home port. The UNSA has ordered all Hermes assets frozen. So far, Titan has rejected the order."

"Understood."

"Message all Hermes businesses to continue doing business as usual, but to increase security."

"Sent."

"Have the Unreported News to dig into the UNSA and put all their secret dealings in the spotlight. Also, break the story about The AWB and China possibly buying our tech."

"Sent."

"Message the Steins about what is going on with the UNSA and tell them they can share the info with the Titan government."

"Sent."

That night the Unreported News reported that the AWB and China were in a bidding war to gain Hermes shielding and engine tech.

The next morning, UNSA called an emergency meeting of all nations. It turned into a feeding frenzy. China denied any involvement, The AWB declared what happened within its borders was an internal matter.

Their representatives declared the Secretary General was a crook and was skimming millions of creds from poorer countries to line his pockets and could not bully them. An hour later the Unreported News broke that story, listing the Secretary General's banking records. The AWB was taking advantage of the spotlight while it lasted.

"That should keep them busy for a while," Jocko said, over dinner.

"We should send the bloc a thank you note," Mal said, smiling.

"How long before the probe is ready?" Jazz asked.

"A day or two, barring anything crazy happening," I answered.

"If the probe proves the theory is correct, what next?" Aunt J asked.

I shrugged my shoulders, "Depending on what kind of FTL speeds we can reach, perhaps send it to Spartan 23. If we find a viable world there, one that can sustain humans, then we could go see for ourselves."

"And if that happens?" Jocko asked.

I thought a moment, "The Hermes Corporation could claim the planet, or planets, or system. We can then support ourselves without Earth. We could export goods back to Sol. Earth would have no control over anyone outside of Earth's atmosphere after that."

"That sounds easy, but we'll be an autonomous planet. How will we rule ourselves? Who will be our leaders? Who will make and enforce laws? This sounds easy, but..." Jocko said.

"I see your point, let's table this discussion until we see what the probe finds."

***

We finished the probe, and Mal installed the ACE comp in her. The shakedown cruise was local, and we tracked her with a hammer. Mal tweaked on the fly, but only small adjustments were required. All the equipment operated perfectly, and we extended and retracted The Gantry a few times with no problems.

"Do you think one light year will be too much?" Mal asked.

"No, I want a known distance to time our speed as well."

"How long do you want the probe to stay at the end point?"

"I think 15 minutes should be enough to take some readings and return."

"OK, I was just making sure you didn't change your mind."

"Nope, I'm good with those numbers."

Mal had programed everything into the probe, which we named *Hope*.

"OK, she's out in open space, ready when you are," Mal said.

"Send her."

"She's headed outbound, accelerating… she's disappeared. Hopefully she's crossed into FTL."

"Now we wait." I said.

***

"Admiral, Message from *Major*. Troops are massing along the AWB borders and corporate ships, both sea and air, have blockaded them. The Legion is watching for any ships heading down from space toward the AWB. The Secretary General is being called upon to resign amidst investigation of his skimming funds from the UNSA."

"Understood."

Two hours and seventeen minutes after *Hope* left, she reappeared on our scans, and downloaded information from her trip. We all stood looking at the readouts from *Hope's* trip.

"Did she make the one light year mark?" Mal asked.

"According to these coordinates she did," Jade answered.

"Am I reading this right? she made the one light year trip in roughly one hour, and her return trip also lasted one hour?"

"Yes," Jazz said, "But that's not the most interesting part, she was not running at max speed."

"Are you sure?" I asked, looking over the numbers.

"According to these numbers, she was only running at …"

she laughed.

"What's so funny?"

"I almost said 'Warp One'!" We all laughed.

"OK, but it's more like a harmonic band, like Harmonic Band One." I said.

"Bring *Hope* back, let's examine her inside out and see if there is anything we've missed. Mal, if you'll dig into the ACE reading to verify, Jazz and Jade look over the telemetry readings. Once all that is complete, and we're satisfied with the answers, we'll talk about Spartan 23."

We spent the next two days checking and rechecking everything. Jazz and Jade did a VR flight using the flight data and said everything checked good. I found nothing mechanical or electrical wrong. Mal said the ACE acted and reacted perfectly.

The family sat in our galley having coffee. "Does anyone have anything to add to the reports?" Everyone was shaking their heads. "So, we are in agreement we should proceed with Phase 2, which is sending *Hope* to Spartan 23."

"That seems to be the next logical step," Aunt J said.

"According to your readings it will take *Hope* a little over 20 hours to reach Spartan 23. How long do we give her to scan the system?" Jocko asked looking around.

"For this first trip, let's take an 8-hour system pass, scanning as much as possible in that time. That will have *Hope* back here in roughly 48 Hours, and should give us enough information to tell us if we need to go back for a more thorough look or move on to another candidate," I said.

Everyone agreed. "Let's get her prepped for her trip to Spartan 23, and we'll send her as soon as she's ready."

Hope slipped into FTL the next afternoon on her way to Spartan 23.

CHAPTER 23

"Mal, does our ACE network have control of all the satellites around Earth?" I asked.

"I'm not 100 percent sure. I'd have to check. If we don't, we could be in a short amount of time."

"Check please, if we do not have control, let's get control, it may come in handy."

"OK, I'll get on it."

"Also identify which ones are military and which ones are strictly for civilian use."

"On it."

"Sir, the Secretary General has been indicted and taken into custody."

"Understood."

"You also have a comm from Reuben Stein."

"Put him through."

"Good afternoon, sir, how are you?"

"Fine James, and you and yours?"

"All doing well. What can I do for you?"

"More political pressure is being applied to the Titan government. They have asked for a political 'Win' from the Hermes Corporation to show the voters they are looking out for their interest."

"What are they asking?"

"Access to your tech."

"What did you tell them?"

"I told them I would deliver the message but made no promises."

"Well, we will need friends in government shortly, the

UNSA is making threats that will affect everyone outside of Earth."

"I was afraid that might happen."

"Here is what we will offer them, shield tech, power tech, and engine tech to all emergency service vehicles and emergency service buildings. I'll leave it up to you as to how much, how fast you offer those favors. Make as many friends as you can while we can."

"I think that is creds well spent. I'll dole out bread crumbs. We'll be in touch."

"Thank you, Sir."

"*Vee*, message Jocko and ask him to meet me in the galley."

"He said to give him 30 minutes."

"Acknowledged."

I was sitting in the galley drinking coffee when Jocko arrived. He pulled a cuppa and took a seat. "What's on your mind, Nic?"

"I just got off comms with Reuben. The Titan government wanted some of our tech, although not stated as such, to continue to hold off pressure from Earth."

"It was bound to happen eventually and I'm surprised it wasn't sooner."

"I'm thinking we should make the same concessions to Conclave and Mars, if we get assurances, or at least some political capital in return. I'd like you to handle talking to Conclave."

"I can reach out to them and see what kind of promises we can get from them. What exactly are we offering them?"

I told him what we were offering Titan, a piece at the time, and I wanted to do the same with everyone else. He might even want to coordinate with Reuben, so no one felt left out or slighted.

"I like that idea, I'll comm him. The longer we can keep the wolves at bay, the better for us."

***

"Sir, you have a comm from Leo with Executive Yachts."

"Put him through. Leo, how's business?"

"Great! Sales are up, which is why I'm calling you."

"Oh?"

"Yes sir. I remember you telling me about corporations that bought ships with your tech on them then tried to reverse engineer it. I think we sold one of our units to one of those type of people."

"What makes you think so?"

"The sale was way too easy. He didn't want to see anything, didn't want a test flight, didn't haggle. He seemed in a hurry to get the deal done and be on his way."

"OK, send me the ID number of the ship and we'll keep a watch on it."

"Sending the info now." *Vee* gave me a green light on my HUD.

"Got it, thanks Leo."

"*Vee*, where is that ship headed?"

"Vectoring toward Mars at 2 NES."

"I guess he was in a hurry, keep an eye on her let me know when she reaches her destination."

"Yes, sir."

"Send Mal all info on that ship as well as a copy of Leo's Comm."

"Done."

***

"I see we may have some excitement in the making." Mal said in my ear.

"Maybe."

"I checked all Defender protocols and they are operational and sending telemetry."

"Good, let me know if anything out of the ordinary happens."

"Will do."

Something was tickling the back of my brain, but nothing had percolated to the surface yet. I went down to Mal's shop to see what he was up to.

I stuck my head in. "Beer anyone?"

"You buying?"

"We'll call it a business meeting, and expense it."

"Well, call this meeting to order and let's go," he said, coming to his feet. "Did you call the girls?"

"No." I answered.

"Are you trying to get us killed?"

"So, you're saying I should call them."

Mal just shook his head, "You're just baiting me aren't you."

I smiled, "*Vee*, message the girls to meet us at the Dew Drop."

The girls were there when Mal and I arrived and I ordered a pitcher of beer as I went by the bar.

"What's the occasion?" Jazz asked.

"Meeting," Mal said.

"What are we discussing?"

"Beer, and how to get the corporation to pay for it."

"Well, as long as it's important," Jade said.

"How long before *Hope* is due back?" Jazz asked.

"A little over 8 Hours." I answered.

"I *hope* she brings good news." Jazz said, smiling. Everyone groaned.

"No matter what the news we are going to have to hire a whole new division," Mal said.

I nodded, "all the earth science or rather, planetary science, people. Best case, if we find a habitable world, we will have to know how habitable the planet is. What crops will grow there, what animals will do well there? We'll have far more questions than answers."

"Have you given any thought of where we will get these people?"

"I'm not sure where the best people will be. Maybe some NASA people who haven't sold out to the corporations would be a good place to start."

"*Vee*, compile a list of the top planetary scientists, especially those who have worked on growing crops in space or other planets. Include in that list agricultural scientists with papers on planetary theories of growing crops."

"And animal husbandry," Jade added. We all looked at her.

"I'm not just another pretty face, you know," we laughed.

"And animal husbandry," I added. "Cross anyone off the list that is in the corporation's pockets."

"There are four names who fit the parameters. One on Titan, One on Mars Station, and two on Earth. All four have published theories and papers on the subjects requested."

"Run deep security and financial background checks on the four candidates."

"Understood."

"Sir, you have an incoming comm from Aaron Stein."

"Put him through to all four of us. Aaron, how are you?"

"Doing well. And yourself?"

"Fine, how can I help you?"

"I wanted to let you know we are being sued for having a monopoly."

I chuckled, "Under which company for which invention?"

"All of them."

"Who is bringing the suit?"

"The UNSA."

"Fine, tell them we'll not sell to Earth."

"They claim that their jurisdiction covers all the Solar system."

"Does it?"

"In some ways, yes."

"Do they have a case?"

"Possibly, it would depend on the court that hears the case."

"OK, do your lawyer thing, keep them chasing their tails for as long as you can."

"All right, I'll let you know when things change."

"Thank you."

"So, they are attacking on a different front," Jazz said.

"So, it would seem," I answered.

"Maybe we should do the same," Jade said.

"How do you mean?" I asked.

"Why don't we hire one of those political campaign companies that makes opponents look bad and us look good?"

I nodded, "That is a great idea. *Vee*, comm Reuben."

"James, what can I do for you?"

"We were just talking to Aaron about a new lawsuit."

"Yes, I heard."

"We'd like to hire a company that puts out opposition info on political opponents. We need someone to make us look good, and Earth, and Earth corporations, look bad."

"That should be easy enough."

"Budget?"

"Open."

"I'll comm you back."

"When you find the company, have them coordinate with Aaron and Joshua."

"Will do."

"*Vee*, have the Unreported News help with our propaganda."

"Yes, sir."

***

Hope arrived right on schedule and docked with *Hermes*. Mal downloaded all the info she had gathered. We sifted through the massive amount of data and found there were actually eight planets in the Spartan system, as well as a large asteroid belt. Three of the planets were in the Goldilocks Zone.

"The speed held consistent, at one light year per hour," Mal said.

"We could go faster, according to these readings," Jazz said.

"Look at the time stamps," Jade said.

"Time remained constant. One hour passed here and one hour passed on the ship, there was no time dilation."

"It must be because of the FTL bubble, time is a universal constant." I answered.

"I thought so," Mal said.

"What?"

"I had *Hope's* ACE shape the gantry emitter to push the bow wake as if there were no gantry. She still slipped into FTL with no problems."

"So, any of our ships can go into FTL?" Jazz asked.

"It would seem so," I looked at the data. He was right. "I was so focused on the gantry I forgot we could shape our grav fields. Forest for the Trees. I'm glad you caught that."

"You would have eventually."

"Let's go," Jazz said.

"Go where?" I asked

"Where have we been talking about, Spartan. We could take *Loki*, she can land on the planet if we want to. She can also make things we might need."

I looked at Mal, he shrugged his shoulders. "The first trip we'll take in *Loki* will be one light year out and see how we handle it. Then we 'll talk about a longer trip."

"Let's talk to Aunt J and let her know what we are planning and how long we'll be gone."

"*Vee*, pull up plans for planetary probes, add our tech to them, and send the updated plans to the ship engineers for suggestions. Once they have completed their review have 20 more of the probes made, ASAP."

"Yes, sir."

We found Aunt J in her office and told her what *Hope* had found and what we were planning. "So, you are going one hour out, take readings and come back."

"Correct." I answered.

"No side trips, so we know everything went OK," Aunt J said.

"No side trips," Jazz answered.

"OK, we'll hold the fort, I expect you back in two-and-a-half hours, then we'll talk more."

"Yes, Ma 'am!" We all said, laughing.

"*Vee*, have *Loki* prepped for departure, and message Buck to report to *Loki* for a short trip."

"Done."

Buck met us onboard *Loki*. "*Loki* is ready when you are, Admiral," he reported.

"Thank you, we'll be leaving shortly."

We left Hermes headed for open space. Jazz and Jade took the helm. I went to the galley and made coffee. Mal was looking over his programs for the emitter projections.

Buck joined me in the galley, "where are we headed, Boss?"

"Test flight, one light year out and back."

He stared at me for a moment, "Seriously?"

"Yep," I nodded.

He thought for a moment, shrugged his shoulders, "OK."

I chuckled, "just 'OK', huh?"

He smiled, "well I know you can get a little crazy, but not with Jazz and Jade onboard."

"True," I said. "We have tested the FTL theory and it all worked with an unmanned fight, now we are checking everything out in person."

"Wow, another first! The first crew to go FTL. My grandkids are going to love this story."

"You need a girlfriend first."

"Working on it."

"We have arrived in open space, ready for FTL," Jazz announced.

"On the way," I answered. "I guess we'd better get to the bridge, wouldn't want to miss anything." Buck followed.

I took the captain's chair. "*Loki*, you have the helm."

"*Loki* has the helm."

"Plot a course one light year away from Earth towards the Spartan system, leave when ready."

"Plotted, leaving."

The view from outside did not change much. The stars were still there. They weren't even blurred.

"We are in the first Gravitational Octave of FTL, current speed one light year per hour," Mal said.

"Confirmed," Jade replied.

"Let's keep her at this speed for this trip and verify all of our data," I said, everyone nodded.

Buck brought coffee for everyone while we waited for the first leg of our flight. Looking through the armored glass, the distant stars looked no different, but local space was a blur.

"What if we run into something?" Jazz asked.

"One theory says we would be pushed around it, another says we are not in the same universe with the other object. I say the shields will handle it, or I hope so," I said, smiling.

"The truth is probably some combination of all those theories."

"I take comfort knowing you have no more idea than I do," Buck said. Everyone laughed.

"One minute to the plotted location of one light year." *Loki* announced. We all watched through the armored glass. "We have arrived at the one light year destination."

"Well, that was rather anticlimactic," Jazz said. None of us could tell any difference between moving through FTL and not. The only indicators were an up-tick in the gravitonics.

"Time and the distance verified," Mal said.

"Confirmed," Jade seconded.

"Power usage?" I asked.

"A steady 12 percent," Mal answered.

"*Loki* report ship systems status," I said.

"All systems are operating normally, all boards are green."

"Does everyone concur?" Everyone gave me a thumbs up.

"*Loki* return us to our point of origin."

"Plotted, enroute."

The return trip was the same as the one going out, which is just how I liked it, boring. We docked with *Hermes* and went to have dinner with Aunt J and Jocko.

"Since you are back, I take it everything went well," Jocko said.

"Smooth as silk," I answered.

"What are you planning as your next step?" Aunt J asked.

"A few things actually. We are having planetary probes built for further planetary surveys. We will send *Hope* back out to see if we can take her into a higher octave of FTL. We will visit a scientist on Titan who specializes in planetary exploration and settlement."

"Sounds like a good plan, what happens first?" I got up and pulled another cup of coffee, "We are having the probes built as we speak. We'll send *Hope* back out tomorrow, or whenever Mal is satisfied with his program." Mal nodded. "Once the probes are complete, we'll take *Duty* to Spartan and deploy the probes. When we think we have enough data, we'll take the data and visit the scientist on Titan."

"Why don't you take the scientist with you? You could work enroute and answer questions on the spot."

"Good idea, but if we are going to do that, we need to make a trip to Titan and interview him. While we are there, we'll check on our ongoing projects. Jocko, did you want to come to Titan and see Bill?"

"No, I'll stay with Aunt J." We chuckled, he smiled.

***

Mel programed the *Hope* ACE to go into FTL and then move up into the next octave. Travel out one light year and back. She left, and we kept a watch on the clock. She was back in 30 minutes.

"How fast is that, four light years an hour?" Mel asked

"I think so, not a bad jump in speed for our first octave. All right, you guys go over the data, I'll make the run to Titan, and see if this guy wants to go for a ride."

"*Vee*, message Lt. Adams and Buck that we'll be leaving for Titan this afternoon."

"Sent… acknowledged."

When I arrived at *Loki*, Lt. Adams and his security teams were already aboard. We touched down at Hermes headquarters 30 minutes later. I stopped into the office and was briefed on the ongoing projects. The corporation was running smoothly… hire good people to get good results.

"Mandy, can you get me an appointment to meet with Dr. Andi Hargrave at Titan Technical Institute?"

"Yes, sir, do you want to meet him there or here?"

"Here if possible." Shortly Mandy told me that Dr. Hargrave would be here at 10 am tomorrow.

I walked over to the Steins had for an update. "No real change Sir, they are filing paperwork, we are counter filing paperwork. However, the public relations firm Dad hired is making life difficult for Earth. Hermes' approval rating is up 20 percent and the UNSA and company is down 30 percent."

"I like the sound of that."

"The Unreported News has also been hitting them hard. There may even be some indictments coming from some of their reporting."

"Good, let's keep after them, don't give them any breathing room."

I went over to see Al. His factory printer was lacking work, so I gave him some. "Al, I want to build an automated autonomous agricultural machine, more than one, actually. One that will clear land, one that will plant crops, and one that will harvest crops, all on a large scale. The one you build to clear land; have it use gravitation to do the clearing."

"Interesting challenge, how big would the farm be?"

"I thought a moment, "a thousand acres per farm."
"I'll get right on it."

***

The next day I was in my office awaiting my appointment, "Mr. Hermes, Dr. Andrea Hargraves is here when you are ready." She said, smiling.

"Show her in, please," I said smiling. I got up and met her as she entered. "Dr. Hargraves, thank you for coming."

"Thank you for having me."

"Coffee?"

"Please."

"Mandy will you have the galley send up coffee, please?"

"On the way, sir." I nodded my thanks.

Coffee arrived, and we both fixed a cup. "What can I do for the Hermes Corporation?"

"I've read your papers on planetary exploration and development, and we have something we think you might be interested in. Before I share anymore with you, you must sign an NDA."

"Of course, that's standard procedure anymore." Once she signed the paperwork, I pulled out the data binder on the Spartan system. There were no references to names or locations.

She took the binder and read. She looked up at me and thumbed through pages. "How many planets?"

"Eight, three in the Goldilocks Zone."

"This data is from a probe?" I nodded.

"Any radio signals from the system?"

"None."

"Any signs of life?"

"Nothing major, but this was just a fast scan."

"This must be new, no one is talking about this kind of

discovery."

"No one outside of my top people and you have seen this."

"Amazing, what do you want from me?"

"I want to know if we can colonize these worlds, and how we should go about it."

"I need more information; how long does it take for your probe to send you the information?"

"Well, we were wondering if you would like to go out with us on our next trip."

She stared at me, "go out with you?" I nodded.

"If anyone but The Hermes Corporation had asked me, I would have thought them crazy."

"I'm sure you could find some who think I am."

"That aside, how long will we be gone?"

"That depends a lot on you, and what you need to do your assessment."

She nodded, "how long will it take us to get there?"

"That is classified, but days, not years."

"You've broken into FTL! It's safe? You've done this yourself?"

I nodded, "It's safe."

She leaned back in her chair, her eyes closed. I took a swallow of coffee and waited.

"My God! Mankind will never be the same. When news of this breaks, what was once impossible is now possible."

"And groups will kill for this technology, literally." I fixed her with a hard stare.

"I saw the video of the attack on your headquarters, so I believe you. When do we leave?"

"As soon as you can plan to leave, and when I say plan, I mean quietly, the less anyone knows the better for all concerned."

She thought a moment, "I can be ready to leave tomorrow afternoon, but I'll need some things."

"Give me a list and we'll make sure we have them ready. Don't worry about computers or equipment. I will provide all of that to you." I gave Mandy the list, and told her to get the best available, no matter the cost, and she had everything by the next morning.

I told Buck that Dr. Andi Hargraves was coming with us. The look on his face was priceless when she showed up. Buck just stared, open-mouthed.

She walked by, "Close your mouth dear you'll catch flies," she said, and winked at him. His mouth chopped closed. I had to leave the room before I busted a gut.

CHAPTER 24

Loki docked with *Duty* well away from the *Hermes,* out in open space. We didn't want the good doctor to see all of our secrets. Not yet, anyway.

Jazz met us at the Lock, "Dr. Andrea Hargraves, this is my wife, Jazmine."

The ladies shook hands, "Jazz."

"Andi."

"If you'll come with me, I'll show you to your quarters."

"Buck will you take all of her equipment to her office please?"

"Yes, sir."

I went to the bridge. "Any trouble?" Mal asked.

"None that I know of. Are we ready to head to Spartan?"

"Whenever you're ready." I looked around the bridge and took my seat. "*Duty* plot an FTL course to the Spartan system, first octave, depart when ready."

"FTL course to the Spartan system plotted, first octave, enroute, ETA 19 hours, 40 minutes."

"Report ship status."

"Ship operations normal, all boards are green."

"Very well."

Mal stepped up beside me. "We have all 20 of the planetary probes aboard, but I still need to tweak their programing a little. They won't get a full ACE comp, but they'll get the job done."

Jazz joined us, "Andi is settling into her quarters, she'll join us for dinner."

I nodded, "Is Buck still following her like a lost puppy?"

"Yep, he's got it bad."

"Her?" Mal asked.

"Andi is Dr. Andrea Hargraves," Jazz said.

"Oh," he said smiling.

"You two better not mess with him about it either."

"What? Who?"

"Don't even try it, you know what I mean."

"Honey, we would never." She gave us "The Look".

***

We ate in the main galley that evening with the crew. Andi was sharing some of her theories with us and what she hoped to accomplish, once she had gathered information about the planets.

"This ship is amazing," Andi said.

"It's a wonder to think we are in FTL on the way to another solar system."

"Yeah, it's kind of new feeling for us too. If you hang around with these two long enough, you kind of get used to new things happening," Buck said.

Andi looked at me, "what would you like to see happen on these new worlds Mr. Hermes?"

"I want to settle which ever planet we can the fastest. Then get it started supporting all our space operations. That will take people who want to settle dirt side. We'll help them get started with a homestead and all the equipment they need to work it."

"How fast do you think this will happen?"

"I'm not sure, but as soon as possible."

"I'll do what I can to help you accomplish what I can."

"That's all I can ask."

"How long before we arrive?"

"Some time tomorrow, then we'll launch our probes and begin gathering more information."

She shook her head, "I'm not even going to ask how far we have come or where we are going. It doesn't matter anyway, as long as I'm in on this discovery."

"You are in on it, and when we make it public, you'll be able to publish."

"I look forward to it."

***

We reached the Spartan system the next morning and moved straight to the largest planet in the Goldilocks Zone — the orbits close enough to the star to be warmed, but not scalded by its radiation.

What was amazing was, it was a green and blue planet, just like Earth, but 25 percent larger. Where the Earth had one moon, this planet had two, with 60 percent of its surface covered by oceans, rather than Earth's 75 percent.

"Unbelievable!" Andi said, looking at the displays.

"Are we ready to launch the probes?" I asked.

"All probes are ready and standing by," Mal answered.

"Launch the first two probes for this planet."

"Launching. The first thing we'll be scanning for is radio waves or other signs of civilization."

I nodded, "start our main ship scans of the whole system." One probe started its search pattern north to south, the other east to west. "Feed all info from the probes to the science department. Time for them to go to work."

"Gladly." Andi replied and left the bridge.

"No man-made radio waves present in this system," Mal said.

"It would have shocked me if there were, but we had to check. Let's launch the other probes for the rest of the system's planets. We can get them mapped and gathering information while we wait for info on the first one."

Mal nodded, "Launching probes."

"*Duty*, move us to the asteroid belt, sub-light speed. We may as well make money while we wait."

"Roger, moving to asteroid fields, sub-light, ETA 30

minutes."

"Once we are there, find a nice-sized rock to land on and start mining operations."

"Understood, Admiral."

When we arrived in the belt, we launched seeker drones to map the area up to one hour's travel around us, and the mining bots and crews went to work. *Duty* landed on a large centrally located rock that had its own gravity, though not much. The Smelter/Refinery crew opened *Duty* and started operations.

"I didn't know what to expect, but this wasn't it. The atmosphere on Haydock is almost exactly like Earth," Mal said, reading his screens.

"What did you say?"

"I said the atmosphere was like Earth's."

"No, what did you call the planet?" Mal smiled, "Haydock. We can't keep calling it number one."

I laughed, "I guess not. OK, Haydock it is, but if anyone asks, you named it. The second largest one we'll name Hermes."

"Good idea, I like it."

"OK, so the air is the same, which is amazing, what about the oceans?"

"Not as salty, and there are plenty of fresh-water lakes and rivers."

"Wildlife?"

"From tiny to very large on land and in the oceans. But no signs of civilization, or intelligent life."

"Large predators?"

"I'm sure there are, with all the wildlife."

"Yeah, stands to reason."

"We need air samples so Andi can tell us if it's ok to go down without enviro-suits."

"Already took samples awaiting results."

"As soon as Andi gives us the green light, we'll take *Loki* down. Our force shields are also enviro screens, so in theory we could go now."

"Yes, but that would force us to go through

decontamination procedures when we get back, which I'd rather not do."

"Yeah, you're right, I don't like that idea either."

We had been at normal mining operations for almost a week and were getting good ore. This part of the belt was rich in metals of all types.

"Message from Andi, she has some results she'd like to share," *Vee* said.

"Where and when?"

"Now, in her Lab."

"On the way, notify Mal, Jazz, and Jade."

"Jazz and Jade are out on a flight."

"Of course, they are. OK, just Mal, then."

"Done."

When I arrived at Andi's lab, she was watching the screen showing a flyover of the surface of Haydock.

"It looks like Earth," I said.

"It does, so there are universal constants at work. Carbon-based life. Photosynthesis-based plant life. Water, air, soil, like Earth but in varying degrees. It has produced very similar results. To be honest, I never expected the results to be this close."

"So, what's our next step?"

"We need to go down for a closer look, and direct samples."

"Have you talked to Doc about the air samples?"

"I have, from all tests so far, we can breathe it, and there are no harmful pathogens detected."

"All right, gather what you need, we'll go when you're ready."

"Give me an hour, and I'll be ready."

"*Vee,* assemble a security team on *Loki,* have them bring Andi a shield belt. Recall Jazz for a trip to Haydock. Everyone be ready to leave in one hour."

"Done."

Shortly thereafter, Jazz flew *Loki* over the surface of Haydock. We were all enjoying the view of the new world. "Find us a large open area with a river that has low banks. There was wildlife everywhere, and as *Loki* was operating on gravitonics she made no noise. The wildlife, mostly, didn't run. Most of the animals we saw were four- and six-legged. That took some getting used to.

Jazz finally found us a good place to land, a wide open area with a river running through it. "Make a few low passes, we want no surprises."

"Roger." After making several passes, Jazz sat us down one hundred yards from the river. *Loki* kept her shields up for protection and enviro-shielding.

"*Loki* keep up your scans, warn us of any approaching wildlife."

"Yes, Admiral."

"Lt. Adams set a perimeter so we can take samples. We have our shields so none of the locals can hurt us."

"Roger." The security team took the lead, and we took our first steps on to Haydock.

There were sounds of wildlife all around us. The science teams took samples. There was nothing in the air that our nanites could not handle, and nothing was having an adverse effect on us.

"There is a group of large mammals approaching the river to your left." *Loki* announced. The security guards on the left side shifted, looking toward the potential threat.

A small group of six-legged beasts came into the open, heading toward the river. They appeared to be six-feet-tall at the shoulder, with long curved forward-facing horns and looked to weigh 1,500 to 2,000 pounds.

"If anything makes a move on us, Hammerhead it." I announced. The animals looked our direction but continued on their way to the river where they stopped to drink.

"There is another group of mammals stalking the first group. They are on the other side of group one." *Loki* reported. We kept watching group one but couldn't see group two yet.

"If they attack and flush group one toward us, use your

shield gravitonics to anchor yourselves. They'll either go around us or trip over us, but they won't hurt us."

Group one exploded from the river, running straight at us. Everyone anchored their shields. The ground was vibrating as the animals ran toward us, then dodged around us, never slowing down.

We could finally see what was chasing them. They reminded me of giant wolverines, but these were the size of a small cow, and they, too, had six legs. They were fast, and when they saw us they gave up chasing Group One and headed straight for us.

The wolverines ran full speed into the shield, which didn't move. Two of them were killed outright, the other two we hammerheaded.

"Red blood," one guard said.

"Get samples of everything." I said. The science team nodded and went to work.

"At least we know the hammerheads work on them," Mal said. We spent an hour on the ground gathering samples in sealed containers. Then we returned to *Duty* for analysis.

It only took two days for Andi to report to us. "The good news is, we can live here, breathe the air, drink the water, and grow crops. We can eat the wildlife and fish we've seen so far.

The bad news is we will be considered prey animals to the indigenous wildlife, and everyone who visits will have to have a nanite treatment to stay healthy."

"So, we need biologists. Well, all the sciences, to study Haydock and its wildlife."

"Exactly."

"We also need an agricultural department to farm. We need to produce our own food ASAP. Earth will cut us off sooner rather than later. Thank you, Andi, we'll let you know what we decide, please continue your study of the planet," I said.

The four of us sat eating lunch, "What do you think of bringing *Hermes* here? With the new scientists, ag-equipment and farmers?" I asked.

"Let's talk to Aunt J and Jocko first and see what they say," Jazz replied.

"Good idea, let's leave *Duty* here and take *Loki* back to talk to them," Mal said. "You and Jazz go; Jade and I will stay here to keep everything going. Also, talk to Aaron about what we need to do to claim planets, and, or a solar system, for the corporation."

"Yeah, I didn't think of that. I mean they can't do anything about it, but we could register it all the same."

"The UNSA will lose their minds," Jade said, laughing.

"How long do you think you'll be gone?" Mal asked.

"Not sure ... four to six weeks, maybe. We'll need time to gather the scientists and equipment, and discuss moving our entire fleet to the Spartan System. Whether we bring *Hermes* or not, we'll bring at least one of the Super Haulers loaded with supplies. Either way, we'll bring back as much ag-equipment and as many specialists as we can."

"We'll continue mining operations and planetary research while you're gone. Don't start any trouble while we're not there to help," Mal said, smiling. Jazz and I left that afternoon, heading back to the Sol system and *Hermes*.

***

After we arrived, we swung by Conclave Station to get an update. "*Major*, give us an up-date on our situation, please."

"Our propaganda campaign worked to gain a measure of public support, but behind closed doors the government's position has not changed. They are still applying pressure to take over the corporation under the guise of planetary security. So far they have not totally stopped selling supplies off world, but prices have risen dramatically. The effect has been a slowing of supplies moving from Earth."

"Local governments are under pressure to stop doing business with Hermes, but but so far nothing overt."

I thought for a moment, "Recall the Super Haulers once they are full. Tell them to go dark and meet at *Hermes*. The same for the Super Tankers."

"Done."

"Well done *Major*, keep it up."

"*Loki,* comm Reuben."

"Good afternoon James, what can I do for you?"

"Good afternoon. I want to buy seed for planting crops. Not hybrid seeds, but natural seed that will reproduce."

I could hear the curiosity in his voice. "Tell me more of your requirements."

"I want seed for all major food crops, 10 tons of each, you'll probably have to use multiple sources to get it all. I would also like to keep who's buying it a secret. If they find out it's going off Earth, someone will sabotage it."

"How soon do you need it?"

"The total shipment is to be picked up in four weeks, on Titan, I'm sure it will cost extra, but that's no problem, just pay the extra cost. Also, please find us an ag-equipment manufacturing company that has a full line of equipment. It should be a good one that needs creds due to problems with the big corporations. If you can, buy it, including any patents.

"Once we own it, I need one of everything they make, delivered to Titan."

"Is that all?" he said, chuckling.

"For now," I said, smiling.

"OK, I'll comm you when I have news."

"Thanks and out."

"*Vee*, comm Aaron."

"Good afternoon, Nic.

"Good afternoon, I have a quick question that probably does not have a quick answer."

"Most legal questions don't."

"Let's say, hypothetically, that someone goes to a new

solar system, and claims it for their corporation. How does one register it, or does one have to?"

"Hypothetically, is this someone going to be an independent world, and if so, will he have his own government?"

"Independent. Corporate rules that may morph into a government."

"If it is an independent system, it requires no registration, but might want to let the Earth government know at some point, so diplomatic conventions can be observed."

"That's what I needed to know, thanks."

"Anytime."

"*Loki*, take us to *Hermes*."

"Enroute to *Hermes*, ETA 45 minutes."

"Message Aunt J that we'll be there in 45 minutes."

"Sent."

Aunt J, Jocko, Jazz, and I ate in our apartment galley on *Hermes*. We showed vids of the Spartan System and its planets while we ate.

"All that unspoiled land!" Aunt J marveled.

"It is beautiful," Jazz said.

Jocko sat there, taking it all in, "what're your plans for developing it?"

"We've ordered seed and ag-equipment to farm so we can feed ourselves when Earth cuts us off — which was the driving force for us going there. Al is also printing us some farming equipment. We will need plenty of people to settle and work the land. We can automate a lot, but we'll still need people on site. We plan on taking *Hermes* there, but we don't want to force anyone to go. If they don't want to leave the solar system, we'll send them back to Titan or Conclave Station.

"How do you feel about going to the Spartan system?" I asked. He looked at Aunt J.

"Julie?"

"There is nothing for us back on Conclave, I think we should go. Besides, someone's got to keep the kids out of trouble," she said, smiling.

Jocko chuckled, "There is that. I think we should go too. If I may." Jocko said, looking at me. I nodded. "Let me do some groundwork and then let the people know we are going to Spartan."

"I would appreciate that."

He nodded, "let's talk specifics. If someone goes to Haydock to farm the land, what do they get? What's their incentive?"

"We'll set them up to farm and live, and we get a percentage of the yield. After a time, they get title to the land. Each farm will be one thousand acres. Each ranch will be ten thousand acres," I said.

"What percentage, and for how long?"

I shrugged my shoulders.

"30 percent for 10 years," Aunt J said.

I nodded, "Sounds fair."

"We will need more scientists specializing in agriculture ... will you see what you can find for us?" I said.

"I'll make some calls. What type of government will you have?" Jocko asked.

"Corporate rules to start. We'll see what happens after that. We will be an independent system, though. Earth Corporations will not get a choke hold on Spartan."

He nodded, smiling. "When do we leave?"

"If we get all of our supplies on time, maybe six weeks."

"Then I'd better get started selling the move — which in all honesty won't be that hard."

***

Jocko started his campaign for us to move to Spartan. He made sure that everyone knew that Earth would cut us off from supplies. He showed vids of Spartan and the planets there. He also let everyone know that if they farmed or ranched, they could become landowners.

He put around the deal we would be offering. It was being well received, and the Black Ice Legion was all for the move. One place was much like another to them. It was just another deployment.

We also decided that when the fleet moved to Spartan, Commodore Smythe would remain in the Sol system to monitor and protect our interests. He would also keep *Hope* with him in case he needed to send a message and could not come himself.

"Message from Reuben, they have ordered all seeds through multiple vendors. Shipment should arrive on Titan before the deadline. We have narrowed the ag-equipment manufacturing companies to buy down to three. Will advise."

"Acknowledge."

I put our ship design team to work on designing a fully self-contained house, including shields and defensive arms, one that we could land on Haydock to support a farming family. Sheds or storage buildings would also be part of the package to store all the needed supplies and equipment. Once they had a design, we made a vid showing the buildings being landed and the farm started.

Later in the week I got another message from Reuben," We have identified a company that fits your criteria. We are beginning negotiations to purchase."

As we walked along the promenade, passersby asked us when we were leaving for Spartan. "I guess Jocko's propaganda is working." Jazz said.

"Yep, looks like."

It only took Reuben four days to close the deal on the ag-equipment manufacturer. They were filling our order from stock, even if they had to pull it out of vendor show rooms. The equipment should be on Titan by our deadline. As our order arrived there, I had the items stored in the Hermes warehouses under our shielded dome, planning to pick it all up at one time.

We recalled all ships to *Hermes* to prepare for the decision.

In the end the decision to go was no big deal. When everyone found out they could be back in 20 hours, and we would make regular trips, most of them decided to go to see the new world.

All the seeds, and it was a lot, made it within the four-week deadline, as did the ag-equipment. We dispatched a cargo ship to pick up our order and return to *Hermes*. They included Al's gravitational land clearing machine in the shipment. We also picked up six scientists or Agro-specialists to go with us.

"*Hermes,* recall all ships to dock to prepare for departure."

"Yes, Admiral."

"*Hermes,* lay in a course to the Spartan system."

"Course laid in, standing by to execute." I was guessing it would take an hour to get all our ships on board.

"Admiral all ships have docked, and everyone is accounted for." I glanced at the clock, it had taken only 40 minutes. I guess people were ready.

"*Hermes* take us to open space."

"Enroute to open space."

"*Hermes*, status of ship?"

"All ship operations are normal; all boards are green."

"We have arrived at open space."

"Very well, engage FTL and take us to the Spartan System."

"Engaging FTL, enroute to the Spartan System. We have entered FTL, all ship operations are normal, all boards are green, ETA Sparta 20 hours."

FROM THE AUTHOR

Thanks for reading!

I hope you enjoyed the story, if you did please leave a review it will help my exposure and sales. I try to read all the reviews, good and bad, it helps me to improve my writing. You can follow me on Amazon, Facebook, Goodreads, and other sites. My home page is Jameshaddock.us stop by for a visit. Thanks again.

All the best,

James

OTHER BOOKS BY JAMES HADDOCK

The Derelict Duty

Nic Haydock, "Nac" to his friends, because, as they said, saying he had a knack for fixing and improving mechanical devices was the understatement of all time. After spending 10 years on Titan where he went through rehab and attended college, he was now returning home to Conclave Station. A freak meteor storm had virtually destroyed the rock-tug his family called home, killing his parents and taking his arm and leg. Reuniting with his lifelong friends — Mal, a computer genius, and Jazz, a natural born pilot, he started a mining and shipping business. However, while repairing their rock-tug, they stumbled upon a way to control artificial gravity, creating a gravitational force field. The massive and powerful Corporation found out about the new tech, and realized it will change the balance of power, something its managers can't allow to happen. Everyone wants this new tech and are willing to do anything to get it. When his friends are almost killed, Nic begins to take it personally and starts using their tactics against them. It soon becomes a no-holds-barred shooting war that spans the Solar System.

Duty Calls

Duty Calls continues the story of Nic, Mal, Jazz and Jade as they fight to hold what belongs to them. The Corporations are becoming more aggressive in their effort to steal their inventions. Our four friends are matching the corporate's aggression blow for blow. The fight has already turned deadly, and the Corporation has shown they aren't afraid to spill blood. Nic has shown restraint, but the gloves are about to come off. They've gone after his family and that's the one thing he will not tolerate.

From Mist and Steam

Searching the battlefield after a major battle Sgt. Eli finds a dead Union Army messenger. In the messenger's bag is a message saying the South had surrendered, the war was over. Along with the Union Messenger was a dead Union Captain carrying his discharge papers, and eight thousand dollars.
Sgt. Eli decides now is a good time to seek other opportunities, away from the stink of war. While buying supplies from his friend the quartermaster, he is advised to go to St. Louis. Those opportunities may lie there and a crowd to get lost in. Sgt. Eli, becomes Capt. Myers, a discharged Union Cavalry Officer, and strikes out for St. Louis.

The war has caused hard times and there are those who will kill you for the shirt you are wearing. Capt. Myers plans on keeping his shirt, and four years of hard fighting has given him the tools to do so. Realizing he must look the part of a well-to-do gentleman, he buys gentleman clothes, and acts the part. People ask fewer questions of a gentleman.

What he isn't prepared for is meeting an intelligent Lady, Miss Abigale Campbell. Her Father has died, leaving the family owned shipping business, with next generation steam-powered riverboats. They have dreams of building steam-powered airships, but because she is a woman, there are those who stand against them. Capt. Myers' fighting is not over, it seems business is war. They decide to become partners, and with his warfighting experience, and her brains the world is not as intimidating as it once seemed.

Hand Made Mage

Ghost, a young Criminal Guild thief, is ordered to rob the ancient crypt of a long dead Duke. He is caught grave robbing by an undead insane Mage with a twisted sense of humor. The Mage burns a set of rune engraved rings into Ghost's hand, and fingers. Unknown to Ghost, these rings allow him to manipulate the four elements — earth, wind, fire, and water.

When he returns to the Guild to report his failure, everyone thinks he has riches from the crypt, and they want them. While being held captive, Ghost meets Prince Kade, the fourth son of the King, who has troubles of his own. Ghost uses his newfound powers to escape from the Guild, saving the Prince in the process.

Spies from a foreign kingdom are trying to kill Prince Kade, and Ghost must keep them both alive, while helping the prince raise an army to stop an invasion. Ghost finds out trust too soon given is unwise and dangerous. He is learning people will do anything for gold and power. As Ghost's power grows, his enemies learn he is a far more deadly enemy than any they have ever faced.

Mage Throne Prophecy

A routine physical shows Captain Ross Mitchell has a flesh-eating virus that specifically targets the brain. Prognosis says he'll be a vegetable by week's end. Having survived numerous incursions in combat around the world, Ross decides he's not going out like that. He drives a rented corvette into a cliff face at over 200 MPH. The fiery impact catapults him toward the afterlife.

Instead of finding the afterlife, he finds himself in a different body with an old man stabbing him in his chest. He fights free, killing the old man before passing out. He wakes to find he's now in the body of Prince Aaron, the 15-year-old second son of the King. In this medieval world, the Royals are Mages. The old man who was trying to kill him was a Mage "Vampire". Instead of blood, the old Mage was trying to steal Ross/Aaron's power, knowledge, and in this case, his body. When Ross/Aaron killed the old Mage, his vampire power was transferred to him.

He now has the memories, knowledge, and powers of the old Mage. Ross/Aaron must navigate this new environment of court intrigue with care. His older brother, the Crown Prince, hates him. His older sister has no use for him. The King sees him as an asset to be used, agreeing to marry him to a neighboring Kingdom for an alliance. Before the marriage takes place, the castle is attacked.

Someone is trying to kill him but is finding it most difficult. Where Mages fight with Magic, Ross/Aaron fights with magic and steel. It's hard to cast a spell with a knife through your skull or your throat cut. As Ross/Aaron travels with his fiancée toward her home for the marriage to take place, they are attacked at every turn. Someone doesn't want this wedding to happen. Ross/Aaron has had enough of people trying to kill him. With Aaron's knowledge, and Ross' training, they take the offensive. The Kingdom will never be the same.

Wizard's Alley

Scraps, a gutter child, is sitting in his hiding place in a back alley, waiting for the cold thunderstorm to pass. Suddenly, lightning strikes in front of him, and then a second time. The two lightning bolts become men—two wizards—one from the Red Order, the other from the Blue.

The Red Wizard, chanting his curses, throws lightning bolts and fireballs. The Blue Wizard, singing his spells, throws lightning bolts and ice shards. So intense is their fighting, they become lightning rods. It seemed as if God Himself cast His lightning bolt, striking the ground between them and consuming both wizards in its white blaze. Scraps watched as the lightning bolt gouged its way across the alley, striking him.

Rain on his face awakens Scraps. The only thing left of the fighting wizards is a smoking crater and their scattered artifacts. He feels compelled to gather their possessions and hide them and himself. The dispersed items glowed red or blue, and he notices that he now has a magenta aura. Magenta, a combination of both red and blue, but more powerful than either.

Scraps then does what he has done all his life to survive. He hides. And unknowingly, he has become the catalyst for change in the Kingdom.

Cast Down World

In the summer of 2257, the asteroid Wormwood was closing in to strike Earth a glancing blow. Even a glancing blow would be catastrophic. Earth's governments and militaries united to try to shift Wormwood's path. Earth launched every nuclear missile she had and succeeded in changing its path, just enough to miss her surface. In doing so, shards from the asteroid, caused by the nuclear blasts, struck the earth. In those shards were spores that caused a change in all forms of life. Wormwood also changed Earth's magnetic field, affecting weather patterns and causing earthquakes and tidal waves.

The devastation caused society's collapse. Only the strongest survived the Great Dying. In the years that followed, mutations began to appear in animals and people. It was a time of lawlessness, where the only law was the one you could enforce. Cities and larger towns became walled city-forts. Some chose to live outside the city-forts as ranchers, farmers, and scavengers. They enforced the law with violence, and the law of the old west returned. Out of this came the Peacekeepers, modeled after the legendary Texas Rangers. They were empowered by the city-forts to be judge, jury, and executioner. They were a group of hard men: hated, feared, and respected.

This is the story of Price—a human mutation, raised in the frontier wilderness—who becomes a PK Scout.

Lord of the High Reaches

His human father named him Cam, as he and his clan were chameleon cats. Kol-ha is what the clan called him, which means shame in clannish. Being a half-breed, Cam was not allowed to take the test to become a clan member. Cam decides that rather than he not being worthy to be part of the clan, the clan is not worthy of him. Taking nothing, he leaves the clan to find his place in the world. Though ignorant to the ways of the 'outside' world, Cam is a quick learner. His first lesson is the outside world is at war, and he is inadvertently drawn into it. Saving the life of a nobleman's son, from an invading army's scouts sets him on a path to meet the King of the Eastern Kingdom. As a reward Cam is given lands and becomes a pawn in the King's chess game. Cam sees it for what it is and decides he doesn't want any part of the King's game. Fate, however, has a different plan. Cam discovers two moored airships in a plague-stricken village with a single survivor, La-mar. He also finds new weapon innovations, and information that will change the balance of power in the Kingdoms. With La-mar's help, Captain Cam finds himself and his ships back in the King's chess game. This time it's with more than one King and Kingdom playing, and they're playing for blood. When they kill some of Cam's friends, he spoils their chessboard when he starts playing by his rules of fang and claw.

James Haddock, retired Army Warrant Officer with 22 years of service, is a full-time author, and RV'er. He and his wife enjoy travelling, seeing the wonders of America. He loves reading sci-fi, watching sci-fi TV, and movies. He'll get an idea or see a picture, and think, that would make a great story. Writing as a "pantser", to him, is like reading a new story. He has no idea where the story is going to end up. He gets excited when he picks up a pen to write and looks forward to writing many more stories.

Made in United States
Orlando, FL
11 August 2024

50269832R00171